IN SILICO

MICHAEL J. ANDREWS

ISBN: 0615847773
ISBN 13: 9780615847771

Library of Congress Control Number: 2013914144
A Step Ahead Publishing LLC, Raynham, MA

PROLOGUE

"I don't usually go back to a guy's apartment on the first date. Especially one that I met on the Internet," Liza said playfully. "You're not some serial killer, are you?"

"Do I look like a serial killer to you?" Scott asked as he opened the door. The main door to his apartment brought them into his kitchen. Warmth engulfed them, fending off the icy chill from the New England evening. Scott felt around on the wall for the switch. He clicked it on and the room was immersed in fluorescent light. An old gas oven and dirty white refrigerator rested against one wall, a tiny cherrywood kitchen table on the other, handed down from his grandmother's attic in Maine. The floor was layered with linoleum that was once white, but now had dulled to a brownish yellow tint.

"Jesus Christ, what are those doing in here? Maybe you are a serial killer," Liza said as she stared at a pair of handcuffs resting on the counter in his kitchen.

"Those aren't mine," Scott said, chagrined to see them.

"Oh, is that what you tell all your victims?"

"They're my roommate's. Remember? I told you he's a correctional officer at the correctional facility in Bridgewater."

"Oh yes, I forgot." Liza nodded, showing her relief. Closing the distance between them, she wrapped her hands around his

iii

waist and moved her lips to his until they were practically touching. Their lips locked. Scott's hands wandered up to Liza's breasts, while hers worked to unbuckle his belt and then unbutton the jeans he was wearing. She was so efficient, he had a moment's wonder if she was a pro. She pulled her lips away from his, and they drifted to his ear as he kissed her neck.

"Why don't you show me your bedroom?"

God, I can't believe my luck, Scott thought. He took Liza's hand and began to lead her out. She suddenly pulled away from him and snatched the handcuffs off the kitchen counter.

"Ever use these?" she asked playfully.

Scott's jaw dropped at the question. "I can't say that I have, but there's a first time for everything."

Once in the bedroom, she pushed him onto the bed and climbed on top of him. With tantalizing slowness she removed her blouse. The soft scent of her perfume consumed him. Her face was ripe with anticipation, and she had her lower lip seductively pressed between her teeth. Scott unhooked her bra, cinched in the front. Her breasts were small, her nipples pebbles. He pulled her toward him and his lips felt her for just a moment before she pulled away. Liza took his hands and began to handcuff them to the bed, his right wrist first. Scott winced as the cold steel was secured on his wrist.

"Not so tight."

"You think that's tight? You haven't felt anything yet." She rubbed his inner thigh with her calf as she secured the cuffs around his left hand. However once his second hand was secure, her focus instantly shifted to his pants pockets.

As she began to tug one open he asked, "What are you doing?"

"What does it look like I'm doing?" she answered flatly. Her body language and facial expressions had changed completely.

Gone was the look of seduction, replaced with one of annoyance. "Did you really think I'd be this easy on a first date? Next time you'd better take it a bit slower with girls you meet on the Internet."

Liza pulled out his wallet and tossed it into her purse. She quickly put her bra back on and began searching a large oak chest of drawers for valuables.

"Give me my wallet!" Scott shouted furiously, suddenly realizing what was happening and that he was helpless to do anything about it. "Wait until my roommate gets home!"

"I'll be long gone by then," she chuckled.

Suddenly an unfamiliar voice filled the room. "Looks like you two have done half the job for us."

Their heads whipped to the doorway. In it stood a hulking figure with his arms crossed, his six foot five inch frame blocking much of the light from the rest of the apartment. He flipped the switch next to the doorway and the tall floor lamp in the corner of the room responded by brightening the room.

"Who is this, your accomplice?" Scott asked defiantly.

Liza didn't respond, but her frightened face had the answer pasted on it. The man entered the room and from behind him emerged another intruder. He had a roll of duct tape, and despite being as large as the first, he moved with the agility of someone much smaller. Before Liza could move, he grabbed her arms and threw her onto the bed.

"Get off of me!" she shouted as she struggled to free herself from the man's grasp. He grabbed her bare arm with one hand and her leg with the other and flipped her over with ease. Showing long practice, he wrapped the duct tape around her hands to pin them behind her back.

"Sit her up," the first man said in his thick Russian accent.

"No problem, Boris." He yanked her up and sat her up next to Scott on the bed. Then he promptly left the room.

Liza's dark hair had fallen over her face, and her chest was heaving as she sucked in oxygen.

"You really should lock your door. You never know who could just walk right in," Boris commented as he turned his attention to Scott. "But look, Yuriy and I, we don't want to cause a problem. We just want one thing."

Scott's anger wilted and a cautious fear began to surface. He'd realized Liza just wanted to take his valuables and run. However Boris and Yuriy exuded a more malevolent intent. "Well, whatever it is, just take it and get the fuck out."

"Ahh, I wish it were that simple."

Boris reached into the back of his pants and took a small hand-gun out. Upon seeing it, Liza started to scream. Boris instantly advanced on her and taped her mouth shut. Strands of her hair were also caught and now stretched across her face, trapped in place by the tape.

"We can't have that," he said.

Yuriy returned to the room with a black leather bag. He unzipped it, took out the computer inside and turned it on. Scott recognized the thin, silver laptop as the one he carried to and from work every day.

"This is what you do for us tonight. You give us access to the source code for…" Boris paused as he pulled a piece of paper out of his pocket. Scott spied the name of the company he worked for and the name of the software Boris was trying to get into. "Give us access to the source code for this ViroPredict. Then we leave you and your friend here alone."

Scott was floored. "How do you know about ViroPredict? How do you know that I work for SimSci?"

"We watch you. We follow you all week and know where you work. Now please give us the source code."

"I don't have access to the source code," Scott said uneasily.

Boris tried to stay calm. "Don't try to stall. I know your room-mate will be home within the hour. Unlike you, he knows how to defend himself, and that's a problem I don't want to deal with."

"I told you. I don't —"

Boris' eyes bulged slightly as he raised the gun above Scott's head and savagely pistol-whipped him. The weapon struck Scott right on his hairline above his left temple, and his skin broke open. Stunned, he looked down and saw his blood dripping off of his head and down onto the green pillow case. Suddenly, his stomach began to churn, as if he'd just rode the world's largest roller coaster. I've got to find a way out of here, he thought.

"I'm telling you the truth," Scott said, an edge of fear in his voice. "I don't have access to the source code. I'm just a research scientist!" As he spoke he frantically scanned the room for a weapon. His eyes landed on the aluminum baseball bat resting in the corner of his room.

Boris' gaze followed Scott's. He went over to the baseball bat and picked it up halfway up the barrel. Old grip-tape hung from the handle, slowly peeling off after years of use. He turned back to Scott, and pulled his head up by his dirty blond hair so he was staring into Boris' beady dark eyes.

"I don't believe you. I know you work with the software."

"No, please, why would I lie about—"

Boris took one end of the bat and pressed it up against Scott's chest. With tremendous force, he began to push it hard into his sternum. Scott's grunts and groans filled the room. He struggled to free himself from under the bat, but with both of his hands cuffed, his efforts were futile. As Boris wrestled with him, the small piece of paper that he had in his hand fell to the ground. "Give us the source code!" Boris shouted as his cool demeanor slowly began to unravel.

A giant vein running down the middle of Scott's forehead bulged and his eyes watered as he tried to catch his breath. Boris pressed harder. Suddenly, Scott felt the air leave his lungs as his ribs punctured one of them. His torso convulsed as he tried to inhale air, desperately trying to fill his lungs.

"What's wrong with you? Give us the source code!"

Scott tried to breathe but couldn't. After a few moments he was able to mutter a few words. "I can't!"

Between the agony and terror on Scott's face, Boris saw something else. Something in his eyes was more telling than words. Scott was telling the truth.

"If you can't give it to us, then who can?" Boris asked.

"Vijay can! Will and James can!" Scott cried as he began to cough.

Boris stood over him like a lion amused with his prey before a kill. He watched as Scott choked up blood, and smiled as it ran down his cheek from the corner of his mouth.

"Vijay? Vijay who!"

"Kalam...Vijay Kalam!" Scott replied. The pleading in his eyes was replaced with a look of desperate hope that his disclosure would end the punishment being meted out to him. Yet the pressure on the bat only increased.

Liza started screaming through the duct tape.

"Shut her up!" Boris shouted.

Also annoyed, Yuriy calmly yanked his own gun out of the back of his jeans. He aimed carefully at Liza's head as it thrashed wildly. With twin roars, two bullets penetrated Liza's skull with neat holes in her forehead.

With revulsion, Scott felt Liza's body slowly slump over against his. Blood began to ooze out of the bullet holes and onto his shoulder. Suddenly everything became surreal to him. He knew he was next. He desperately tried one final time to dislodge the bat, but his muscles couldn't muster the strength to relieve the pressure.

Boris could tell that Scott had shared everything he knew. He pulled back the bat and began striking Scott mercilessly in the chest with it. The rain of blows quickly crushed his ribs and in turn punctured his other lung. Sounds around Scott became muted, his vision blurred.

As Scott faded out of consciousness, the last thing he saw was the rage in Boris' eyes as he delivered blow after fierce blow to his chest.

CHAPTER 1

The auditorium was filled with over nine hundred people, all here to listen to Will Woltzberg's presentation at the International Symposium on Infection Prevention and Disease Control. Their specialties varied from virologists and biomedical engineers, to medical doctors and computer programmers.

Will wore a navy Brooks Brothers pin-stripe suit tailored for his six foot two frame. His dark hair was parted on the side, and the lights on the stage served to highlight the peppering of gray. A sea of unfamiliar faces awaited Will. Years ago my knees would be jelly, he thought as he settled in behind the podium. But after a peregrination spanning generations, he had a firm grasp on the subject matter.

"My name is William Woltzberg, and I'm chairman and CEO of Simulation Scientific, or SimSci. For the past twenty-five years my company has been researching how computers can help scientists predict how viruses will react to a range of variables that exist in their environment. Today we are pleased to release SimSci's ViroPredict version 1.0. In the ViroPredict Viro module, through powerful computer-based simulations, this one-of-a-kind software can not only predict how a virus's surface proteins and genetic makeup will evolve, but it will predict when those changes will take place, given the variables in the environment. Moreover, it will also determine the conditions that will produce the fastest and slowest viral mutations. This functionality is not limited to viruses currently being carried by humans. We can simulate all viruses across all species. Of course, the simulations are performed 'In Silico.' As I'm sure most of you know, 'In Silico' means that an experiment is performed by a computer, as opposed to 'In Vitro,' where an experiment is performed in a test tube or other laboratory setting and 'In Vivo,' which is when an experiment is actually performed in a living being."

Will hardly needed to explain, because he knew everyone gathered was an expert in their field. "With this data we can monitor and predict how existing viruses will mutate and when. Since we will know when a virus will mutate, we will have ample time to study the genetic makeup of the virus, and produce a genetic match so that vaccines can be created and administered. What may be the most remarkable aspect of this software is that all results have a confidence level of slightly over ninety-nine percent. During the past five years we have formed a partnership with the Center for Disease Control as well as the National Institute of Health. Both have reviewed much of our work and have been pleased with what they have seen."

Will paused for a moment to take a drink from the glass of water on the podium, as well as to let his audience consider what he'd just said. His eyes met those of a woman in the audience. Her blue eyes glistened like sapphires as she listened intently to his words.

"Over the next hour, I'll go into greater details regarding the research that demonstrates not only the accuracy of these simulations, but I'll share with you a current strain of the common cold and show you how it will mutate within humans in the continental United States over the next ten years."

During the next sixty minutes the group sat listening to Will discuss the extraordinary accuracy that SimSci's software had when predicting how, where, and when viruses would mutate.

"For those of you in academia, we are excited to discuss with you the opportunities to collaborate with the research teams at your universities. For those of you in the drug and vaccine industry, we wish to form partnerships to produce the vaccines people will need to fight off these ever changing viruses. With your help, we will make the world a safer place to live. For those of you who are interested in working on a dynamic team, come see me and we can discuss the opportunities here at SimSci. We are always looking for talented people for our workforce. My brother James and I will be attending the dinner that's taking place later, and we'd be happy to discuss anything and everything with you. Thanks for your kind attention tonight," Will concluded.

Applause filled the hall as Will left the stage. Once out of view, he immediately looked for his younger brother James. James' six-four athletic frame stood out, literally a head above other people in the hall. His dark blue sports coat with its white dress shirt and form-fitting, neatly pressed jeans gave him a European look. "Hey, kid, come on."

The two brothers headed out of the conference hall, then through the hotel lobby to the hotel entrance. Lighting around the entrance chased away the darkness, but the same couldn't be said for the Chicago winter. Will crossed his arms in front of his chest to conserve heat. Nearby, a bellboy assisted an elderly woman get out of the passenger seat of a silver Lexus as the driver waited impatiently.

While Will Woltzberg was CEO of Simulation Scientific, James was the VP of Scientific Modeling. The presentation that Will had just made represented twenty years of both their lives.

3

"He shoots, he scores!" James motioned as though he was shooting a basketball. "That went great. Your delivery was flawless. I wish you could write code that good."

"Thanks," Will said, ignoring the crack. "What were the reactions of the people that you spoke to?"

"Very positive. I spoke to a professor from the Bradley Department of Computer Engineering at Virginia Tech. He's leading a research group right now that's been working on how the human body reacts to different chemicals found in foods. He thinks that some of the same algorithms we are currently using could be adapted for his work."

"Wonderful!" Will wasn't interested in the potential profits that could be realized from his software. From his first day in college majoring in biology, Will had wanted to make the world a better place. He wanted his name spoken in the same breath as other people who had changed the world. He used his passion for science as a means to this end. Now with the ability to virtually eliminate nearly any pandemic before it even began, his dream was about to be realized. He knew that his brother shared his vision for the company.

Besides the impact ViroPredict would have on disease control throughout the world, it would also produce enough profits for both he and James to become extremely wealthy. For his part, Will had been very happy living modestly. Like anyone he did treat himself once in a while. But not James. He had an eye for the finer things in life and didn't hesitate to buy them on a whim. That wasn't Will's only pet peeve about his little brother. He was financially savvy, but balancing risk and reward didn't come as easy as balancing a check book. A series of bad investments and a life-long sports gambling habit left James with a fraction of the savings he should have had. When James had a hunch, he let his money do the talking.

"Another was from BakerHynes."

"*The* BakerHynes?" Will asked, referring to the fifth largest pharmaceutical company in the world.

"Yes, *the* BakerHynes. I have her business card here." James took a card from his pocket.

"Her name is Mindy Hegarty, Vice President of Business Development. They're interested in talking to us, but not here, not now. They want to arrange to come out to our offices in Cambridge."

Will responded by wryly raising his eyebrows. The response got a fist pump and a smile from his brother.

"This is just the beginning. I have a feeling we'll be receiving a lot of interested prospective partners."

The two watched people hurrying in and out of the busy revolving doors for a few moments while they replayed the presentation in their minds. Will's gaze drifted to his brother and he saw that something wasn't right.

"Hey," Will said as he drew eye contact with James, "what's wrong?"

James blinked in surprise, but something else slid out of view.

"Nothing, Jeez, Will, what could be wrong?"

Gone were the days of being able to pin his little brother down and give him Indian rope burns until he confessed. But Will could usually still get the truth out of his sibling if he persisted with his questioning long enough. Immediately Will wondered if James had gotten himself into a fix in the stock market. Just six month earlier, James had found himself on the receiving end of a series of margin calls. Will had to give him a cash infusion to save him from having to liquidate his portfolio. Will didn't want a confrontation between the two to over shadow the success of the evening. Tomorrow, he told himself, he would press the issue.

"Are you ready to go into the dining hall?" Will asked.

"I sure am."

The two brothers entered the hotel and followed the signs to the function room. The vast room held dozens of round tables covered with white linens. As most of the people attending the conference were already seated, the empty seats were sparse. Will went over to a table that had a seat open and introduced himself.

He started a discussion about his presentation and soon it dominated all the discussion at the table. There was no shortage of questions, as all were anxious to find out more.

As their dinner plates were being cleared and the waiter was serving coffee, Will took the opportunity to excuse himself. He had been talking nonstop and he needed a break. He headed back through the lobby to get some fresh air.

As he walked outside, he recognized a woman smoking a cigarette next to the building. It was her brilliant blue eyes that had captured his attention from the podium. She was wearing a dark gray business suit with a light pink turtleneck. Her big blue eyes stood in stark contrast to her black hair. Her long legs and slim waist were as pleasing as her other attributes. She took one final drag from her cigarette and dropped it into a sliver ashtray set in front of the hotel entrance. The two made eye contact as she approached him.

"Monica Rowe, CEO of Sander Pharmaceuticals. I was in your presentation earlier this evening," the woman said, extending her hand.

"It's a pleasure to meet you, Monica. Will Woltzberg."

"I just want to tell you that we at Sander have been aware of Sim-Sci's work for some time. I'm personally honored to be speaking with you right now."

Will studied Monica as she spoke. She exuded confidence, and she knew how to exploit that look. Closer up, Will could see the beginning of wrinkles forming around her eyes, and he estimated that she was in her late thirties. He'd recognized her name, and Sander Pharmaceuticals, of course was the second largest drug manufacturer in the world. She was young to be the chief executive of such a large company, he thought.

"Thanks. It's the result of twenty hard years of software development," Will said, reverting to sales pitch mode. "My brother and I have been waiting for this night for a long time. James and I believe that this software is going to revolutionize the disease control industry."

She laid a hand on his arm. "I think so too. I also think that Sander would make an excellent partner in the commercialization of these vaccines. I would love to discuss that possibility with you over a drink. Would you care to go to the bar?"

This isn't how I thought this night would end, he thought. He was envisioning making small talk with a few more geeky scientists and then heading to bed to get a good night's sleep before the flight back to Boston. I guess one drink won't hurt, thought Will.

The two headed for the bar, found a pair of empty seats, and settled into them. Monica ordered a gin and tonic, Will a microbrew that the bar had on tap.

She was all business at first. "In your presentation today you referenced numerous publications where third party scientists as well as university professors have documented that your software correctly predicted which carbohydrates certain viruses would attach to next before they actually began doing so. Could you tell me more about this?" Monica asked.

"Well, the most recent paper was published in the *Northeast Medical Journal* about nine months ago. We ran a simulation using the exact genetic makeup of the MVMi Minute Virus of Mice. We ran the virus through a simulation that essentially allowed us to view how the virus would mutate over long periods of time in an environment similar to what it would encounter in the U.S. The resulting strain of the virus then surfaced some twelve months later."

Monica listened carefully to Will as he spoke, and then took a sip of her gin and tonic. "This is truly remarkable. Sander is very interested in consummating a partnership with your organization. Let me take a moment to tell you a little about Sander Pharmaceuticals." Will gave a short laugh. "That won't be necessary. I'm very familiar with your organization."

They held patent protection on drugs ranging from cholesterol-lowering medicine to little blue pills that helped men get their motor running "when the time is right." However, what interested Will about the company was that they were the largest producer of the seasonal flu vaccine in the world. Each year the company made nearly a hundred million doses of the vaccine. The size and scope of the production facilities that Monica controlled were second to none. Even better, their corporate headquarters were based in downtown Boston. Sander would be an ideal partner.

"SimSci is very interested in forming a partnership with your company," Will offered. "I'd like to discuss this, but not here. My brother should be a part of this discussion. When we get back to Boston, we'd love for you to come out to our facility in Cambridge."

"I'll certainly take you up on that offer," Monica said, her big blue eyes ripe with anticipation.

Minutes slipped past as the two learned more about each other. As Monica was talking about their worldwide marketing scope, Will finished his beer and checked his watch. He'd already been in the bar longer than he'd wanted. Suddenly, Monica put her hand on his and moved toward him until their faces were just inches apart.

"You're not thinking of leaving, are you? We've only had one drink, and this is the last night of the conference. You don't want to end the night talking shop, do you?"

Will wasn't sure how to respond. He'd not expected such a proposal from any woman tonight, never mind a gorgeous brunette who happened to also be the CEO of one of the largest pharmaceutical companies in the world. The gears in his mind began running at triple speed. Sarah would never know. She's hundreds of miles away back in Boston.

Through eighteen years of marriage, Will hadn't cheated on Sarah. Oh, there had been opportunities, although as the years went on they became less frequent. Had she been faithful to him over eighteen long years? A few years ago he would have surely thought so, but over the past few he wasn't so sure.

When they'd first married 'work hard, play hard' were words Sarah lived by. A successful biologist by day, she would be the last of her friends to leave the bar at night. That changed when she became pregnant with their first child, Logan. Maternal instincts kicked in and she became a nurturing mother. Now that the kids were nearly grown, that had changed. Now he never knew what kind of surprises he was in store for when he got home each night.

As two wily blue eyes hung on his response, Will heard his brother's voice in his mind.

"There's a time and a place for spontaneous indiscretions, and it's called college."

Wise words from a night years ago when Will was faced with a similar decision. The memory brought a smile to his face.

Mistaking the smile for acceptance Monica took Will's hand and began to lead him out of the bar.

"Umm...," Will raised his hand, and Monica paused.

"You're a fascinating, beautiful women, but I'm sorry. I can't join you tonight."

Monica's confidence wilted a bit, but she persisted. She leaned into Will until her lips were nearly touching his ear. He could feel her warm breath as she spoke.

"It's one night. Tomorrow we'll be home. Everything will be just like it was when you left."

The thought of following her back to her room crept back into his mind. How could any man resist? He inhaled deeply and pulled away.

"My wife of eighteen years is at home. She's the mother of my kids. If this were a different time and place, I'd be joining you. But not here, not tonight."

Monica pulled away and got up from her barstool.

"Let's talk when we get back to Boston. I'll be in touch," Will said.

"Not if I am first," she said, placing her hand on his in a final attempt to seduce him. In a silky smooth motion, Will slid his hand out from under hers and stood up.

"Good night."

As he headed up to his room, he thought about all that had happened that night. A lot of offers were thrown my way tonight, he thought as he opened the door to his hotel room. I better stick to accepting the ones that don't get me kicked out of my house.

CHAPTER 2

James pressed the replay button on his voice mail. Three of his office walls were lined with nautical paintings, the forth displaying his diploma from Tufts University. A tall bookshelf rested beside his desk holding scientific literature that was purely for show. His desk was in disarray, papers everywhere. The morning's coffee cup, its contents devoured hours ago, sat on top of a stack of manila folders. The quiet drone of the buildings ventilation system was the only sound he heard as he waited to hear the message again. This can't be happening after all these years, he thought. He had a pen in his hand, and wrote down two words, "Scorpion" and "Nadir". After hearing the message again, he slammed the phone into its cradle.

"You got a minute? I've got news that you really need to hear."

James looked up and saw Will at his office door.

"Sure," James replied, flushing with guilt.

Will closed the door as he came into James' office and sat down in one of the chairs across from James' desk. The family resemblance between the two brothers was strong— both with healthy heads of hair and an athletic build.

At this time of the morning, the sun shone brightly into James office, and it only took Will one look to know that something wasn't right with James. Maybe he'd already heard the news, Will thought.

"Did you hear what happened to Scott Bredahl?"

Yet James was too distracted to reply. He glanced at the phone, as though the message would replay aloud by itself.

"Hello in there...." Will said, trying to get his brother's attention.

"No, what happened?" James asked.

"He was found dead in his apartment. Murdered."

"Jesus Christ," James replied as his eyes suddenly focused squarely on Will and his mouth hung open in disbelief.

"He was found with a known prostitute and drug addict."

James wheeled back clumsily in his chair. "The guy was as silent as a mouse in the office. I would've never guessed he was picking up hookers and blowing lines with them every night. Gotta watch those quiet ones."

"Oh wait, it gets stranger." Will explained. "The police found him and the hooker dead in his bed. But that's not all they found. They also found his laptop at his feet with the power on."

"Nothing like a little porn to set the mood...."

"I don't think that's what they were doing. He hadn't even logged in. But hold on, it gets even stranger. They also found a piece of paper with the name of our company and 'ViroPredict' on it."

"Hmmm....that is bizarre," James said feeling prickles of alarm.

"That's what the cops said when they showed up here today wanting to ask Vijay and I some questions." Vijay Kalam was Sim-Sci's lead programmer and Scott's direct supervisor.

"Do they think that what happened is related to SimSci?" James asked, tapping a pen on his desk.

"They didn't come right out and say that, but they are considering it a possibility."

12

"It sounds like the kid was into some kinky shit. But what people do outside of the office doesn't have anything to do with this company. I mean, all they found is a piece of paper with our company name on it," James thought out loud. "Maybe it fell out of his briefcase or something."

"Possibly, but it sounds like too much of a coincidence to me. I called Charles Madre to see if he could get me any additional information. He still hasn't called me back."

James' heart rate jumped at Will's words. Detective Charles Madre was one of Will's best friends and a homicide detective in the Cambridge Police Department. They'd known each other since high school, and remained in touch since then despite their careers veering in different directions. James knew Charles very well. He was very passionate about his work, and took pride in solving cases. If he got involved in the case, he would work tirelessly to ensure that no stone was left unturned. With the Scorpion suddenly resurfacing after all these years, James didn't need any law enforcement snooping around in his business.

Their conversation was interrupted by James' office phone. James looked at the caller ID and all the blood drained from his face.

"Do you need to get that?" Will asked.

"No," James said, his voice barely audible.

"Everything okay?"

The phone rang again.

"Yes."

As the phone rang a third time, James felt like each ring was louder than the last.

"Would you tell me if it wasn't?" Will persisted.

James was relieved as his voicemail picked up. "Look, everything's fine, seriously."

James grinded his teeth when he was nervous. He felt himself doing it and quickly stopped. His older brother knew about this bad habit. He pasted on a smile that wouldn't fool a total stranger, never mind his brother. As Will rose from his chair, an uncomfortable silence thickened the room.

"I'll let you know if I hear anymore about Scott Bredahl," he said. "Oh, and when you're finally ready to tell me your big secret, just let me know."

CHAPTER 3

Replying to an email, Monica Rowe's fingers were tap-dancing on her keyboard when Nancy O' Keefe knocked on her door.

"Are we still on for three?" she asked, glancing at the clock.

Monica couldn't believe that it was already three in the afternoon. Her day was flying by and she hadn't even begun to do the things she'd put on her calendar.

Monica's day often started at five in the morning and could last until midnight or later. People from all over the organization were constantly vying for her attention and awaiting her decisions. The pharmaceutical industry was cutthroat, and they had to keep ahead. Luckily, no one in it was more competitive than Monica.

"Yes, please come in."

Nancy sat down at the conference table Monica had in her office and waited for Monica to finish her email. Nancy O'Keefe was VP of Business Development at Sander Pharmaceuticals. As striking as Monica was, Nancy wasn't concerned with physical appeal, not even bothering with a little concealer under her eyes. Her duties included studying new opportunities, including new lines of business and potential acquisitions of existing businesses. Today they'd be discussing the latter. At last Monica rose from behind her desk and sat down at the conference table with Nancy.

"So what did we find out about SimSci?" Monica asked.

"We found quite a bit. Let me start with the organization in general. It was started twenty-one years ago by the current CEO and VP of Scientific Modeling, Will and James Woltzberg. The initial funding was from bank loans that they obtained. Initially, their main source of revenue was contract R&D for various pharma and biotech companies domestically." Nancy's blunt fingertip indicated the list. "They used the profits from these operations to fund their internal R&D projects surrounding viruses and leveraging computers to track changes in viruses over a number of years and in various environments. Eventually their staff grew in size and included a number of biologists and chemical engineers who were working with computer engineers to design the software that's known today as ViroPredict. From the articles that I've read, the software has a demonstrated history of accurately predicting the way that viruses will mutate. It's the real deal and no competitors are even close to their capabilities in this field." Nancy paused, allowing Monica an opportunity for questions. Monica remained silent, and Nancy continued.

"Will and James have retained their roles since the company's inception. They're an interesting duo. Their motives for starting the company were never financial. Their goals are mainly altruistic. I was able to track down some personal information on the two and they live quite modestly in the suburbs outside of Boston. They're both married with kids, both on their first marriages."

As Nancy spoke, Monica thought back to a few nights ago to Chicago, sharing a drink with Will. She had tried to seduce him and he'd resisted her advances. She rarely had a man reject her, and she'd been angered by it.

"Regarding other key people in the company, the CFO is a guy named Nick Waters. He…"

"Did you say Nick Waters?" Monica interrupted.

Nancy checked her notes. "Yes, a guy by the name of Nick Waters is CFO of SimSci."

Monica couldn't hold in her excitement. She slapped the table with her open hands.

"That could be our in with this company. I worked with Nick Waters back at Baxter and Baxter." Monica said. "If he's CFO, he must have changed since I last saw him."

Monica had known Nick well. They had both begun their careers at Baxter and Baxter, another large pharmaceutical company. They worked closely on many projects, and Monica knew that he was extraordinarily intelligent and articulate from the hours of nine to five. After work, though, was a whole different story. She'd gone out for drinks with him many times, and more than once had to call him a cab to take him home.

After a few years, rumors began circulating that he had a drug problem, and that it was affecting his work at Baxter. The rumors were confirmed when one of the vice presidents found him in the men's room of a bar with a bag of white powder in one hand and a rolled-up dollar bill in the other. The run-in had informally ended his career at Baxter. Three months later he accepted a position at another company. It was a lesser job title, but it avoided outright dismissal from Baxter. Monica had thought it more likely to hear that he was found dead from a drug overdose than that he'd risen to the level of CFO of a small company.

"He's not the only person at the company you'll know. Do you remember a young virologist who used to work here named Tanner Fitzgerald?"

Monica paused before answering, trying to place the name. Then the connection dawned on her.

"The one who did that incredible work on the flu virus a few years ago— how could I forget? He was nothing short of brilliant. Did he leave us to go to SimSci?"

"Yes, he's one of their lead virologists now."

"That is very interesting, very helpful," Monica said, nodding her head.

"I do have one other piece of information, albeit it's a bit strange. One of their employees was recently found dead in his home, murdered. The official cause of death was cardiac arrest stemming from tension pneumothorax, cardiac arrest in layman's terms. The police think that he was murdered, and here is the strange part. They found a piece of paper with the name of Will's company and the word 'ViroPredict' on it. The cops haven't publicly linked the murder to SimSci, but who knows what they are thinking privately?"

"The paper could just be a coincidence. But you're right. I'm sure the cops have their eye on everyone at SimSci," Monica agreed. "You haven't heard any whispers of people interested in acquiring SimSci?"

"I'm sure there are plenty of companies both big and small that want this technology. But I haven't heard that they are in serious talks with anyone. Besides, the brothers won't sell, so it's probably a moot point."

Monica would do all she could to change their minds. "Ok, anything else that I should know?"

"No, that covers it."

"All of this information is very helpful. In regards to next steps, I'm going to call Nick Waters today and plan a trip out to visit Sim-Sci to meet with him and Will. I'll make this first visit alone," she clarified for Nancy. "Please keep your eyes open for other tidbits about this company, and let's get someone in finance to build a sales model to forecast how much a near monopoly on infectious disease vaccines would bring in."

"I'll keep my eyes open and let you know if I hear anything." Nancy replied as she left Monica's office.

Monica sat back down at her desk and got the phone number for SimSci. After a short exchange with the receptionist, Monica was connected to Nick.

He sounded delighted. "Monica Rowe, to what do I owe this pleasant surprise?"

"Nick Waters, how are you?" Monica asked.

"I'm well. Wow, what in the world has made you track me down?"

Monica knew what Nick wanted the reason to be. I'll have to find a way to let him down easy, she thought. "Your name came up as I was talking to one of my VP's about your company and some of the exciting things that you've been working on. It's been a long time since Baxter and Baxter. I'm now CEO of Sander Pharmaceuticals."

"I know that, I've kept track of you, Monica," he said with unwelcome familiarity.

"So what's going on outside of work these days? Married with kids?"

"No, marriage hasn't been in the cards so far. With everything that I have going on at Sander, I don't have time for a committed relationship," Monica responded.

"I see," Nick said.

Monica could almost see the gears in Nick's head turning in triple speed. Time to throw in the monkey wrench.

"The reason that I'm calling is that I've heard good things about your ViroPredict software. Really good things. You and I go back a long way, all the way back to the beginning of our careers. So I'm going to be straight with you. Sander is very interested in acquiring your company. We are willing to pay whatever it takes to get it."

Nick chuckled before he spoke. "You never did beat around the bush. In this instance I appreciate your forward approach, but

I'm not sure you're going to be able to buy us out. You probably know that SimSci is owned by Will & Jim Woltzberg."

"Yes, I saw Will speak at the conference in Chicago a few days ago."

"Well, they aren't selling this company. It's pretty cut and dried. You could throw a billion dollars and a night with the women of their dreams at them and they wouldn't sell."

That's what I would need to offer you if you owned the company, Nick, she thought to herself. Nick Waters hadn't changed one bit.

"I had the opportunity to speak with Will earlier this week in Chicago after his presentation, and I made tentative plans to visit your offices. I'd like to speak to you about this a little more when I get out there. How does that sound?"

"Monica, I'd love to see you and catch up, it sounds like a deal. You visit our humble offices here in Cambridge, and we can discuss this over dinner. We'll have a few drinks and it'll be just like old times."

"Lunch actually works better for me," Monica said. She had no intention of spending an evening reminiscing about their time at Baxter and Baxter. Worse, she certainly didn't want to endure an evening of Nick trying to get in her pants.

"You can count on seeing me in Cambridge next week," Nick said, almost gushing. "I can hardly wait. This will be just like old times."

Monica agreed, and ended her call. She sat back in her black leather office chair and tapped a pen on a stack of papers piled on her enormous desk. Could Nick Waters be my way in? she thought. I'm just going to have to find out.

CHAPTER 4

"You're avoiding me, like you did Cynthia Grossman after she found out you were cheating on her," Will exclaimed when Charles Madre answered his phone.

"And she was a hell of a lot easier to look at than you are!" he responded.

The two shared a comfortable laugh that old friends can do when they are completely comfortable with one another. The two men had been good friends since high school. They could go six months without talking, but when they finally did, it's like they saw each other yesterday.

"So what's so important that you're leaving messages on my office, cell, and home phone?" Charles asked with mock exasperation.

"If I'm that big of a pain in the ass, I'll take my extra ticket to tomorrow's Celtics' game elsewhere—"

"Seriously, you have an extra seat?"

"No, but next time call me back right away. You never know when I may come across some!"

"You're such a prick, do you know that?"

On the other end of the line, Will couldn't hold in his laughter.

"So what did you really want?"

Will paused for a moment to gain his composure. With his phone on speaker, he was free to get up from his desk chair to look out of his office window. It was a cloudless, chilly day.

"I'm actually calling about something very serious," Will began. "I don't know if you heard, but one of our employees was murdered a few nights ago."

"Really? What's his name?"

"Scott Bredahl. He was murdered in his condo along with a hooker."

"Oh, the double over on the Somerville line. I did hear about that. Didn't catch it, though," Charles said, referring to not being assigned the investigation. "That guy worked for you?"

"Yes, he was one of the best scientists that we had," Will replied.

"Well, it sounds like he partied pretty hard after being in the office with you all day. I guess you didn't manage to suck all the fun out of him."

Will strode over to the refrigerator and grabbed a bottled water. "Listen, I need to know more about what happened that night."

"What was this guy to you?" Charles asked.

"I told you, he was one of the best—"

"I heard you, but come on, Will. Your employee was into some kinky shit. Obviously he pissed off the wrong person. Don't you have more important things to worry about in your little science shop over there?"

Charles never really understood exactly what Will did, nor did he make any effort to. In his mind, Will played with Bunsen burners and dissected frogs all day.

"For one, this guy was a damn good researcher. He'd been with SimSci for seven years, and I knew him pretty well. I find it very strange that he would get himself involved in such a seedy scene. He's just not that kind of peron. Second, a piece of paper was found with our company's name on it. I'd like to know how the hell it got there and what else may have been written on it. Last but not least, along with the two dead bodies, his work-issued laptop was found on the bed in his bedroom when he was found. Pretty strange, don't you think?"

"Wow, you're really upset about this. Let me see what I can find out on my end. Why don't we grab a beer later this week to discuss?"

The two friends consulted each others' busy calendars until they found a mutually agreeable time and date and exchanged farewells.

"It'll be good to catch up, it's been a while," Charles said. "I just hope you don't think you're going moonlighting as a homicide detective. You leave that work to us."

CHAPTER 5

Coffee spilled in Vijay's lap as the plane suddenly hit a pocket of turbulence and began shaking. He applied a small napkin to his suit pants to blot up the coffee before it set into the fabric. The fasten seat belt lights lit up in the cabin, and static could be heard in the loudspeakers.

"This is your captain speaking. It looks like we have hit a bit of turbulence. I'm going to request that you fasten your seat belts and remain seated. Thank you."

Dr. Vijay Kalam closed his eyes and rested his head. He had been in transit for over 30 hours, and this was the final leg of the trip. He was coming home from Hyderabad, India, where he was in the initial stages of a collaboration between SimSci and a group of professors led by Professor Rajaya Kumar at the Rajiv Gandhi University. Vijay had seen some of the modeling prior to the trip and was struck by how good the work was. He was coming home even more impressed. If he could obtain the algorithms that Prof. Kumar's team was currently utilizing in their programs, it could help the progress of what was already the best-in-class software his company had developed.

"May I take that cup from you?"

Vijay's musing was interrupted by one of the stewardess's request.

"Yes, thank you," Vijay replied.

His final destination was Logan International Airport, touching down in Boston at just after one in the morning. He couldn't wait to get home. As thoughts of his wife and young children filled his mind, Vijay closed his eyes and fell asleep.

An hour later, a gentle nudge woke Vijay from a light sleep.

"Sir, please put your tray table and seat in their upright position. We're preparing to land."

Vijay looked up at the same stewardess that had taken his coffee cup earlier in the flight. "Yes, of course. Thank you."

Twenty minutes later, the sound of wheels bouncing on the runway were heard. The plane taxied to the gate, and Vijay began to collect his belongings from the storage area above his seat. It felt good to stand after being seated for so long. Once his belongings were collected, he made his way through the jet bridge into the terminal and down to the luggage carousel. He was relieved when he saw his familiar green suitcase drop onto the revolving black belt. He lifted it onto its wheels and let it roll behind him as he headed to the parking garage where he'd left his car.

As his eyes idly scanned the terminal, they met those of a man standing beside a sign with a newspaper under his arm. His black leather jacket had a large red Russian flag embroidered onto the front. Vijay didn't notice any luggage beside the man, not even a carry-on bag. He must be picking someone up, Vijay thought. But there aren't many people on this flight. Maybe he's at the wrong terminal.

After five minutes of navigating around the airport, he finally arrived at his car. He put his bags in the trunk, got in and began the final leg of his journey home.

The traffic was light from the airport to Cambridge. Soon he was focused on finding a parking spot on the crowded city streets. Even with his coveted resident parking permit, finding a desirable parking spot at this late hour was far from guaranteed. Finally Vijay found a spot only two blocks away. He navigated his car into the spot, not noticing the car pulling over behind him.

Vijay proceeded to the trunk for his luggage and began rolling it to the town house. As strode home, he noticed that he was alone on the icy street. The frigid winter temperature made him wish he'd brought a winter hat and gloves along. It was a dry cold. There wasn't a drop of precipitation in the air. He walked carefully down the sidewalk picking out and avoiding the patches of black ice. As he traversed the slippery landscape, he spotted a black Mercedes parked on the street with exhaust coming from its tailpipe. Two men were sitting in it. He briefly wondered what the two were doing sitting in their car at this hour.

As he walked by, the passenger got out. The man quickly closed on Vijay. Vijay recognized the black leather jacket with the bright red Russian flag embroidered on the front of it, but it was too late. Boris seized him, knocked his luggage out of his hands, and forced his arms behind his back.

"What do you want?" Vijay cried as he struggled with Boris.

As Vijay resisted, he saw the trunk of the car pop open, and Yuiry got out of his side of the car. Vijay looked for help, but the street was dark and void.

"No, please take whatever you wa—" Vijay began before having his mouth covered. Yuriy came over to help Boris and they manhandled Vijay back to the car. It suddenly occurred to him that they weren't just trying to rob him, they were going to put him into the trunk of their car. Ripping free one arm, Vijay used his elbow to hit Boris squarely on the jaw. With the impact, Boris loosened his grip on Vijay just enough for him to break free.

"Hey, stop!" Yuriy gave chase. As Yuriy closed in, Vijay saw the streetlights above him shimmer off of Yuriy's bald head. Vijay grabbed one of the bags at his feet and hurled it at him. Although not hurting him, it slowed him enough for Vijay to get past him. Without a word, Yuriy got back into the car, and Boris gave chase on foot.

A neon sign in the distance glistened like an oasis in the desert. There would surely be someone in the twenty-four hour convenience store below it. But it was blocks away. A bone-numbing wind whipped his face as he dashed toward the shop.

Yuriy turned the car around in the middle of the road. There was no traffic and the car caught up with Vijay in seconds, at nearly the same time as Boris.

"So you want to do this the hard way," Boris said, panting.

As Boris pulled him down by his coat, Vijay collapsed to the ground. His palms hit the cold pavement, followed by his chin.

The fall cut his lip, and he saw his blood splattered on the sidewalk below him. He tried to gain his footing, but Boris tripped him again. Now on his back he found himself staring up at Boris' large silhouette. He saw his arm cock back. He tried to block the blows, but he didn't have a chance. One after another, Boris pummeled Vijay's face. Suddenly out of the corner of his eye, Vijay saw headlights from a car, a chance for someone to help him.

"Please! Help me!" he shouted.

His stomach sank when he realized the car was the black Mercedes. Then he felt the blows raining down on him subside.

"Please take my wallet! Take my bags, take whatever you want!" Vijay pleaded.

Without warning, he felt himself being lifted off the ground. With both arms secured by the men, Vijay kicked Yuriy in the shin. As he gasped in pain, Vijay tried to free his arm, but couldn't. This was what they wanted. Not my money or my jewelry, he thought, they want me.

"Please…" Vijay began but he could say no more as Yuriy covered his mouth with duct tape. As Yuriy carried him toward the car, the pestilent aroma of exhaust from the tailpipe filled Vijay's nostrils. The trunk popped open, and Yuriy dropped him inside.

"We need to get the laptop," Boris said. "It's back there."

Yuriy slammed the car into reverse, screeching down the block backward. He grabbed Vijay's laptop and luggage. Then they sped off toward the nearest highway.

CHAPTER 6

The plastic bag fell to the floor and with it the receipt for the five hundred dollar purchase. With the shoe box in hand, Will sat down on the bed in his bedroom and removed the lid. He loved the smell of a new pair of shoes. He took both of the dress shoes out of their individual bags and inspected them for any blemishes. Satisfied with the condition, he proceeded to make sure that the shoes fit like the ones that he'd tried on in the store. Yes, these were going to work out perfectly.

He went over to the closet on his side of the bedroom and placed the shoes onto the shelf next to his eight other pair of designer dress shoes. For each formal suit Will owned, he owned a pair of dress shoes. But not just any brand of dress shoes. Will settled for nothing but the finest footwear money could buy. Some were made in Spain, like his Mezlan cap toe oxfords, others from France like his Mephisto lace-up dress shoes. But his favorite were his Bruno Magli slip-on moc toe loafers, made from fine Italian leather. Sarah would joke about the closet full of shoes on his side of the room, how he had more shoes than she did. But that was not a worry at all. No sir. For he had the perfect shoe no matter what the need may be.

Will wandered downstairs afterward. "Wow, look at you!" he said as he went into the kitchen and saw his wife. Sarah

Woltzberg had on fashionably tight jeans with a tight fitting pink tank top with the logo of a high-end fashion designer on it. Gone was her light brown shoulder length hair, replaced with an above-the-shoulder cut accented with blond highlights.

"Don't you love it!" Sarah said as she performed a little pirouette so her husband could see all angles of her.

"You look like you're ten years younger with those clothes and that hair."

Will approached and put his hands on her hips. He leaned in so that their lips could touch, but at the last moment she jerked her head away, and slid out of his grasp.

"C'mon on, that's old news. Do you notice anything else?" Sarah asked. Will looked his wife up and down. He had no idea what he was supposed to be noticing, but knew from experience he'd better find something and do it quickly.

"The jeans?"

"Try up here," Sarah said, pointing to her face.

After inspection of the familiar sight Will shook his head.

"My wrinkles. They're gone!" Sarah exclaimed. "I got Botox injections!"

Once she'd told Will, he suddenly saw the changes. They were most prominent around her eyes, where wrinkles were beginning to creep, especially when she smiled.

"I don't know how I didn't notice. I definitely see the difference now that you mention it!"

"Well, surprise!"

It was one in a series of surprises Sarah had given him in recent months. First came the new wardrobe with a young look, then she dyed her hair blond, and now Botox. But the changes weren't just in her appearance. Her behavior had undergone a change as well. Ever since Will had started SimSci, Sarah had mentioned the possibility someday of selling the company for millions and retiring to an exotic tropical location. But as more attention focused on the company, Sarah's questions about selling it had increased. She began to spend money as if a sale was inevitable. Before Christmas two purchases of jewelry appeared on his credit card that exceeded three thousand dollars. Even more troubling were the items she was clearly mulling over. Last month Will had gone into her purse looking for his car keys. Instead he found two brochures, one for a condo complex in the Cayman Islands and the other from NetJets explaining the benefit of buying shares in a private plane. His wife had changed from being a dedicated biologist to an impulsive shopaholic.

But shopping wasn't the only impulsive change in her behavior. She had become quick to fly off of the handle at Will over any little thing. Their wall to wall carpeting had been replaced with eggshells. No matter what room Will was in, he was walking on them.

"Nate called today," Sarah said, referring to the couple's oldest son.

"What's new at Georgetown? Has he found a job for after graduation yet?"

"Georgetown is good, but no job, not yet. But I'm sure he'll find one."

Nate Woltzberg's college graduation was just three short months away and he hadn't found a job yet. He'd chosen to follow in the footsteps of his parents and major in biology. Will was thrilled with his decision.

"You seem awful confident."

"I think he'll be just fine."

Based on the look on Sarah's face, Will thought that she knew something that he didn't about their oldest son. He decided not to press the issue.

"What about Logan, what's he up to? Is he upstairs in his room?" Will asked.

"No, he's supposed to be home in time for dinner. He'd better be home in time for dinner," Sarah said as she began cutting lettuce and dumping it into a large ceramic salad bowl. "I got a phone call from Mrs. Cannon yesterday," she went on. "She wanted to know where Logan's progress report was. It was supposed to be returned to her at the beginning of the week."

Logan wasn't getting a progress report because he was doing well in school. They were sent home to children's parents when the opposite was true.

Will didn't know what to do about Logan. He had been a good kid up until the past few years. He looked up to his older brother Nate, and tried to do things just like his big brother did. Since Nate had gone off to college, though, Logan's behavior had gone straight downhill.

"Do you think everything is all right?"

"I'm sure everything is fine, but this isn't going to continue. I'm going to talk to him when he gets home."

"A lot of good that's done so far," Sarah shot back.

"Well, what do you propose I do?"

"Don't you think it's a little late to ask that question?"

Will shrugged his shoulders.

"You know what I'm talking about. We should've sent him to St. Paul's. I told you once Nate moved out that Logan would need to fill a void. You just ignored me. Told me money is tight. Well, it wouldn't have been so tight if you just stopped thinking you're going to win the Nobel Peace prize."

Now Will knew where Sarah was headed. "Do you think it would've made a difference?"

"We'll never know, will we? Just like I'll never know what it's like to not have to work and retire before I'm old and gray."

"You'll never be old and gray if you keep dying your hair blond," Will commented dryly.

Sarah responded by turning her back and concentrating on her chopping. Will turned his attention to the small television on the granite countertop as sports highlights were shown. The silence was broken by the ringing of the kitchen phone. A thick Indian accent greeted Will from the other end of the line.

"Will, I'm so happy that I reach you. It's Abha, Vijay's wife. I'm very sorry to be calling you at home, but I'm very concerned about Vijay. I have not heard from him, and he was supposed to be home last night. Have you spoken to him?"

"Uhh, no, I haven't heard from him," Will said. "I assumed there'd been a delay in his travel plans, and he hadn't gotten in until late last night."

"I called the airport. They said his flight had arrived on time, and confirmed that he was on it," Abha replied, strain entering her voice.

Will flipped the television off. It wasn't like Vijay to simply not come home. Suddenly he thought about what had happened to Scott and shivered.

"Will, are you there?"

"Yes, look, Abha, I'm sure everything's fine. But just to be certain, I have a friend with the Cambridge Police. I'll give him a call just to be safe."

"Oh, my God," Abha said quietly.

"Let's not jump to any conclusions. I just want to call him as a precaution. I'll let you know after I hear from him."

Will ended his call with Abha and quickly dialed Charles' number. *Something very strange is happening,* Will thought as he waited for Charles to answer. *And it's happening to my best employees.*

CHAPTER 7

From his seat at the bar, Will watched the door to Fourth and One. The tavern was he and James' favorite place to go when they needed to get away. It was well lit, with huge flat-screen televisions mounted on every wall. Sports memorabilia crowded every other space. For Will with all the nostalgia came memories of his parents and of simpler times when he and James were young.

The door to the bar opened, and Charles Madre walked in. He was a heavy-set man with an oversized stomach. He hadn't always been in such poor shape, but the stress of his job and a poor diet caused by the untraditional hours that a homicide detective worked slowly caused his waistline to expand. His face was full, his chin nonexistent. He enjoyed a full head of black hair that was always disheveled, no matter the time of day.

"You dragged me out here, so I hope the bartender already has your credit card for the tab," Charles said as he propped himself upon the barstool next to Will.

"Already handled," Will replied with a wide smile on his face as Charles ordered a beer.

"You're on top of your game. I hope your old lady appreciates you."

"She does, although lately she's been a handful. I swear she's going through some kind of mid-life crisis."

"Aren't we all…" Charles said as the bartender brought his beer to him.

"So what's new? I feel like I haven't seen you in a while."

"C'mon, Will, I've known you too long for that shit to work with me."

Will cracked a smile at his old friend. Corporate small-talk wasn't needed around his old friend.

"Okay, fine, I'll cut the bullshit. I want to know what happened the night Scott Bredahl died. I want you to get on the case. Then you can take me to the crime scene."

"Wow, is that all? Piece of cake," Charles said sarcastically. "Seriously, I can't do that," Charles replied.

"Why not?"

"One, from what I've heard, the case is a mess. A double homicide involving from what you are telling me was a pretty straight-up guy. Worse, I ran into the lead on the case in the hall the other day, and he said the crime scene is utterly clean, no evidence."

"What about the case file, crime scene photos—" Charles waved his hand for Will to stop. "There's nothing. He mentioned that the job looked professional."

Will sat back in his chair, stunned. This was confirming his deepest fears.

"There's something else I have to ask you."

"I'm used to giving the interrogations, not getting interrogated. What now?"

"Have any homicide victims in the past twenty-four hours been a middle-aged man of Indian descent? Last night the wife of one of key employees called me to tell me he hadn't come home from a business trip."

Charles took a healthy sip of his beer. "That's hardly a missing persons case. People miss their flights all the time."

"She called the airline to make sure he was on his flight. He collected his baggage.

"I can double-check tomorrow when I get in, but off of the top of my head, no victim matches that description."

"I would really appreciate it," Will said as he grabbed his beer and hoisted it.

"Here's to one friend doing another a favor."

"Here's to one friend not promising the other anything just yet."

The two clinked their bottles together as Will nodded his head.

"Just find out if Vijay Kalam was murdered."

CHAPTER 8

Boris Kozlov steered his Mercedes onto the off-ramp to Pawtucket. The last twenty-four hours had been ice-cold, with temperatures falling to the single digits. Did he remember to turn on the heat in the warehouse? He hoped that he had. Otherwise, he was going to have a big problem on his hands when he arrived. He looked over at his passenger, who was trying to fish a packet of ketchup out from in between the car seat and the center console. Boris took a hand off the steering wheel and whacked his partner on the side of his head.

"You get that ketchup on this car, and it won't be the only dark red stain on its interior."

The two had stopped at a fast food restaurant to get some food for the person that they were going to see, and Yuriy had decided he also wanted a meal for the ride.

"And watch the french fries. Don't drop those either."

Soon they reached the dilapidated warehouse. Boris looked around the perimeter for anything suspicious. The sun had long since set, and only two spotlights attached to the building illuminated the parking lot. It hadn't been plowed since the early morning snow, and Boris didn't see any tire tracks in the white powdery coating. Comfortable no one was around, he parked his car next to the stairs. He examined the lock on the loading dock shutter as well as the door next to it. Both appeared untouched. He and Yuriy climbed the outside cement stairs, and Boris unlocked the door and searched for the light switch next to it. He could feel the warmth inside, which confirmed that he had in fact turned on the heat.

The warehouse stood empty, with the exception of three chairs and a small table in the middle. From where Boris was standing they seemed tiny, almost like doll furniture in the vast cavernous space. Tied to one of the chairs sat Vijay Kalam.

As Boris came closer, the smell of urine filled his nostrils, and his face wrinkled in disgust. He looked at Vijay and could see the fear in his eyes. In addition to being tied up, Vijay's mouth was duct taped closed. It had remained so since his abduction.

Boris and Yuriy sat in the two seats facing their victim.

"I thought we would give you an opportunity to think. You've had time to think about your family, and think about our request," Boris said. "You must be very hungry. Yuriy, don't we have something for Vijay to eat?"

Yuriy removed the tape from Vijay's mouth and opened up the bag containing a hamburger.

"I do not want that. I will not eat that," Vijay said as he exercised his jaw, now free of the restrictive tape.

Hindus' regarded cows as sacred animals. They didn't kill cows or eat their meat. Yet he'd been in the warehouse all day, tied to the same chair and he hadn't eaten anything since his flight home.

"This guy doesn't want the burger," Yuriy said.

"Fine, let him starve. Is that what you want to do? Starve to death in this warehouse?" Boris asked.

Vijay didn't respond. Boris had carried a black bag into the warehouse with him. He opened it and took out the laptop that Vijay had with him the night that they had abducted him. He put it onto the table and turned it on. When the computer's screen prompted him for a login id and password, he turned the computer to face Vijay.

"Now, we'll try this again. Cooperate this time, and we can let you go. You will see your family again. No one will ever know what you have shared. You will be free. For your sake, let's make this easy on everyone. Please tell me what your login and password is."

Vijay closed his eyes and began to chant quietly in Hindu. "*Om trayambakam yajaamahe sugandhim pushtivardhanam Urvaarukamiva bandhanaan mrityor muksheeya maamritaat.*"

Enraged by the jabbering, Boris rose from his seat and swung his open hand at Vijay, hitting his face with the back of it. "Give us the password!" he shouted.

Vijay opened his eyes for a moment, reeling from the impact of Boris' hand, but then reverted back to his prayer. Boris looked at Yuriy and nodded. Yuriy went out to the car, got another black bag and came back into the warehouse. He pulled a straight razor out of the bag and began to take off Vijay's shoes.

"Give us the password." Boris said.

Vijay did not respond. With his shoes removed, Yuriy then took off his socks. He looked up at Boris, who nodded again. With Boris' approval Yuriy took the straight razor and began to cut the skin on Vijay's right foot. The cut was not deep, just enough to slide the razor under the skin. Yuriy proceeded to slice the layer of skin off nearly half of the bottom of Vijay's foot. Vijay grunted in pain between words of prayer as blood poured onto the floor of the warehouse. Even Boris shivered as he watched. Once the skin flapped down, Yuriy took the flap and ripped it away from where it was still attached. As the skin tore away, Vijay couldn't hold in the agony. He let out a screech that did not sound like it could come from a human being.

"Give us the password," Boris said.

Vijay ignored the demand again.

"Do the other one."

Upon hearing the command, Yuriy repeated the task on Vijay's left foot. As the pain shot up from his feet, Vijay's eyes closed and tears rolled down his cheeks. Beads of sweat began to accumulate on his brow. With a slight frown, Yuriy reached into the bag and removed a large basin and two bottles of cheap vodka. He put the basin on the floor and began filling it with alcohol. Vijay watched Yuriy fill the basin in front of him, as his eyes widened in dread. He knew what was coming. He shook his head and pleaded with Boris.

"No, please!" he shouted.

Yuriy got up and began wiping the blood from his hands with napkins in the fast food bag.

"Then make this easy on all of us and just give us the password," Boris said, trying to take a softer approach.

"I can't."

"Fine, we will give you some time to think about your answer. A little vodka may help the situation," Boris said and turned to leave the warehouse. "We will be back tomorrow."

Yuriy knew what this meant. He lifted Vijay's feet and forced them into the basin of vodka. Blood mixed with the alcohol in the basin, and Vijay screamed as the alcohol seared the bottom of his feet.

Yuriy gathered everything that he'd brought into the warehouse and headed toward the exit. Just before he left, he turned back toward Vijay and muttered two simple words:

"Lights out."

CHAPTER 9

James sat inside La Comida Grande sipping a soda and grinding his teeth. The Mexican restaurant was long and narrow. Large sombreros and colorful ponchos lined the faded orange walls. Behind the bar, the bartender watched sports highlights on a huge flat screen. Only one couple was dining in the restaurant, but given that it was mid-morning, James didn't expect many people to be gorging on tacos and guzzling margaritas. Still, the lack of other people around made James nervous. He'd asked for a seat next to the exit. He wanted to be able to leave in a hurry if the need arose.

It was fitting to have to meet about a project that had been nicknamed the Scorpion in a Mexican restaurant, he thought bitterly. He suddenly remembered that he hadn't called his brother to let him know that he wouldn't be in the office that morning. He took out his cell phone and punched the speed-dial.

"Will Woltzberg."

"Hey, it's James," he began. "I meant to let you know that I need to get the SUV fixed. It's making a strange noise. I'll be in around noon. I can't think of anything too pressing going on this morning, but I wanted to call and let you know."

"I need you to get here as soon as you can," Will said sharply. "We have a major problem on our hands."

"What's happened?"

"It's Vijay, his wife called me. He's gone missing."

"What do you mean?" James asked.

"He disappeared somewhere between Logan and his house on his way home from Hyderabad. The airline verified he was on the flight to Boston, but he never made it home."

This was disturbing news, James thought, "Have you called Charles? Do the police know?"

"When I asked him last night if any recent homicide victims matched Vijay's description, he said there hadn't been."

"Did his wife have any clue where he could've gone?"

"She called me in tears asking me that question."

"It's not like Vijay to just take off and not tell anyone. Christ, he doesn't even go to lunch without letting me know. So the cops are looking for him?"

"His wife has gone down and filed a missing person report," Will continued in a grave tone. "I know it's hard to think about work when something like this happens, but we need to figure out how we continue development of ViroPredict without him."

Just then, a man came into the restaurant. He was alone, well dressed and appeared to be of Middle Eastern descent. James knew this was Nadir without a formal introduction.

"As soon as I get back to the office, we can discuss it," James said, hurrying up. "The car guy is waving me over, I have to go. I'll catch up with you later."

Nadir was wearing a camel-colored suit with a dark handkerchief in the breast pocket. It was clear that the man had money. He spotted James and made his way over to him. He sat down without an introduction.

"You decided to come. That was a wise decision." Nadir flashed a broad smile that stretched from ear to ear. "I'll bet you thought that this matter was buried in the past. A skeleton in a closet with a key that had been lost and long forgotten."

James didn't like his smarmy ways. "What is it that you want from me?"

"The information that I have can destroy your organization. It can destroy your relationship with your brother. It can quite possibly ruin your marriage. Worse, it could put you in jail for a long time." Nadir leaned on the table toward him. "Of course, there are things worse than jail, things so horrible you don't want to hear."

James felt himself shiver as Nadir spoke. "You can't prove that I had any involvement in what you are calling 'Scorpion.'"

Nadir let out a soft, condescending chuckle. "We are both very smart men, James. Let's show one another the mutual respect that we deserve, okay? I won't waste your time and you don't waste mine."

Nadir reached into his pocket and revealed a handful of papers. He handed them to James, who looked them over. His pulse quickened, and he fidgeted nervously in his chair when he realized Nadir had him dead to rights.

"If you weren't involved in the Scorpion, then someone else at your company was. Correct me if I'm wrong, but back around the date on that bank statement and those wire transfers, weren't you keeping the financial records for the company? And at that time, weren't there only seven employees including you and your brother?"

"Can I start you off with a beverage?" A young, dark-skinned waitress came over to the table and offered Nadir a drink.

"Nothing for me just yet, thanks."

Nadir patiently waited for the waitress to be out of earshot before continuing. "Further, isn't it your signature on this wire transfer sending these payments to Ferris Consulting? I recall your friend Jon Ferris as barely graduating high school, yet he was employed as an independent consultant by your firm?"

James' face began to turn red.

"And the eight transactions that made up the 'eight legs of the Scorpion,' well, any half assed investigation will show that those companies were completely fabricated, as were the invoices designed to allow the money to come into your organization in a seemingly legitimate transaction."

"What the *fuck* do you want from me?" James hissed.

"Hold on, I just want to make sure we are both on the same page." Nadir was enjoying watching James squirm. He ran his fingers up and down the edge of the menu resting on the table as all the sordid details came flooding back to him in vivid, crisp, clarity.

"It was a long time ago, and things weren't as sophisticated back then as they are now. But the old fashioned paper trail hasn't changed much. Good old Jon Ferris. Bet you wish you never helped out your good friend now."

Nadir was right. James should've let Jon find another way to launder the money those many years ago. Of course, at the time the deal made perfect sense for everyone. SimSci had been suffering from a lack of revenue. Having already maxed out their credit lines, the company was in dire need of cash to float the business. The immediate influx of dirty money did exactly that in the short term, and the portion that James was allowed to ultimately retain for his part in the scheme helped the business longer term. The transactions helped SimSci at a time when it needed the money most. Even so, it was the first and last time James had ever involved himself in anything like that.

Nadir removed a second set of papers from his suit jacket pocket. They were filled with tiny print that some people would need a magnifying glass to read.

"This is the final piece of evidence needed to put you away for a long time and destroy the business enterprise that you and your brother have worked so long to build. Would you like to look at the list?"

James instantly knew what Nadir was talking about. It was the list of credit cards that Jon Ferris had stolen and then sold. That transaction had generated the large amount of money that was subsequently laundered through SimSci.

"You've made your point," James said, defeated. "Now what do you want from me?"

"If I go to the police with this, you will lose your company and your freedom for some time, and who knows what your family will think of you when you finally do get out of jail? I just want a portion of what you'd lose if I bring this information forward."

"What piece?" James asked.

"I want you to give me control of SimSci, complete ownership."

James was so shocked he couldn't respond. He took a drink of the cola in front of him. If this guy, he thought, hadn't already shown me the evidence that he has, I'd swear this was a joke.

"You realize I only own half of SimSci. What you're asking for is impossible without getting my brother to go along."

"I don't want to get bogged down in the details. I just want all of the stock transferred to an LLC that I will create."

"I can't do that. There's simply no—"

Nadir put his hand up to stop James from continuing. "Please, don't make any hard decisions here and now. Take some time to think about my offer carefully. I will be in touch within forty-eight hours to hear your decision."

With those words Nadir got up and left the restaurant, leaving James in a state of shock.

* * *

Will was coming back from a meeting when he saw James' office door open. He went over to the doorway and popped his head in.

"Is the SUV fixed?"

"What? Oh yes, my SUV. Yes, it's all set."

"That's good to hear. Do you have a minute?"

"Sure," James replied motioning toward the two empty chairs next to his desk.

The office was nearly as big as Will's but only had one wall of windows compared to Will's two. As there wasn't a cloud in the sky, the sun shone in so brightly that the fluorescent lights weren't needed.

"Have you thought about how we are going to manage development of ViroPredict in Vijay's absence?" Will asked.

James was glad the conversation had gone in this direction. He'd been so unnerved by the meeting with Nadir, he hadn't done a thing since he'd come to the office.

"I was just trying to think about what might have happened."

"I can't believe Scott Bredahl was murdered and now something has happened to Vijay. Do you think it's a coincidence?"

As Will spoke, James noticed that the bank and wire transfers that Nadir had given him were sticking out of the pocket of his jacket, resting on the chair across from his desk. His heart began to pound. If his brother saw them, he'd surely wonder why he was carrying bank statements from five years ago. Worse, if he saw the wire transfers, he'd want to know why so much money had been wired out of his company to Jon Ferris.

"I don't know," James said anxiously.

"If this has something to do with this company, I'm going to find out just who the fuck is doing this," Will said emphatically. Agitated, he walked from the doorway over to the seat across from James' desk. He pushed James' jacket aside and sat down. As he did, the papers slipped out farther. James tried not to stare at them as they hung almost entirely out of his jacket. If they were to slip to the floor, they'd fall right at Will's feet.

"Has Charles spoken to Vijay's wife?" James asked, trying to use shear willpower to get the papers back into his jacket pocket.

"Charles hasn't directly, because he's in homicide," Will paused as he adjusted his tie. "Until Vijay returns, I'm afraid much of his work will end up in your lap."

"I figured, but I realize our options are limited." James said vaguely, his attention focused on the telltale papers.

Will recognized his brother's indifference. "Well I can see you're distracted. We have just lost the lead developer for our flagship product and you don't care?" He got up from the chair, frustration written all over his face.

As he did the bank statements fell from James' jacket pocket. James watched helplessly as they fell to the floor in plain view. But Will had already made his way to the office door. As he opened it, Colleen's phone rang just outside. Will took one step outside the office, then turned back to his brother.

"Just what the hell is going on here?"

James thought he was referring to the papers. "What do you mean?"

"I mean with Scott and now Vijay. Do you think someone is targeting our employees?"

"I think you're watching too much television."

51

"Maybe so," Will acknowledged, "but my gut is telling me something is not right. Something is not right at all."

Without waiting for a response, Will marched off. Once he was out of sight, all of James' muscles relaxed and he sat back in his chair, relieved his brother was gone. With no one watching, James rose and collected the papers lying on the floor. He went over to the small shredder beside his desk and destroyed them.

"I wish I could take this whole mess and eradicate it," James said softly. "How am I ever going to get out of this?"

CHAPTER 10

On the fourth floor of the Sander Pharmaceuticals corporate headquarters in downtown Boston, Monica was participating in a video conference with members of the board of directors, who had flown in from all parts of the country. At the head of the table sat Alan Burke, the chairman of the board. His sharp eyes were focused on Nancy O' Keefe as she spoke. He was listening attentively, ready to pounce on any ambiguities in Nancy's remarks.

Nancy had just finished giving an update concerning acquisition negotiations with a company Sander was interested in buying. That was the last item on the agenda for the meeting and Alan thanked everyone for their time. As the participants began gathering their belongings, Alan approached Monica before she left the room.

"Monica, could you hang around for a few minutes? I want to catch up with you regarding your trip."

"Yes, no problem," she responded.

Alan waited for the others to leave the conference room before speaking. Monica rose from her seat at the far end of the table and sat in one next to Alan.

"So what time is your meeting with SimSci?" he asked. The two had exchanged emails earlier in the day discussing her visit to the small company.

"I'm arriving there at one-thirty for lunch with the CFO. He's an old friend from Baxter and Baxter."

He raised his eyebrows, pleasantly surprised by Monica's news. "Really? Well, that's wonderful. I hope there were no bridges burnt at Baxter with this guy."

"Alan, you know me better than that."

Alan conceded the point with a smile.

"After lunch I meet with him and the CEO Will Woltzberg to discuss SimSci's strategic alternatives."

"Please call me later tonight to let me know how the meeting with Will went. I've seen some of the projections from finance." He lifted a light file containing the numbers. "They're quite compelling. Having the ability to simulate virus' mutation patterns months before they occur would allow us plenty of time to produce the vaccines for them. We would be coming to market with the vaccine while our competitors are just beginning to make it. I don't think that I have to tell you how good this would be for Sander. We should be ready to pay whatever it takes to buy this company and its software. Give them whatever they want. We should do whatever it takes to get these capabilities." Alan paused, drilling her with a look that made his employees cower. "I think that I have made myself clear."

"Crystal clear. Look, I have to run or I'm going to be late for my meeting. I'll keep you posted on my progress." She said as she looked at her watch. The two exchanged farewells, and Monica headed to her office to gather what she needed.

The chauffeured ride into Cambridge took twenty-five minutes due to the traffic, and Monica was a few minutes late for her lunch with Nick. The SimSci offices were located in a four-story building sheathed with dark windows. She announced at the receptionist's desk that she had come to see Nick.

As she waited in the reception area, she wondered how he had changed since she last saw him some ten years ago. She doubted the years had been kind to him. She suspected he hadn't cleaned up his alcohol and drug abuse, and that the abuse would show. She was guessing he would have put on thirty pounds from years of consuming beer and fast food. When he entered the foyer, she realized that she was only half right.   "Monica Rowe, it's so good to see you," he said, extending his hand.

She tried not to make it obvious that she was looking him up and down. But she was sure that he was doing the same to her. She'd been wrong about his weight. He'd actually slimmed down since she'd seen him last. She guessed that he stood at about six feet tall, and weighed around one hundred sixty pounds. That would make him pounds lighter than the last time they'd seen one another. She wondered if he'd traded the food and alcohol for a harder, more potent substance. As his weight left, so did his hair. He was completely bald on top of his head. His face also showed his age, and his eyes were sunken in with dark circles under them.

"It's been a long time Nick. It's good to see you."

"It's good to see you too. You look great," he replied.

"So do you." If this was the biggest lie that she told all day, she would have no trouble sleeping tonight. The two exchanged more small talk until she decided to get down to the reason that she was there.

"So where are we going for lunch?"

"I thought we could go to a little sandwich shop right across the street."

Monica extended her arm. "Lead the way."

The two headed out into the cold and once inside they found a table.

"Do you still keep in touch with anyone else from Baxter?" Nick asked.

"Yes, we are actually partners with Baxter on a number of potential drug candidates in various stages of research. Most are only in phase one, but who knows, they may turn out to be blockbuster drugs."

"I see. Well, that's good," he said crisply. "I hope everyone there is doing well. I don't know if anyone ever said anything, but I didn't leave there on the best of terms. Not that I care. I've moved on and have never looked back."

A waitress came over to take their orders. Monica ordered a salad, and Nick a cheeseburger sub with onions, banana peppers, and mayonnaise. If this was how Nick ate on a regular basis, she wondered what he was doing to keep the weight off. The two sat in silence for a moment.

"You really do look good," Nick said as he smiled warmly at her.

This wasn't the direction Monica wanted the discussion to go. She looked down at his hand and saw he wasn't wearing a wedding ring. With most men this would indicate that they were not married, but she knew Nick well enough to not assume anything.

"Oh stop, I've gained a few pounds since you last saw me. And for that matter a few wrinkles too."

"There's no need for modesty. You look great."

There was a pregnant pause as Monica read a message on her Blackberry. "So how is Will to work for?"

"We have our ups and downs. I mean, the man is brilliant. He's got a steel-trap mind, and his thinking is far ahead of everyone else. People at the company really respect him."

"So what do you mean 'you have your ups and downs?"

"I do a lot for this company as CFO," he said with a frown. "I've navigated it through countless financial storms. I feel like he should be doing more for me."

That's the Nick I thought I knew, Monica thought. I've been out with him for five minutes and he's already trashing his boss. He's not going to be someone I can rely on.

"You always were good at what you did," Monica said, flashing her pearly whites.

As they ate, their discussion turned to their old friends at Baxter and how their own careers had progressed since working for the same boss. For each reference Nick made to a possible second meeting, Monica responded with a swift but subtle rejection.

"So what is this meeting with Will about?" Nick asked as the two walked back to SimSci.

"It's pretty much what we discussed a few days ago. After hearing Will's presentation last week in Chicago, I thought it would be good if we could get together and discuss how our two companies could work together. A partnership between us could be mutually beneficial, in my opinion."

As Nick opened the door to SimSci, Monica's attention shifted from Nick to the man standing in SimSci's reception area. Tanner Fitzgerald did a double take, then smiled and turned toward Monica a bit gingerly. He doesn't know if I'm going to remember him, she thought.

"Tanner, how are you?" Monica asked, extending her hand.

"I'm well, thanks. And you? It's been a few years."

"I'm doing very well. Sander keeps me very busy," she said. "But it's easy when you love what you do. I've heard some very exciting things about what's happening here. I'm sure you're playing an important role in all of it."

"Well, I do what I can," Tanner said modestly.

"So how do you two know one another?" Nick asked, not pleased to be sharing the limelight.

"Tanner was one of Sander's best virologists before he left to join your team at SimSci," Monica replied. "No hard feelings, of course."

The group spoke for a few moments while waiting for Will. Finally the doors behind the receptionist area opened, and Will appeared.

"Sorry, a client call ran over. I'm sure you know how those can go." Just as their hands shook, their eyes met for just a moment, before Monica's quickly shifted away. A sudden flare of anger filled her as she recalled the outcome of their encounter in Chicago.

"This way," Will said betraying no emotions himself.

Will guided them to a meeting room, and the three of them chose one of the assortment of dark blue leather chairs. Will took a seat at the head of the table.

"So Monica, you wanted to meet so that we could talk about how SimSci and Sander could potentially leverage ViroPredict in a manner that would be mutually beneficial. I know we started that discussion in Chicago, but I thought it made sense to continue the dialogue in a more formal setting."

Monica could feel her face turning red as she was flooded with a mix of embarrassment and anger. She was hoping it didn't show.

"Yes, we are very interested in ViroPredict. But we are interested in joining forces in a meaningful way. We think that there's significant value to be created if we combined companies. I'd actually like to share our thoughts on the synergies we'd—"

Will held up his hand to interrupt her. "Whoa, whoa, we are getting way ahead of ourselves. Nick mentioned you might want to talk about buying us out. SimSci isn't for sale. We've been an independent company since our inception, and we're not about to change that now."

She'd expected the objection. "I understand you'd want to maintain control of the company. That makes perfect sense. What we would do is maintain SimSci as a standalone subsidiary and allow you to retain your status as president and CEO."

"No, we aren't on the same page, Monica," Will said confidently. "It's not about me maintaining my title. SimSci isn't for sale, regardless of what my title is after the deal is consummated."

"I understand your first instinct is to reject my offer."

As soon as the words were out of her mouth she felt her face burning up again. I should have just recorded myself at the bar and just pressed play.

"But you have to think about the financial resources I can offer you. Not only in terms of R&D dollars that will go toward improving the product, but also the dollars that will go to you personally through the purchase price. The money would be life-changing. You and your family would be able to do everything you've always wanted to do. You'd have everything you've always wanted."

Will shook his head. "This isn't about the money."

Monica shifted in her chair. This was not going to plan. Nancy had said these guys wouldn't sell SimSci, and she was spot on. But I'm not going to just roll over, she thought. Maybe she could skin this cat in a different way.

"I understand your desire to remain an independent company. What if we were to make you an offer for the rights to ViroPredict? We could—"

"You want to buy our best in class, flagship product? The one that generates eighty-five percent of our sales?" Will asked.

Monica could see that this approach was dead in the water too. She looked over at Nick, who hadn't said a word during the entire discussion.

"Well, I think you know what Sander's position is. It sounds like the timing just isn't right at the present time."

Will tried to be conciliatory. "I thought we were going to be meeting today to discuss new fields that ViroPredict could be used in. Had I known this was the direction you were headed, well…"

"No need to apologize, I understand completely." Monica said as she rose from her seat, a move that prompted the men to do so as well.

"I guess this is going to be a quick meeting," Nick said.

Both Monica and Will flashed disapproving looks at him. The three headed for the conference room door and then back toward the foyer. As she reached the door, she extended her hand to Nick and Will.

"Think about my offer, and if you reconsider, you know how to reach me," she said and turned to leave.

Will had turned her down twice in as many weeks. No one does that to Monica Rowe, she thought as she walked to the waiting town car. She tightened her scarf and her pace quickened as the frigid wind whipped around the parking lot. But if Will wasn't going to let her get her hands on the software, how could she get it? Although Nick would be willing to sell his own mother for the right price, he wasn't reliable or trustworthy.

The town car stopped at a red light outside a rehab clinic. On all four corners of the intersection she could see people holding signs asking passing commuters for their spare change. Suddenly she had an idea. What about Tanner? He was very loyal during his time at Sander, and he was bright enough to get the job done right without getting caught. But would he play ball? Monica would just have to find out.

CHAPTER 11

The traffic leaving Cambridge at rush hour was especially bad and James shouted in frustration as the Greyhound bus in front of him jammed on his brakes. Will was going to be pissed that I'm so late, oh well, I've got a lot of shit to deal with right now. I better call him. After two rings Will answered.

"Where are you?"

"Stuck in traffic, I should be there in a few."

"Just another day for James Woltzberg…What do I tell you? Set your clock ahead fifteen minutes and you'll be on time for everything," Will said sarcastically.

"A meeting ran late at the office," James explained.

"But you've been late your whole life."

"Which is exactly why you should be used to it by now. Do me a favor and give me ten God damn minutes."

He finally pulled into the darkened parking lot, grabbed his gym bag from his trunk and his ice skates and stick from the back of his car. The sting of the cold February air made it the perfect evening for ice hockey. Johnson's pond was full of middle aged men dressed in winter clothing with hockey sticks and ice skates, warming up for a friendly game. He walked down to the bank of the pond and began to put his ice skates on.

"Look who decided to join us," Charles Madre shouted from the ice.

"Wouldn't miss a chance to skate circles around you."

"Watch it, Woltzberg, or I'll have the unies harass you on your way home," Charles replied, making reference to the uniformed police.

The other men on the ice were all friends of Will and James. They had known some from as far back as high school, but most they'd met in an indoor ice hockey league.

James looked around the pond and was surprised to see that they were the only people on the ice that night. He did notice one other man in the park. He was walking with a slight limp and had a tiny beagle on a leash. The dog couldn't have been more than a few months old. Something about the man struck James as out of place, but he couldn't put his finger on it. Instead he turned his attention to the pond.

As James skated onto the ice one of the men passed him the puck.

"Take a couple quick shots to warm up," he said.

A few broad strides and a crisp wrist shot was all he needed.

"Right in the nine hole!" James said, poking fun at the goalie. "I'm ready when you guys are."

All of the men were in their late thirties and early forties and were all around the same general skill level, so the games were typically pretty competitive regardless of who was on what team. Although there was plenty of trash talking before and after, once the game began the conversation was minimal.

Thirty minutes into the game, James rotated out of the action to take a break. He watched his breath turn to fog as he took a seat on the bank of the pond. Although he would deny keeping track of his statistics, he was pleased that he had recorded an assist on one of the goals. As he rested, he looked over and saw that the man who he'd seen with the puppy nearly half an hour ago was still in the park. Now he was sitting on a black metal bench watching the men play hockey. His dog was curled up snuggling against his leg, trying to shield itself from the cold. It struck him as odd that the man would still be sitting on a park bench thirty minutes later. But there was something else that James found even stranger. It was a cloudy, dark, moonless evening, with the only light being supplied by street lights throughout the park. But despite the darkness, the man was wearing sunglasses.

Suddenly he felt his stomach knot up. Could that man be watching me? he thought. Could Nadir be having me tailed? He thought back to the money-laundering scheme. At the time, Jon Ferris had told him very little concerning details that weren't important to James' role. "The less I know the better," he recalled telling Jon. But now Nadir was trying to blackmail James. He wondered if the man sitting on the bench was doing more than taking his pet out for some fresh air.

"James, you're in."

James slowly got up and joined the game, despite his mind being in another place.

The men played for another forty-five minutes before they decided to call it a night. All of the men sat on the banks of the pond as they cooled down and took off their ice skates. A few of the men discussed going out to grab beers at a local bar when they leave the pond. Despite the idle chatter, James couldn't shake the nervous feeling that he had. He looked back over to see if the man was still sitting on the bench. Sure enough, he was watching James and the other men.

"James, are you joining us?" one of the men asked, referring the post game festivities.

"No, I'm afraid not."

"Will?"

"I'm going to pass as well."

"Two peas in a pod," the man replied as they headed for their cars.

Soon Will, James, and Charles were the only ones left sitting by the pond.

"How's that case file coming?" Will asked.

"I'm trying, believe me, but when you have a double homicide that happened less than a week ago, it's not like they are just lying around. If that thing were to just disappear, there would be questions," Charles replied.

"I need to know what happened that night."

"And believe me, I am trying to help you, but you're going to have to be patient." A hint of frustration found its way into his tone.

"What about the search for Vijay? Has there been any progress there?" James asked, trying to change the topic to calm everyone's nerves.

"I'm afraid there has. After his wife filed the missing-persons forms, his car was found less than a mile from his house. There were no signs of a struggle, nothing substantive for us to work with. I'm good friends with the lead investigator on this one, so information should be pretty easy to come by."

"This isn't good enough," Will said irritably.

"You think you can do it better Magnum PI?" Charles said, his voice rising.

The three men were silent for a few moments as they removed their skates and replaced them with sneakers.

"On a lighter note, now I get to go home to see what Sarah impulsively bought today," Will said.

"I haven't heard you mention any big purchases in a while. Have there been any good ones? Not sure you're going to top the Lexus," James said, referring to the car Sarah bought herself a few months ago.

Will flashed a broad grin. "This one might."

"Oh, boy I can't wait," James said.

"Botox."

"She got Botox injections?" James asked, eyes wide with surprise.

"That's right, no more pesky wrinkles on her forehead or around her eyes."

James chuckled. "What did you say when she told you?"

"She came right up to me and asked if I noticed anything different about her, and I commented on her jeans. I couldn't even notice. It didn't go over well."

"I wonder what's next."

"I don't know, but I sure hope that this midlife crisis thing ends soon. It's gone on long enough for me," Will said as they walked over to his car.

"Well, keep me posted. Sarah's only three years older than Cindy, so I'm due for this behavior soon. I want to know what I'm in for." James put his skates and stick back into his car.

"Why do I always have to deal with these problems first? Will asked.

"Because you're the big brother."

As Will drove off, James exchanged farewells with Charles and got into his own car. Before he left the park, he looked over to where the man was sitting on the bench. He was gone. Could he already be in his car, ready to follow James home?

Suddenly James looked over both shoulders. Maybe he's about to give you some incentive to cooperate with Nadir, James thought.

But his paranoia proved to be unwarranted. James started his car and was about to drive away when he looked back one final time.

The man had left something behind. Tied to the bench was the small dog that the man had been walking. It had been left to freeze to death in the cold winter night.

CHAPTER 12

As the sun set, Omar sat on an Islamic prayer rug inside of a mosque in Cambridge. He was joined by a handful of other Islamic men who had come to the house of worship. All of them were on their knees, their foreheads touched the ground as they performed the centuries-old tradition of prayer at sunset. Despite trying to focus on his prayer, Omar couldn't help but think ahead to the upcoming meeting with the two Russian goons.

He rose to his feet, signifying the end of the prayer. He turned away from Mecca as he rolled up his maroon wool prayer rug.

As he was leaving, one of the men who had joined him in prayer called to him.

"Brother Omar, how are we progressing?"

"Good, brother Ghalib, but I'm not done, and there remains much work to do. I will inform you when the time has come."

"Yes, please do that. The infidels in this country must feel the blade of our sword as we spill their blood in their own streets. When this day comes, then our goal shall be achieved."

Omar nodded in reply and left the mosque. He had a lot of important work to still accomplish. He walked to Central Square and hailed a cab.

"Fifty-one Speridakis Terrace," he said.

Ten minutes later, the cab was turning down a dead end street lined with triple-decker homes the entire length of the street. The cab stopped and Omar saw the number fifty-one in silver decals on the black mailbox affixed to the white vinyl siding of the house. He climbed neglected wooden stairs leading to the porch and rang the bell for the second-floor apartment. As he waited, a mangy tan cat appeared from behind a pair of rubbish barrels. It approached him and he gently kicked it aside. It's back arched, and it quickly scurried away. Moments later he could hear the sounds of footsteps inside. The front door opened and Boris greeted him.

"Come in."

Boris led Omar up the stairs. The two entered the small apartment, and Omar took a seat at the kitchen table. Yuriy heard the two men enter and came into the kitchen to join them. Omar had no desire to engage in small talk. They'd been given a mission to complete.

"How are we progressing with the programmer?"

"He's still not cooperating. We have given him every opportunity to do so. We have also provided him plenty of reason to cooperate. He refuses," Boris replied.

This was the news that Omar was afraid that he would hear. He rose from his seat and walked over to the single window in the kitchen. The house was so close to the one next to it he could see into the neighbor's kitchen. Inside a woman was washing vegetables at the sink while watching a small television on the kitchen counter. An afternoon talk show host's voice floated on the air from the television into the apartment. Omar closed the window.

"I see only one option remaining."

"Yes. If that's what you want us to do, we will do it," Boris replied.

"Time is of the essence. We must proceed with this mission. When do you think you will be able to move forward?"

"I will have it done tomorrow."

"If you have any questions, you know how to contact me. Good luck."

Omar headed for the door. These men were useless. I never should've relied on Europeans to do this.

"You do not appear to be satisfied," Boris said as Omar opened the door leading to the stairwell.

"I want the job done as soon as possible. You do this, then we are all happy."

After Omar left, Yuriy shook his head in disbelief. "This is a lot of work for a simple computer program. Can't we steal another?"

"He must have a buyer. They must have someone who really wants this one. I don't know. But it must be worth a lot of money to someone for us to go through all of this to get it. Fucking Arabs," he gave the refrigerator a firm kick. "Who knows what they're going to do with it?"

CHAPTER 13

The three beeps from the microwave told Nick that his dinner was ready. He got up from his leather recliner and headed into the kitchen for his Chinese leftovers. Once back in the living room he put his plate down on a brown folding table, pushing aside a bottle of vodka as he did so.

His mind kept replaying the meeting with Will and Monica a few days earlier. He'd watched with some fascination as Will rejected a buyout without even hearing the offer. He wondered exactly what SimSci was worth. He'd speculated in the past that it was worth around fifty million dollars, but with the release of ViroPredict, the value of the company had risen tenfold practically overnight.

Nick felt that over the past ten years he'd been a vital part of the success of SimSci. He'd worked with various banks to obtain financing. He'd also provided other valuable financial guidance to Will and James as they struggled to keep the company solvent while incurring millions of dollars of expenses to develop ViroPredict. As the only two shareholders, if they were to sell the company, they would reap profits equaling hundreds of millions of dollars. When they were negotiating Nick's most recent contract, he'd requested a nominal amount of stock options, but Will wouldn't agree to it. Those two pricks don't appreciate all of the work I do. He took another shot of vodka and finished his last bite of General Tso's chicken before pushing the folding table aside and reclining in his chair.

Nick tried to relax but couldn't. His mind kept circling back to his situation. Finally he couldn't take it anymore. He rose from his seat and went into his bedroom.

Shades were drawn on the two windows in the small room. Nick fumbled with the lamp for a moment before it flooded the room with light. The place was in disarray. Magazines, bills, and Powerpoint presentations were scattered across the floor. A pile of unfolded laundry sat atop the unkempt bed. One of Nick's suits worn earlier that day was strewn on the floor beside the bed. An open box of Q-tips lay on the floor, its contents spilled haphazardly across the other debris on the floor.

Nick made his way to the bureau. He opened the top drawer and took out a small plastic bag of white powder and a small mirror. He went back to his chair in the living room and poured a little bit of powder out of the bag. He reached into his wallet, which had been tossed onto the floor beside his chair, and took out a credit card and dollar bill. After getting the cocaine into a straight line he rolled the dollar bill up, blew his nose into a napkin to clear his nasal passage, and snorted the line. Despite the drug taking effect almost instantly, he still found himself thinking about work. I'm using this crap to help me relax and its Will's fault. I'm tired of being on edge, tired of working hard with nothing to show for it. Those sons of bitches should be paying me what I'm worth. It's time that I start to look out for my own best interests, not Will Woltzberg's.

CHAPTER 14

The sun was ablaze as it slowly set in the western sky. As Paul Francis motored past Hope Town in a twenty-five foot Criss Craft motor boat he thought about what was in store for the rest of the evening. The sun in the Bahamas had been brutal. As he rarely spent this much time out in the daylight and almost never out on the water, he took lots of precautions to keep himself protected. He used the cap on his head to partially protect him and carefully applied the Max Block Sunscreen to all of his exposed skin every thirty minutes. In addition to the hat, a blue and white Nautica shirt, beige cargo shorts and boat shoes rounded out Paul's outfit.

After a lazy yawn, he decided that judging from the speed at which the sun was setting, he'd best get going before the last bit of daylight was lost. As he drove along in the calm water, he approached a large speed boat. Paul was familiar with the type of boat he was looking at. It was forty-seven feet long and cost hundreds of thousands of dollars. From a distance he saw that the two occupants, a voluptuous blonde in a tiny bikini and a middle-aged man. They were sitting down, drinks in hand enjoying each other's company. Paul could see the name of the boat printed in large black letters.

Ares' Getaway

Paul chuckled as he recognized the reference to the Greek god of war in the title. He wondered if the owner on the boat was able to fit his ego on board. As he closed in on the larger boat, the motor in his boat stopped. In the calm water he slowly floated to a stop just a few feet away.

"Everything okay over there?" the man asked, clearly agitated at the interruption. Paul stumbled over to the side of his craft.

"I need your help, please, my chest, please...I think I'm having a heart attack!" he cried as he stood clutching his chest with one hand and using the other to hold himself up against the side of the boat.

The man's lack of a response made his desires clear. If he didn't have to help, he wasn't about to. Yet the woman jumped to her feet to see what was happening.

"Oh my God, Vince, we have to help him."

Vince turned to her and muttered something under his breath. His chest and arm muscles were well defined, clearly a result of hours in a gym.

"Please, can you take me to the shore? I'll leave my boat here. The..." Paul's voice tailed off as he grabbed his chest and doubled over in pain. After a few moments he regained his composure and finished his statement. "The Coast Guard can retrieve it."

The woman pleaded again, until finally he relented. He yanked out a floatation device on a rope designed to keep the two boats from touching one another.

After a few minutes of jockeying the boat, the two vessels were nearly touching. Vince reached his arm out to Paul, who struggled to rise to his feet. Unable to reach him, Vince stepped out of his boat and onto Paul's. Still clutching his chest with one hand, Paul took the man's hand and slowly rose to his feet.

As he held the man's hand, Paul reached down into the pocket of the cargo shorts he was wearing. As he pulled the hammer out of his pocket, he jerked Vince's arm violently forward, causing him to lose his balance and fall into his boat. Paul's arm thrust forward and the hammer landed with deadly precision.

The man's body went limp. The woman let out an ear-piercing scream. But no one could hear it out here. Despite having one leg permanently damaged during Operation Desert Storm, Paul moved with cunning speed. He quickly climbed onto the other boat and advanced on the blonde. Still in shock, the woman realized too late what Paul was trying to do. He closed the gap and delivered a blow from the hammer that no human skull could withstand.

Paul took a moment to catch his breath once the pair of boaters was dead. He sat in one of the chairs on the boat and opened the cooler beside it. Not only was the couple nice enough to go down without much of a struggle, but they also left an ice-cold beer for him when he was done with them. How nice. As he opened the beer, he saw the other party favors that the couple had left. On a table was a bag of marijuana and a smaller plastic baggie full of cocaine. Although Paul rarely missed an opportunity to enjoy a cold beer, he never indulged in any other type of drug. He needed a sharp mind for his line of work.

After finishing his beer, he went back over to his boat and took the man's body in his arms. Pushing with uncertain footing beneath him, he dropped the man's body back in the speed boat. As far as he was concerned, they could drift until they reached shore in Borneo.

He couldn't wait to take these ridiculous yuppie boating clothes off. As he began to head south, he knew he'd have great news for one jealous husband tonight. He took the photos of Vince DeRosa and Nikki Folatti of Cranston, Rhode Island out of his pocket, tore

75

them up, and threw them into the tropical water. He did the same with the piece of paper that he'd written Vince's boat's name and model on. Finally, he threw his hammer and gloves overboard.

The sun was now gone from the sky and the lingering light it left behind was slowly fading. Maybe someone would find the boat. They'd be shocked by the lethal efficiency of a hammer. He didn't care. He'd be on an early morning flight off to Atlanta.

CHAPTER 15

The activity in the R&D laboratory at SimSci was as busy as ever. Each researcher would take the genetic material from viruses currently in existence or that had existed in the past and run those viruses through ViroPredict. The scientists would then run simulations on each virus, the output of which would show the billions of possible ways that it could mutate over time. In just hours ViroPredict could predict how viruses would mutate in different environments for the next hundred years. Then using the genetic makeup of viruses that have caused substantial harm to humans in the past as a guide, the program would flag the viral variations that represent the biggest risk to humans for the virologist to investigate further. With nearly two thousand viruses currently in existence, and a nearly infinite number of potential mutations over time, the team at SimSci had plenty of work to do.

Will, as part of the group of researchers studying viruses flagged as the highest risk mutations, worked closely with lead virologist Tanner Fitzgerald. Tanner had been with SimSci for nearly five years, and his role was similar to that of Vijay, only instead of writing code for ViroPredict, Tanner studied the results of the program. He also worked with Vijay to revise the algorithms and other logic that was the fundamental basis of the ViroPredict software.

Despite having a brilliant mind, members of the opposite sex enjoyed his physical attributes more than the mental. Although he enjoyed all of the benefits that his good looks provided, he also took his work very seriously. People at SimSci enjoyed working with Tanner, whose soft smile and body language made him very approachable.

He was reviewing mutations when one in particular caught his eye. He looked at the genetic makeup of the virus, and the environmental variables that had caused this variation. It took him over four hours to review and understand all of the variables that had gone into the simulation that created this virus, far longer than he'd normally spend.

"Jesus Christ," Tanner muttered to himself after being satisfied that all of the data was correct. He sat back in his desk chair his brows knitted in thought. He could only think of one word to describe what he was looking at – terrifying.

Will was finishing up a call with the University of Delaware's computer engineering department. The university had reached out to SimSci to explore the possibilities of using ViroPredict in a study that the students in PhD program were conducting. He had just ended the conference call when Tanner appeared in the window outside his office. He had his hands full of paper. Will waved him in and the two exchanged greetings.

"What's up?" Will asked as Tanner took a seat across from his desk.

"I think that I have some data that you should take a look at."

Will took the sheaf of papers and began flipping through them. Tanner sat quietly for a few minutes as Will read through the work, occasionally popping an M&M from the bowl on his desk.

"Tanner, what is this? Is this a joke?" Will exclaimed at last. "There has got to be a flaw in the model. This can't be right."

"I checked all of the data. If there is a flaw in the model, I didn't see it."

"Have you ever seen results like this from ViroPredict?" Will asked.

"Never."

Silence followed as Will scanned the data a second time.

"Look, I don't have time to really dig into this right now. Leave it here with me and when Vijay gets back, he and I will look at it."

"Well, I can take it to Lisa. She can—"

"Tanner, I said leave it with me!"

Will's voice rose to an imperious command and Tanner's mouth hung open. He'd never heard Will shout before.

Moments later Will realized the tone he'd taken and quickly calmed down. "Look, Tanner, I'm sorry, I...There's a lot going on here right now, and I think the stress is starting to get to me. What do you think needs to be done to ensure that this information is correct?"

Tanner offered a tentative solution.

"Umm...I need Lisa and her team to double check some of the algorithms in the software. I just need them to make sure there are no bugs causing these results."

"Yes, look, I think that's a great idea. Take the information back with you and let me know what they find. Thanks, Tanner, and again, I'm sorry for that outburst." Will said.

Tanner took the stack of paper and scurried out of his office without saying a word.

CHAPTER 16

No matter how many times he stared into the mirror surrounded by the bright light bulbs, Nigel Drake was never comfortable with the setting. He was much more comfortable having the camera follow him through the jungle. He often used the back of a Jeep as his dressing room. His impatience was compounded by the woman standing by to his side, applying makeup to his face. Today he was preparing to shoot a clip for his cable television show. Fans of the show knew him not as Nigel Drake but as Nocturnal Nigel. His adoring fans made "Nocturnal Nigel's Wildlife Adventures" the top-rated show on cable television. It focused almost exclusively on animals who roamed the land while most people slept. While some of the footage was shot during the day in a studio, the majority of the program was filmed at night to catch these creatures in their natural habitat. After its first season, Nigel's on-camera persona, striking good looks, and expert camera work made Nigel's program an instant sensation. He had the rare combination of the looks that could make him a daytime soap star and the brains to have been able to obtain a PhD in zoology. Today he was preparing to shoot a segment about how viruses can be transmitted from one species to another.

"Hold still, I want to apply cover up under your eyes," the woman said as he squirmed in the chair. Sighing, Nigel did as he was instructed. Behind his back he heard the door to his dressing room open.

"The man needs a little more blush to highlight his pretty blue eyes so all those MILFs watching Nocturnal Nigel with their kids can get hot and bothered."

Nigel recognized the voice immediately, that of Marcel Jarden, his field producer and camera man. Despite his face never appearing over the airwaves, his role in the success of the program was as important as Nigel's.

"Shouldn't you be doing something other than harassing me just before a shoot?" Nigel asked.

"I actually didn't come in here to take you off your game before you head out there. I've got something I want to run by you."

"Better make it quick."

"I think we have the location for our next shoot. How does Thailand sound?" Marcel asked.

"Thailand? What are we looking for? Bats? Haven't we done that already?"

"We have, but it was all the way back in the third season. It's time to recycle this idea and give it another go."

Nigel waited for a final powder puff before replying. "Hey you're the producer and you've managed to get it right so far—"

"Nigel, you're on in five," a voice said as his dressing room door opened.

"Okay, Thailand it is. I can't wait. Now let's go out there and get this shoot finished."

He took one last look at himself in the dressing room mirror— he was gorgeous— then headed out to the shoot.

* * *

"Good morning, Nick. Sorry for not being around for your calls yesterday, it was a very busy day," Monica said.

When her phone rang, she'd been waiting for another call, but when her secretary told her it was Nick, she knew she had to take it.

"No problem. That was quite a meeting we had here with Will a few days ago. He's stubborn, isn't he?" Nick asked.

He wasn't beating around the bush, she thought. "Well, I don't know if stubborn is the right word. Let's just say he's committed to his company."

"Fair enough," Nick conceded. "Since we had that meeting, I'd been thinking about what you're trying to accomplish, and I think that maybe I can help."

"Anything you can do to suggest to Will that the company would be better off under the Sander portfolio of companies would be helpful."

"I had something a little more effective in mind. With the proper incentive, I think I could create an environment where Will would find it would be in his best interest to sell. Why don't we grab dinner and a few drinks one night and I can walk you through my thoughts?"

He was so eager to stab his boss in the back. "I'm actually booked solid all week with client dinners. But you've piqued my interest. Could you elaborate?"

"I don't want to spend the rest of my life in an office crunching numbers. I'm looking for a big payday, one that will allow me to unburden myself from this nine to five grind. Do you know what I mean?"

Monica heard his cryptic message loud and clear. "So what you are saying is that you're exploring the possibility of a consulting engagement with Sander Pharmaceuticals. Is that what you're suggesting?"

"Yes, a consulting gig, exactly."

"And specifically what services would you render for us?"

"No company can survive if their finances take a sudden turn for the worse. In the economic environment we are in today, banks' loan requirements are increasingly stringent. If something were to happen and SimSci began to violate their loan covenants, well, they would be forced to seek strategic alternatives or not be able to make payroll. As CFO, I am responsible for the finances of the company. I would hate for our finances to suddenly take a turn for the worse, but sometimes it simply can't be avoided."

Monica understood what Nick was proposing. As CFO, Nick could create, or fabricate, a financial situation so dire that Will and James would have no choice but to sell. In return for his work, he would look for a giant payday from Monica after SimSci is acquired by Sander. It could work, Monica thought. But she knew Nick too well. If something were to go wrong and he were caught, he wouldn't hesitate to spill his guts. Even if things went perfectly, Monica wasn't sure he could be trusted.

"That's a very interesting way to look at things," she said neutrally. "But Sander isn't interested in engaging in activity that could be considered unethical, or worse, illegal."

"Illegal is a strong word. I don't think anyone is suggesting doing something illegal," Nick said defensively.

"I always enjoy hearing from you. If anything else comes up, don't hesitate to call again," Monica said.

Before Monica could take the phone away from her ear, she heard Nick slam the phone into its cradle. She calmly put the phone down and chuckled to herself. Good old Nick Waters, she thought, you haven't changed a bit.

CHAPTER 17

The agony was unbearable. Vijay couldn't move his feet without pain shooting up his legs. The tissue was beginning to get infected, and he tried not to think about the permanent damage being done. His clothes had not been changed, nor had he had eaten in three days. He reeked of stale urine and excrement. Slowly Vijay was becoming weak. He was losing his will to live. He thought about his two kids, Rahul and Ganesh, and it brought a faint smile to his lips. Then he thought about his wife and the anguish that she must be going through not knowing where he was or what had happened to him. He desperately wanted to see them all again and to hold them in his arms.

The utter darkness was suddenly breached by light as the door to the warehouse opened. He couldn't see who had entered the warehouse, but he suspected that he knew who it was.

"Today is a big day," Boris said. His voice was full of optimism and excitement, as if he were speaking to a four-year old about to get their first bicycle. He turned the lights on in the warehouse, flooding the room with brilliance.

When Vijay's eyes adjusted to the light, he saw Boris' hulking six-five frame standing above him. His black leather jacket was partially unzipped, revealing an aqua colored T-shirt. Vijay stared at the Russian flag on Boris' jacket as he tried to avoid eye contact with the man. To Boris' left, Yuriy turned on Vijay's computer. Vijay did not think that he could take another sequence of torture like the last time. But he knew that he couldn't give them what they wanted. If he did, millions of innocent lives would be in jeopardy.

"I hope you're enjoying your stay. I trust that you found the seat comfortable?" Boris asked, grinning as he spoke. Vijay didn't reply, and his eyes dropped to the ground.

"How are your feet doing?" Boris asked as he squatted over and picked up one of Vijay's legs. Vijay moaned in pain as he did so.

Boris winced as he examined the bottoms of Vijay's feet. "It looks like we may have ourselves a serious infection. Stupid man. This could all be, how do you say, avoided."

Vijay continued in his silence. He had nothing to say to these monsters.

"It smells like you could really use a shower," Boris went on. "I tell you what we do today. We're going to work with you. We want to be friends. We're going to untie you. We want this to be over as badly as you do. Now you help us do that."

Boris nodded at Yuriy, who untied Vijay's hands from behind his back. As Yuriy was doing so, Boris gave Vijay a firm warning.

"Please don't try to do anything crazy. Remember there are two of us and one of you." He looked down at Vijay's feet again. "Besides, I'm not sure you could run away even if you wanted to."

As Vijay's wrists were freed, he shook his arms feeling prickles of pain from the numbness.

Boris let him enjoy his new-found freedom for a few moments before speaking. "We want you to put your hands to good use," Boris began as he pushed the table with the laptop computer toward Vijay. "We untie your hands, we untie your feet next. Then we bring you onto the street where you call for help. That's what we do for you today."

Boris studied Vijay as he added, "You just use those free hands to log us onto your computer and the program."

Vijay continued to simply stare at the floor. Boris tried to remain calm. Finally he grabbed Vijay by the hair and forced his head up.

"You listen, and listen now. We need the password. Just give it to us."

He let go of Vijay's hair and pushed his head down.

"Nothing is going to get through to this stubborn man," Boris said, looking over at Yuriy.

Vijay quietly began to pray. He knew that for all the good in the world, there was bad that came with the good. And the bad elements had caught up to him. He knew that it was just a matter of time before they would. Every morning he would pray that this day would never come. He had made up his mind many years ago that he wouldn't give in to the evil. He was willing to die for the good. If he shared what he knew, it could mean death on a scale that the world had never seen before. He began to pray louder, expressing his hopes for his family.

"Stop, stop with your prayers," Boris screamed above Vijay's prayers. "God will not help you. Only one thing will save you. Give us the password."

Finally he couldn't take it anymore. He walked behind the chair. Vijay could sense Boris's movements, and how grave the situation had become. He felt his bowels involuntarily release their contents. He was now praying at the top of his lungs. Boris reached into the back of his pants where he had a gun concealed from sight and placed the muzzle at the back of Vijay's head.

As he felt the pressure of the steel muzzle, Vijay could no longer control his larynx and vocal cords to use them to form words. His prayer was now groans that contained no discernable words. They were the sounds of a man who knew that he was about to die.

Suddenly, Boris let out a scream at the top of his lungs as he pulled the trigger twice, releasing two bullets into the base of Vijay's skull.

CHAPTER 18

Colleen Alpert stood outside Will's office waving wildly as he tried to finish an online demonstration with a group of professors from the University of Southern California. He'd given them a quick overview of the capabilities of ViroPredict, using the phone to speak and the Internet to transmit images of the software. The complexity of the program didn't lend itself to an hour-long demo, and as was usually the case, the professors had many questions.

Will had motioned to Colleen a number of times, holding his index finger up to her to indicate that he would only be a few more minutes. But she kept shaking her head, indicating to Will that whatever she was trying to tell him must be quite important.

"Gentlemen, I really appreciate your time today, and I really hate to cut this discussion short, but something has just come up here that requires my attention. Let's schedule a follow-up discussion for next week so that I can answer more of your questions. Again I thank you for your time."

Colleen looked pale and upset when Will opened the door.

"Will, the police are here."

Now he understood why Colleen was so anxious. Without a word, he walked down to the foyer to see them. Could they want to ask me more questions about Scott, he wondered. Or was the purpose of their visit to deliver grim news about Vijay? Will entered the expansive foyer and saw Charles with a uniformed officer.

"Will, thanks for coming out to meet us. This is Officer Jacob Madre," Charles said curtly.

The look on Charles' face was grim, and Will braced for the worst.

"We regret to inform you that Vijay Kalam was found dead this morning. I'm sorry."

Will struggled to find the words to respond. Out of the corner of his eye, he saw the receptionist put her hand in front of her mouth.

Vijay was dead, just like that. His head filled with visions of Vijay in a dark basement pleading for his life. Will quickly shook off those thoughts. He was the second SimSci employee to be found dead in the past few weeks. This was more than just coincidence, Will realized. Someone was targeting his employees. He felt a shiver run all the way down his back. Just as Charles was about to say something, James emerged from the back offices. He looked at his brother and then at the two officers.

"What's going on here? Charles, what are you doing here?"

Charles introduced his partner again, and he repeated the news. Hearing the announcement a second time, the receptionist began crying uncontrollably.

The two brothers looked at each other, but neither said a word. Finally, Will gained his composure. "What happened? Where was he found? How did he die?" he asked all in one breath.

Charles' eyes darted from Will to the receptionist, then back. "I think we should talk in private."

Will led Charles, Officer Madre and James into a conference room and closed the door.

"What happened, Charles?"

"He was found alone in an empty warehouse. It looks like he had been there for a few days. He died as a result of twin gunshots to the head."

"An empty warehouse?" James asked, a look of horror on his face.

"He'd been tied to a chair inside an empty warehouse. We don't know right now how long he'd been there, but we believe whoever abducted him brought him there immediately."

"How did you find him?"

"We didn't find him. The landlord did when the adjacent tenant complained of a horrible smell coming from the unit next door. The landlord said he thought a cat or a skunk had gotten trapped."

"Jesus Christ," James said.

"I don't want to make this any more difficult for you, but as a friend I want to give you as much information as I can. He had been tortured before he was killed. When we found him, his feet looked like eggplants with the skin peeled off. They were swollen and raw."

"Jesus, Charles," James said as he covered his mouth in shock.

Charles' face shut down, becoming impassive like a cop. "I think you've gotten the idea. I'll spare you the rest of the details. Our job now is to find the vile being that did this. I know how important this is to you, Will, so I've demanded that I be placed on this case. I'll be investigating Vijay's death."

Will nodded his head in relief as Charles continued. "I can tell you that this doesn't look like a random act, especially when we combine this with the Bredahl death. But we still have a lot of work to do before we can share any hard leads."

"Understood," Will said as he looked at James. "We need to let the rest of the office know." James nodded, and the group left the conference room and headed back out to the receptionist desk. When they arrived, they found the receptionist with tears streaming down her face.

"Please make an announcement over the loudspeaker. I need everyone in the cafeteria in five minutes. Please do not say a word about what you have just heard. To anyone," Will said.

His receptionist blew her nose to chase away the sniffles before making the P.A announcement. The Woltzberg brothers headed toward the cafeteria, and the officers followed. Will waited a few minutes as all of his employees had trickled into the large lunch room. Many were talking and joking among one another until they entered the cafeteria and saw the two police officers standing beside Will and James. Cold perspiration matted Will's brow as he began.

"Thank you all for gathering so quickly." Will told the assemblage. "There is no easy way to say this, so I'm going to just go ahead and say it. The search for Vijay has ended, and unfortunately, it has not ended well. The police found Vijay's body this morning."

The expressions on his employees' faces ranged from horror to shock to sadness. As he looked around the room, the spectrum of emotions that he saw was overwhelming, and he began to feel his own eyes swell up. He felt a tear run down his cheek as he continued. "We will all remember Vijay as a wonderful employee, co worker, researcher, and most important, a wonderful friend. Without his contribution to this company, we would not be where we are today."

His words brought tears to several people in the cafeteria. So much sadness on the faces of everyone in the room angered him. Whoever did this needs to be brought to justice, he thought.

"In regards to finding the monster that did this to our friend, the police will conduct an investigation and find this person. If other law enforcement resources are needed, they will be utilized. We will find this animal."

Yes, Will thought to himself as he looked over at Charles, *we* will find him.

CHAPTER 19

Bundled in a winter jacket and boots, Will stood at his brother's front door and rang the doorbell.

James opened the door and welcomed them in, but he wasn't alone. Doing its best to scare off anyone who dared approach the house, James' new pet beagle was barking at the top of its tiny lungs.

"What in the world….Where did this little guy come from?" Will asked as he bent over to pet the little dog.

"It's the one that we saw at the pond a few nights ago. I just couldn't let it stay there," James replied.

"I thought you were going to bring it to the pound."

"I was, but then I felt the little guy shivering and I decided that I would keep him instead."

"Well, it looks like we have a new member in our family. What did we name him?" Will asked with a warm smile.

"Scorpion," James said.

A look of confusion crossed Will's face.

"It's a long story. Let's just say it reminds me of an old friend."

The group walked into James' house. The house was small compared to most homes, but average for the congested City of Cambridge. The front door brought them right into the kitchen.

James' wife Cindy was pouring a glass of wine on the small Formica countertop. The wall-mounted cabinets above it were made of solid wood stained with lacquer. A hinge was missing from one, causing the door to hang at an angle.

"Would you two like a drink?" Cindy asked.

Will and Sarah responded in the affirmative, Will with a rum and coke and Sarah with white wine.

"Are you going to wait for the cabinet to fall apart to fix it?" Will asked, turning to his brother.

Before James could respond, Cindy chimed in. "Oh please, that's the least of the problems with this house. The whole thing is falling apart."

"Why don't we come in here where everything's in working order," James said, motioning toward the living room.

Will and Sarah obliged, and found their way to the couch.

Despite the television playing in the background, there was an awkward silence in the room as no one really knew what to say, even though they all had the same thing on their minds. Sarah finally broke the silence.

"I read in the paper that the services will be on Monday at the Stony Brook funeral home over in Somerville."

"Yes, I saw the same thing. I didn't catch the time, though," Cindy replied. "I would expect everyone from the company to be there."

James and Will had shared the news of Vijay's death with their wives, and this was the first time that the group had gotten together since they'd learned of the murder.

"Do you think he was involved in something illegal?" Sarah asked.

"Yes, could he have been involved in something?" Cindy asked.

"We've known Vijay for years. I simply refuse to believe that he was involved in any nefarious activities," Will replied. James nodded his head in agreement.

"What does Charles think?" Cindy asked.

"Officially he's not ruling out anything. But we've talked privately and he thinks that Vijay's murder may be linked to Scott's." Will took a deep breath before his next statement. "He believes that it may have something to do with the company."

That drew looks of concern from the women, and caused Sarah to gulp down her remaining half glass of wine.

"What do you mean? What about the company could possibly lead someone to do something so horrible?"

"That's what we've been trying to figure out since we got the news," James said.

"He'd just gotten back from India. Hadn't he been traveling there a lot over the past few months?" Sarah asked.

"Yes, but that was business related. He was working with a few universities over there. They were going to partner with us to improve our software," James replied.

"That's what he told you. Maybe there were other reasons for those trips. He did get abducted coming home from one."

Will waved away that notion. "I just can't believe that's the case. He was a devout Hindu. He seemed very happy all of the time. He loved what he did, and he loved his family."

Suddenly a loud buzzing erupted from the kitchen and Sarah instinctively grabbed Will's arm.

"It's just the timer on the oven," Cindy said as she got up.

"I think I need some fresh air. I'm going to go out to the back porch for a few minutes," Will said following Cindy into the kitchen. He opened the sliding door to go out onto the porch. As he stepped outside, he was quickly reminded how cold it was this winter evening. He looked out into James' small backyard as he continued to think about what had happened to Vijay. A single pine tree stood in the middle of the lawn. Will watched its branches sway in the breeze. He wondered if the motive the police suspected was right. He couldn't believe that Vijay's murder was related to SimSci. SimSci was just a tiny software company. They weren't designing missiles for the U.S. government or spy planes for North Korea.

Will had been outside for a few minutes when Sarah opened the sliding door to get him.

"Dinner is on the table. Is everything okay?" she asked.

"Yes, I'm fine, just thinking," he replied.

As he headed inside, he closed the slider door. He pushed the lever on the door to lock it, and was surprised at how easily it moved. After locking it, he tried to tug the slider open and it slid open as if nothing had changed. He closed the door again and headed into the dining room.

"You should really get that slider fixed," Will said as he took his place at the table.

"I told you the whole house was falling apart," Cindy said.

"So, how are the rest of the employees reacting to the news?" Sarah asked, changing the subject.

"I guess you could say that they're reacting as well as can be expected under the circumstances," James replied.

"It was so hard to share that news yesterday. To see the reactions on their faces was something that I hope that I never have to do again," Will said. "We're also taking measures just in case the police are right about the crime being related to the company. We'll be hiring a security guard to keep an eye on things during business hours for the next few weeks."

"Do you really think that you need one?" Cindy asked, alarmed.

"I don't know, but when we were speaking to Charles yesterday, he suggested that we get one just to be safe."

"I've got a better way to keep everyone in this family safe," Sarah announced.

It was just a matter of time, Will thought.

"We can sell the company to the highest bidder. Then everyone will be safe. Hell, the four of us can have our own remote island that no one can get to," Sarah said.

"Now is not the time for you to get onto your soapbox," Will said, his eyes locked on Sarah.

"Cindy, this lobster casserole is really amazing," James said trying to lighten the discussion.

"Oh, I'm sorry, I forgot. Anyone who doesn't have the same opinion as you shouldn't dare speak. You don't care about my opinion. You haven't for a very long time."

Cindy and James exchanged uncomfortable looks as Sarah went on.

"Actually, I don't even think you've cared about *me* for a very long time. You don't even notice me anymore. I'm just your roommate, you know, the one that cooks you dinner and happens to be the mother of your children."

"I don't care about you? I don't notice you? When I try to notice you, you ignore me!" Will jumped up from his chair. He was seething. "You're buying these skin-tight jeans and layering on makeup just to go to the supermarket. You even got Botox injections! I know it's not for me. Whenever I touch you, you act like I have the plague!" He threw down his napkin. "Enjoy your god damn dinner. I'm out of here!"

James' mouth hung open and Cindy's face was bright red as Will grabbed his jacket and stormed out of the house. Moments later, the trio inside could hear the sound of a car peeling out and roaring down the street.

Left behind, Sarah drew up her lips in a grim line. "That bastard," she said quietly.

CHAPTER 20

Monica closed the internet window on her computer, drumming her fingers on her desk. She'd just read an article about Vijay Kalam. She knew that she should take the opportunity to call Will Woltzberg with her condolences. Yet only a few days had passed since she'd been out to speak to Will in his office, and she didn't want to seem pushy.

"This better be important, I'm going to be late for my drinks with Chloe Cunha, the CEO of Endless Pharmaceuticals."

Monica turned and saw Alan Burke standing in her doorway. "It's important," she said moving toward the large meeting table in her office. She took a seat, and Alan chose one directly across from her.

"We haven't had a chance to sit down and discuss my meeting with Will Woltzberg the other day."

"Oh, how did it go?"

"Not good. I was stonewalled. He isn't interested in selling."

"So he's going to play hardball. I don't know if he realizes who he's playing against," Alan said, shaking his head. "What are our other options? You said you know the CFO?"

"I've considered that approach, but he just can't be trusted. He's a loose cannon. He always has been. But I did run into one of their virologists while I was there, a guy by the name of Tanner Fitzgerald. He started his career here."

Alan's eyes lit up. "How well do we know him?"

"He's very bright. I did work with him a bit while he was here. He's in his early thirties. He's very confident, and seems trustworthy."

"He could be someone we can work with. You're closer to the situation than I am, so I'll let you feel him out and get back to me. I also have an idea of how we can angle our way in to this organization."

"Do tell."

"I went to college with Will's wife, Sarah. She and I took a number of classes together, because she was a biology major as well. After college we ended up working on a few drug trials that our respective companies partnered on. I know her well enough."

The look of surprise on Monica's face matched her feelings. Alan rarely offered to get involved in nuts and bolts work.

"Really? Just how well do you know her?"

"Not as well as I would have liked, if that's what you're implying. She was an attractive woman back then. I'll bet she still is. We kept in touch after working together, but I haven't seen or heard from her for at least five years, maybe longer."

"So I take it you never really got what you wanted out of the relationship?" Monica wasn't afraid of broaching the subject of sex with her boss. She knew of his obsession with women and how prolific his sexual encounters were. He made no effort to conceal any of it from her, in fact the opposite was true.

"In college she was all too involved in her studies. Then she met the man she would eventually marry. The time was never right. But I think I could break through that tough outer shell if the time was right."

"When did you two last talk?"

"Some years after we worked together, I tried to get her to join Beta Pharmaceuticals before we sold out. She politely declined the offer, one that was quite generous. I think she may have realized that I was looking for more than a competent biologist," Alan replied with a sly smile.

"How can we use this to our advantage?"

"I don't know yet. I will call her, feel her out. Who knows, maybe there are other factors at play that we can leverage."

"I wonder how happy her marriage is," Monica remarked. "Will is a stuffy suit, that's for sure."

"We had a real connection when we worked together. If it's not going well, I may be able to get a sense of that from her..." He stopped short. "It's certainly an angle I can work. I swear she had a little crush on me."

"Feel her out. Maybe you can rekindle that spark, if there ever was one," Monica said through a broad grin.

"What are you saying? That my ego may be exaggerating how much she was into me?"

"You men and your egos, you never know..."

"Well, I guess we will just have to find out, wont we?"

* * *

"Will, do you have a second?"

Will looked up to see Lisa Oshry standing just outside his office door. With the loss of Vijay, Lisa had stepped into the role of lead programmer for ViroPredict. The decision to assign the work to her was one of necessity, one that Will had struggled with. He knew that she was smart enough to take on the work, and when she applied herself, she was truly brilliant. But he also knew that all too often her personal problems and boisterous, candid personality would interfere.

"Sure, what's up?" He replied.

She came into his office and closed the door behind her.

She had on a pair of loose-fitting jeans and old running sneakers. A plain baby-blue collared golf shirt topped off her outfit. Every day was casual Friday for Lisa.

"I'm not going to sugar-coat this, I'll get right to the reason that I'm here. I have to leave SimSci, effective immediately. Today is going to be my last day," she said.

Will tried not to show the disappointment that he felt. Losing both Vijay and Lisa would severely slow additional enhancements to ViroPredict.

"I'm disappointed to hear this. Can I ask you what has led to this decision?"

"Sure. I don't want to leave. I'm very happy here, you're great to work for and everyone here is great to work with. But things have gotten a little too intense here for me right now. What happened to Scott and Vijay is pretty creepy. It's bad enough I've got creditors after me everywhere I turn. I don't want to have to watch my back for some psycho killer."

Her last statement took Will by surprise. Had she just implied that by taking on Vijay's role in SimSci that she might be next on some killer's hit list?

"I understand," Will began. "You do what you have to do. I understand your reasoning. This is a very difficult time for this company. What happened to Scott and Vijay was horrible."

Lisa nodded in agreement.

"What is the mood right now, you know, with everyone else out there?" Will asked.

"I think everyone is very afraid. No one really knows what's happening. You know how rumors and speculation can cause people to freak out. Naturally people are wondering if somehow what happened to Vijay and Scott is connected to work."

"I can understand everyone's concern. All that I can say is that I have confidence in the authorities and their ability to conduct this investigation and quickly find the people who've done this."

The two spoke for a few more minutes regarding the administrative paperwork that needed to be done to finalize Lisa's departure as well as what work she was doing and how it would proceed without her. Their discussion took the better part of an hour, and when they were finally done and Lisa was about to leave Will's office, he called her name just before she'd opened the door. She turned back around to look at him.

"Is there anything I can do to convince you to stay?"

"I'm afraid not. I think that it's time that I move on."

"Once all of this blows over, I want you to know that there will be a job for you to return to at SimSci."

"Thank you. I'll keep that in mind."

Once Lisa had left his office, Will rose from his chair and headed two offices down to see his brother. James' door was open and he was at his desk absorbing the data from a stack of papers.

"Got a minute?" Will asked.

"Sure," James replied without looking up.

Will sat in one of the chairs and picked up a foam football from the floor and gently lobbed it to James. James liked to keep the football in his office, and sometimes held informal meetings while playing a game of pass in the hallway.

"Lisa Oshry just gave her notice, effective immediately," Will said.

That brought his head up. "Jesus Christ. Did she say why?"

"She's scared. She said that she doesn't want 'some psycho killer' stalking her," Will said, making quotation marks with his fingers as he spoke.

"That's what she said? Wow. I wonder if everyone out there thinks that."

"If that's the case, we could have more people leaving. As it is, I don't know how we are going to replace both Vijay and Lisa. We've just lost our two best ViroPredict programmers at a time that we need them the most."

James shook his head in grave concern. "It'll take months to replace them. Six months of lost development gives our competitors time to study the software and make up lost ground. We can't afford that."

"It's clear that you and I will need to pick up some of the workload. Are you comfortable with that?" Will asked.

"Of course I am. I just don't know if it'll be enough." James replied with a perplexed look. "Maybe we need to consider other options. Maybe we should get Monica Rowe and Jack from Champi and Lefkowitz together for a discussion. Maybe we should at least consider it."

James was referring to Jack Ferbert, an investment banker who kept in touch with both Will and James. Although SimSci had never had the need for the outside funding that an investment bank typically helps secure, they'd used Jack as an advisor a handful of times when they'd contemplated small fold-in acquisitions. Will knew that James wasn't implying that Jack be used for either of those purposes in this instance. He was contemplating a discussion concerning an outright sale of SimSci to Sander Pharmaceuticals.

"I don't think I'm ready for that yet. We've been through some rough patches before, and we've worked through them. Remember when the bank canceled our credit line?" Will asked.

James chuckled grimly at the irony of Will's words. It had been the bank's decision to cut their line of credit that forced James to get involved in the money laundering scheme now called Scorpion. "But back then we weren't getting the attention we are now.

We didn't even have a saleable product. Now we have legit interest from one of the biggest companies in the world. I'm not saying we sell tomorrow. I'm just saying we should listen to what Monica has to say."

"Now you're starting to sound like Sarah," Will said. "You know how I feel. I've put too much into this company to see someone else come in and take it over. Not when we are on the brink of such large-scale success."

"Okay, look, I'm just throwing it out there. We're in this together, bro. I guess the first step forward is to get as many resumes in here as possible and try and fill those positions ASAP."

Will nodded in agreement and got up to leave. As he opened the door James called his name. Will turned and instinctively put his hands out as he saw the foam football leave his brother's hands.

"We'll pull through this." James said as he smiled reassuringly at his brother.

Will tossed the football back. "I hope you're right."

CHAPTER 21

Although the sun couldn't poke through the clouds, that didn't stop it from driving the temperature past ninety degrees. Perspiration matted Nigel's brow as unfamiliar faces passed him outside the Don Mueang International Airport in Bangkok, Thailand.

"We picked the wrong time of year to come here. It's like sixty-five degrees back in California. This is going to be a long ride." Nigel said as he turned to the man behind him. In front of them was a large black Jeep with mud stuck to the sides of it. The driver got out, came around to the sidewalk where Nigel was standing and extended his hand.

"Dr. Nigel Drake," Nigel said as he gave the man a firm handshake.

"Jao Willapana, I will be your guide for this trip. I'm looking forward to working with both of you."

"Marcel Jarden, very nice to meet you," Marcel said as he shook Jao's hand.

"I'd like to welcome you both to Thailand. We're approximately two hours away from the Uthai Thani Province, where we will be picking up a local guide who is very familiar with the park that we're heading into. I'll transport you to our destination as well as translate everything that our local guide has to say. If you have any concerns during our trip, please let me know. Now if you don't have any questions, I suggest we begin our journey."

"I think we're ready when you are," Nigel said.

Jao nodded and headed toward the driver's side of the jeep, and the two Americans got into the vehicle, Nigel in the front and Marcel in the back. Jao started the jeep and turned onto the busy street.

"So have you ever been to the Haui Kha Khaeng Wildlife Sanctuary before?" Nigel asked.

"Just once before, but I'm not very familiar with it. Not like the locals. This is one reason we'll be picking up a local who is familiar with it. He will know the area much better, particularly the area of the park into which we are heading," Jao said.

"Ah, I see." Nigel said. "But you've done work like this before?"

"Oh yes, I've been involved with many wildlife film crews. In fact, the other times I've visited the Sanctuary, I was doing jobs like this one."

"Well, I hope you know what you got yourself into with this one. This is going to be a dirty one for sure." Marcel said.

"I brought many clothes for this journey," Jao said as he looked back at Marcel, smiling.

As they drove, Nigel thought about the work that lay ahead of them. This shoot was a little different from many of the episodes that he'd shot in the past. Instead of shooting at night, this episode was going to be taped entirely during the day. However, Nigel and Marcel were going to still be working in the dark as they were doing an episode containing footage of two species of bats. Bats spend most of their lives in dark caves. Based on the episode that they'd shot a few years ago with a different species of bat, the two men knew that the environment that they were about to enter was going to be hot, dark, and dirty.

Idle chatter occupied the group's time during the two-hour drive to the small village that they would be staying at while they shot the program. Once they arrived, Nigel got out and stretched his legs. It felt good to be out of the Jeep. Despite its size, after packing in all the luggage and camera equipment there was little room left for the three passengers. As he stood six feet five inches tall, long cramped car rides weren't Nigel's favorite part of the job. After stretching his legs, he turned toward the Jeep and looked at his reflection in the window. He ran his fingers through his hair to comb it back into place after the windy ride.

"This is where you will be staying. We're about forty-five minutes away from the Sanctuary. May I suggest that you unpack and make yourself comfortable?" Jao said.

"That sounds good," Nigel replied. The hotel was a one-story building that looked quite rundown, but Nigel had slept in worse places in the past. The building had approximately thirty rooms and each room faced onto the parking area. He spotted a few other cars, along with a small amount of adventurist tourists arriving at the hotel. He was beginning to get his belongings out of the Jeep when he felt a drop of rain on the tip of his nose. Then he felt a few more on his arms.

"Do you feel that?" he asked Marcel.

"Sure do."

"It looks like we're in for a torrential rain storm," Jao said as he pointed to the sky off in the distance.

Nigel saw dark clouds rolling and tumbling in their direction. Shooting the introductions, reviewing the talking points for each shot, as well as lunch and other breaks from the filth of the cave all would take place outside. If the weather didn't cooperate, it would delay their first day of filming.

"Do you think it's going to just be a passing storm?" Nigel asked.

"I don't know. I'm afraid we'll need to wait and see."

That wasn't what Nigel wanted to hear. "Well, let's get this stuff inside and we'll play it by ear."

The men began bringing their belongings into the hotel. Just as they were coming out of their rooms for a second trip, the skies above them opened up and heavy rain soaked the three men. They all dashed to the Jeep to grab the rest of their belongings. From underneath the cover of the hotel's awning the three men gathered to discuss what to do.

"It looks like at a minimum we need to wait until this storm passes. Let's give it forty-five minutes." Nigel said.

The other men nodded their heads in agreement. Nigel looked up at the sky and saw nothing but more dark clouds heading their way. He'd been hoping to get a lot of work in today, and spending the day in a hotel room wasn't where that work would get done.

CHAPTER 22

"Brains and beauty in one tight package. You still have it, Sarah Collins," she said, referring to her maiden name as she looked at herself in the restroom mirror. She couldn't help but admire how good she looked for a woman in her late thirties. She was wearing an ivory top covered with sequins tucked tightly into tight black pants. The top had thin straps, and between the cleavage it showed and the way it clung to her breasts, it was becoming one of her favorites. She looked like she was ready for a full-blown night on the town. Once she was finished applying a subtle touch of blush to her face, she headed out. As she returned to her seat, she leaned forward exposing just enough of her breasts for the man sitting across from her to wonder what the rest of her top was concealing.

The table was located in the rear of a sparsely lit Italian restaurant in Boston's North End. The walls were all dark red brick, and photos of Italy were hanging from various spots on each wall. A smaller room off to their right held a bar.

"So now where were we?" Sarah asked.

"Well, like I'd said before, I don't see any reason why I can't make this work on my end. You do what you have to do on yours, and let me know that we're good to go."

"We've always been able to do great things together. I don't expect this time to be any different," Sarah said as she sipped her martini. "Can I just tell you how excited I am to be out to dinner tonight? It's been so long since Will's taken me out, I feel like I need to really make the most of the occasion."

Alan Burke smiled from across the table. "Since we are confiding in one another, let me confess how pleased I am to be out with such a beautiful woman."

Sarah could feel herself blushing.

"So where's Will tonight?"

"Where do you think? He's at work, said it's going to be a late one. Some sales demo for a potential client on the West Coast. He told me not to wait for him for dinner, so I'm not." Sarah took the cherry from her martini by the stem and placed it sensually on her tongue. Will did not know what he was missing.

"Well, it's his loss."

"It's been his loss for a long time," she complained. "And I'm not talking about just missing a few dinners."

Alan offered a look of genuine intrigue as he rested his elbows on the table. His eyes were live with interest, his head tilted at an angle.

"So I take it he's missing something big?"

"Yes, me!" she said with a wink. "I mean, he's stopped noticing me. It started over a year ago. I've always tried to look good for him when he gets home from work."

Their waiter came over and they both ordered another drink.

"Some nights I even put on these short little silk nighties. Do you know that he doesn't even look at me? I mean really *look* at me, like a man looks at a woman. He looks at me like I was his business associate or at best an old friend."

"That's not how a good husband should be treating his beautiful wife."

"You don't have to tell me that."

Sarah's cheeks were turning red as she spoke, the product both of the frustration she was feeling and the alcohol she was consuming. As if on cue, the waiter returned with their drinks. The glass had barely touched the table before Sarah began tossing it back.

"I know sometimes men need something new after being married as long as we have. They like variety, it's a primal instinct. I tried to give him that! The new lingerie, the new hair, Christ, I even tried to look younger by getting Botox injections!"

"By the way, your hair, is gorgeous," Alan said.

"So then what is it? What is his problem? Why doesn't he notice me?"

"Some men are very foolish creatures," Alan said casually. "They always look for the next big mountain to conquer. For some men those challenges are women, and each is represented by a notch in their bed post. For others it's work, landing that blue chip client or running the competition out of business. For your husband it's probably the latter. At least I hope it's the latter with such a beautiful wife at home."

As he spoke he gently took Sarah's hand in his, then slowly squeezed it.

His touch was electric to Sarah. It made her feel good, sexy, *alive*. A flurry of thoughts entered her mind, but they were so forbidden, she instantly pushed them away.

"Hello? Everything okay over there?" Alan asked.

Sarah forced her mind back to the present and back to Alan. Suddenly she felt a wave of guilt wash over her. "Yes, I'm sorry. What were you saying?"

"I was saying we should get a couple of menus. I think some food would do you good."

"I actually think I'd best be going." Sarah said, flustered. What am I doing with this man? she thought. Here I am meeting an acquaintance I haven't seen in years and suddenly I'm telling him the secrets of my marriage?

"You really need to get some dinner in you before you get behind the wheel," Alan pleaded as Sarah put her coat on and grabbed her purse. "What about our little arrangement?"

"I'll call you!" Sarah said, looking for her keys as she headed for the exit.

* * *

"Thanks for meeting me. Would you like a drink?" Monica asked as she sat inside a bar two blocks away from SimSci.

"I'll have a beer," Tanner responded. "It's not every day that I'm invited out to meet the CEO of my former employer."

"Well, when I saw you the other day in the foyer at SimSci, I thought it would be good to reconnect for a couple of reasons."

Tanner took a sip of the beer, curious as to why Monica had asked to meet him. She'd called him at work yesterday, asking him if he had time to meet her outside of work for a "candid discussion." He expected that she wanted to recruit him to come back to Sander. If that was the reason for the meeting, she was wasting her time, but he knew he couldn't blow her off. "I was surprised to see you there. I assume you were meeting with Will?"

"Yes, I had gone to lunch with Nick Waters. Then he and I sat down with Will."

"Well I hope the discussion went well."

Monica put on her best troubled look.

"It was actually quite troubling. It's why I asked you to meet me somewhere other than my office."

"Troubling?" Tanner asked, perplexed.

"Back when you worked at Sander, you seemed to be an honest, genuine person. You seemed like someone who wanted to do the right thing. That's why I called you. What I'm about to tell you must be kept between the two of us. Understand?" Monica asked.

"Sure, yes, I understand."

From behind them a bass drum began to thump steadily as a live band warmed up.

"We first contacted Will regarding ViroPredict some months ago. You see, we were very impressed with the software's potential when we first heard about it. We wanted to learn more, so Will put us in touch with Vijay."

Monica paused, and Tanner nodded his head. "Vijay was the best programmer we, umm, had. You heard about what happened, right?"

"Yes, it's horrible. Did you know him well?" Monica asked as she finished her drink.

"Yes, he and I worked closely together. We spent much of our workdays together."

"I'm sorry," Monica said, leading up to her story. "Vijay had been working with a very small group of programmers and virologists within Sander. As the study got under way, Vijay introduced us to Scott Bredahl, and we were told he'd be our go to person in terms of addressing any questions that we had. After a few weeks of testing the software we found a number of instances where the software didn't accurately predict what actually happened in nature."

"You mean, you found instances where ViroPredict wasn't working?" Tanner asked.

"Yes. First, we mentioned them to Scott. A day later, Scott was found dead. Naturally, we allowed a few days for the grieving process before contacting Vijay with our concerns. We brought those same examples to Vijay just before he disappeared. He didn't have a chance to explain them to us before he...was murdered."

"So are you saying that you mentioning these issues to Vijay and Scott and them disappearing is more than a coincidence?"

"What if they uncovered something when they looked into our questions? Something Will didn't want anyone to know."

Tanner flashed a look of skepticism at Monica. "You're accusing Will of killing two people over flawed software?"

"I know it sounds crazy— heck, it still sounds crazy to me when I hear myself say it. But two people disappearing is simply too much of a coincidence."

Tanner thought back to a few days ago when he'd discovered something unusual in a simulation run by ViroPredict. He recalled with vivid clarity the acrimony in Will's voice during their discussion. Could the programming in ViroPredict be fundamentally flawed?

"Let's pretend for a moment you're right about the software having major problems," he said slowly. "Why would he murder two people in cold blood over flawed software? To me that doesn't add up."

Monica shrugged. "ViroPredict is the only viable product Sim-Sci has. Sure, they do a little contract R&D, but that's not enough to keep its doors open. Will has placed a huge bet on the success of ViroPredict. With it, the company is worth hundreds of millions of dollars, and Will can cash out by selling SimSci to a company like Sander. Without it, the company would probably close its doors."

"But Will isn't in this for the money," Tanner countered. "He tells people all the time that he envisions a world where people dying from viruses is a thing of the past."

Monica gave him a wry look. "That's what he may say publicly, but how many people do you know that would pass on the opportunity to pocket a couple hundred million dollars?"

As the two spoke, Tanner watched as people trickled in for the night's entertainment. At any moment their discussion could become drowned out by the sound of guitars wailing and drums pounding.

"I'm finding all of this a little hard to fathom. But I'll assume you are right about the software issues and Will murdering Vijay and Scott. One question still remains in my mind. Why are you telling me? What do you expect me to do about it? If I were you, I'd be going to the police."

"I can't go to the police yet. I need more proof that the software is fundamentally flawed. If I go to the police and I'm wrong, and then it leaks out, the damage to Sander's reputation would be irreparable. It would be the stereotypical big pharma trying to squash its small start-up competitor. This is why I'm reaching out to you."

"Do you want me to somehow test it?" Tanner asked, still unsure exactly what Monica was about to ask of him.

"No, there's no need for you to test anything. I want you to get ViroPredict's source code for me. Then I can have some of my programmers find the flaws in it and prove my theory."

Tanner sat back in his chair, stunned by the request. The source code was the engine that ran ViroPredict. If the software was functioning properly and he handed the source code over, he'd be handing Monica hundreds of millions of dollars. But if it was the missing piece of evidence Monica needed to put away a sociopath, then he knew he needed to do it before someone else died.

"This is a lot to ask. I need some time to think about it."

"I completely understand. Take some time, but remember, we don't know who else may be in danger. Someone at my company could be next on his list."

Once again Tanner thought about his exchange with Will the other day in his office. He felt himself shiver as he wondered if he might be the next person in danger.

CHAPTER 23

As Nick walked into Raff's Pub, he surveyed the bar. It ran the length of the interior, with around a dozen empty stools to choose from. In the center of the room sat two pool tables. The doors to the restrooms were in the back corner. All of the patrons were sitting at the bar despite there being a half dozen tables to choose from. As usual, he recognized nearly everyone there. He was pleased to see the one person that he had come to see, and he took a seat next to him at the bar.

"What's up, Fletch?" Nick asked as he sat down at the bar.

"Oh shit, Nick, what's going on?"

"Not much. Just coming down here to get out of the house for a little."

Fletch was sitting at the bar with his friend whom Nick only knew by his first name, LeSean.

"Are you coming here to shoot some pool, or just to grab a beer?" Fletch asked.

"Both actually," Nick replied, understanding Fletch's cryptic question.

"Well, let's go outside for a smoke."

As the two were walking outside, Nick's eyes met those of a woman sitting at the end of the bar. She was in her late thirties,

Nick's age, with short brown hair and big brown eyes. She was with another woman that he recognized as a regular.

Nick already had the money ready in his pocket, so the transaction took just seconds as the two smoked. The two finished their cigarettes and then headed back inside. Instead of going back to his bar stool, Nick headed to the men's room. This will give me the lift I need tonight, he thought as he quickly snorted a little coke once safely inside the bathroom. As he checked himself in the bathroom mirror, he tried to remember just exactly how he and Fletch came up with the term "playing pool" to refer to an eight-ball of coke. No matter, he thought. Let's get out there and enjoy the night.

As he returned, he could already feel the effects of the drug. He sat back down next to Fletch and began to drink his beer. The three men exchanged idle chatter about the Celtics' chances in the playoffs.

As the night went on more drugs and alcohol pumped through Nick's veins. He was feeling pretty good, like he could party all night long. After finishing his seventh beer, he got up to go outside to have another cigarette. He had just lit it when the door to the bar opened and a woman walked out. She was the one who had caught his eye earlier. She had a cigarette in one hand and was fishing for a lighter from her jacket pocket with the other.

"Cold enough out here for you?" Nick asked as he handed her his.

"On days like this I'd like to live in Florida."

"I'm Nick," he said as he extended his hand.

"Kelley."

"I think I've seen your friend in here before, but I've never spoken to her."

"You're talking about Reilly. She's here quite a bit. She dates the bartender, has for a couple of years now."

"Makes sense. And you are keeping her company tonight?"

"It's Friday and we decided to go out for a change. She was in a fight with her roommate, and I was getting cabin fever spending every night alone."

"Well, I don't think you guys are the only ones who had that idea. This place is more crowded than it usually is," Nick said as he finished his cigarette. "I'm going to head in. Don't stay out here too long. It's cold. What are you drinking?" he asked.

"A Long Island Iced Tea," she replied.

"A what?"

"You're not from around here, are you?" she asked, laughing.

"Guilty as charged."

"Just ask for a Long Island Iced Tea. The bartender will know what you mean."

Nick took her at her word and headed inside to buy the drink. As he sat back down, he saw Kelley's friend staring at him from across the bar. A few minutes later, she came back into the bar and looked around before spotting him. He raised the drink to her and she came over to get it.

"So what is in a Long Island Iced Tea?"

"A lot of vodka, some gin, tequila, rum, and lemon juice."

"Whoa, that sounds like it packs a punch."

"But it tastes really good. Want some?"

"Sure." He took the glass from her and tasted the drink.

"Not bad. It's funny, I've never even heard of this drink before."

"It sounds like you need to get out more often," she said with a big smile.

"Why don't you sit down here and finish this drink?" he asked, motioning to the barstool next to him.

"Okay."

The two spent the next two hours talking to one another. The bartender finally approached.

"C'mon guys, time to go. We're leaving," he said motioning to Kelley's friend.

Nick looked at his watch. It was one in the morning. His eyes then scanned the room. They were the only ones left at the bar.

"I really can't drive home," Kelley said, looking woozily at Nick. "Could you bring me back to my place? It's about ten minutes from here."

"Sure," Nick replied, and the two began gathering their belongings.

Halfway through the ride to Kelley's apartment, a new song began playing on the car stereo. Kelley turned up the radio and started saying something to Nick, but he couldn't hear her. He shrugged his shoulders and pointed at his ear. She leaned across the car and put her mouth up to Nick's ear. He could feel her breasts rubbing up against his arm as she leaned into him.

"I love this song," she said.

As she spoke, he could feel her warm breath on his ear and her hand landed on his leg. Despite all of the alcohol that he had consumed, he could feel himself getting very excited. Focus. Let's get us to the apartment before I wrap this car around a telephone pole. The entrance to her condo complex finally appeared in the distance, and Nick swerved into it. He pulled the car into one of the spaces in the parking lot outside. Not quite between the yellow lines, but good enough for me, he thought.

"You should come in. You don't want to drive home at this hour, and I really need someone to have a drink with," she said as she took the keys out of the ignition and put them in her pocket.

"Okay. That sounds good."

As he walked beside her, she lost her footing a few times and stumbled into him. He wasn't walking all that straight himself. But the two managed to navigate the way to her apartment.

They had barely gotten inside when she took her jacket off and proceeded to help Nick take his off as well. She moved closer in until their lips were just inches apart. Nick didn't waste the opportunity. After a short kiss, Kelley pulled away and threw Nick's jacket onto her kitchen table.

"I'm not ready for this party to be over," she said, her big brown eyes locked with Nick's. She led him into her bedroom and pushed him down onto the bed. Then she opened her nightstand drawer.

"Want to feel better than you've ever felt in your entire life?" she asked as she pulled out a bag of blue pills.

"What are those?"

"They're OC's."

He knew that OC was short for Oxycontin, a powerful pain medication frequently given to people with chronic pain, often in advanced stages of cancer. When taken the right way it provided a feeling of euphoria much like heroin.

"What are you going to do with that spoon?" Nick asked as he watched Kelley.

"We're going to crush one of these pills up, then snort it like coke. It's the quickest way to get high." Kelley looked up at Nick. "You've never done this before, have you?"

"I'm afraid not."

"This is going to knock your socks off."

Kelley crushed the pill and snorted a line of powder. She handed the dollar bill to Nick, and he proceeded to snort the two lines of powder that she'd laid out for him.

"After blowing those two lines, you're going to want to fuck all night," she said as she pushed him down onto the bed and began to kiss his neck.

CHAPTER 24

Inside a large conference room in the headquarters for the U.S. Department of Homeland Security, the discussion was being led by the Deputy Secretary, Colonial Leonard Webb. The meeting included representatives from three of the major branches of the department including Science and Technology, Health Affairs, and Intelligence and Analysis. On a large screen at the front of the room were pictures of Will and James Woltzberg. The pictures were exact matches of the ones on their driver's licenses.

Leah Peterson sat at the center of the round table, impatiently chewing on the blue cap to her pen. As a field agent, she loathed large meetings, but at the same time she recognized the importance of this one. Her chewing slowed and she listened attentively as Leonard continued.

"The technology core to ViroPredict has many applications both good and bad to the U.S. I think it's fairly obvious to everyone in the room what the benefits of such a technology would be. Pharmaccutical companies with access to this technology would be able to create and produce enough vaccine for the entire country before harmful viruses kill a single person."

Leonard paused as he saw a number of individuals around the room taking notes. As the pens slowed down, he continued where he left off.

"But it's the negative aspect to this technology that brings us here today. Our intelligence group has recently picked up some "chatter" during their surveillance of individuals thought or known to be part of a terrorist cell. We believe that a group is currently trying to get access to this software. We don't know why for certain, but various groups under the Homeland security umbrella have worked together, and it's believed that this terrorist cell wants to use the software to discover the right mix of variables needed to create a particularly deadly strain of an existing virus. Once they identify the conditions needed to create the strain, they'll put the live virus in those conditions and then allow it to mutate. Once they have a virus with the desired genetic makeup, they will knowingly infect members of their organization. This new breed of martyr would be carrying a weapon that no metal detector or bomb-sniffing dog could ever find. Once infected, they would proceed to spread the virus by visiting places in the country where there are many high-risk individuals, such as hospitals, schools, public transportation, and sporting events. Instead of becoming suicide bombers in the traditional sense, they would kill by spreading the virus to thousands of innocent people and then let the virus kill them. Instead of hundreds or thousands of people dying instantly from a bomb, people would die slowly once the virus is contracted. The terrorist infected would still die, bringing many people with him just like a traditional suicide bomber, only slower. As the virus spreads, he or she would not just kill the people that they come into contact with, they'd be killing people that come into contact with the person that they originally infected, and so on. This uncontrollable pandemic would become much more deadly than a conventional suicide bomb."

The note taking had nearly stopped. He saw shock on the faces of hardened intelligence agents. They had never encountered a threat like this before.

"Do we think they're technologically advanced and organized enough to carry this out?" Leah asked.

"We absolutely believe that they have the means to carry out this operation. After 2001, we have to operate under the assumption that they have the ability to carry out any operation that would harm our country." Leonard paused to see if there were any other questions. No one else spoke.

With the click of a mouse, Leonard changed the images on the large flat screen at the front of the room, and the pictures of Scott Bredahl and Vijay Kalam appeared on it.

"The situation has been further complicated by the recent deaths of the two people that you see on this screen. Scott Bredahl and Vijay Kalam were both employed by SimSci. Scott was a scientist, and Vijay was SimSci's Director of Software Engineering and one of the key developers of ViroPredict. Scott was found dead in his apartment with his work-issued laptop open on his bed with him. Vijay was abducted in the city of Cambridge, Massachusetts, and was found dead less than a week later. He had been tortured before he was killed, shot execution style in the back of the head."

Leonard paused, this time to take a sip of bottled water. He looked around the room to see if anyone had any questions, and then proceeded to change the image on the giant screen. The next image was that of a man with dark skin and a long beard.

"The chatter that we have intercepted has been from the cell phone of this man. His name is Omar Al-Tabari. We believe that he's part of the terrorist cell interested in the technology. We have been tracking his whereabouts via a GPS tracking on all cell phone calls that he makes. Based on his calls, he has never come within five miles of Simulation Scientific or the homes of the deceased. We believe that he has been working with another group, but we have not been able to identify who this group is or what their role might be. This is one of the reasons that we need to bring field agents into the investigation.

"Regarding the potential terrorist plot and their ultimate goal, if they were able to get their hands on the software, find a potentially deadly virus, and infect themselves with it to spread in highly populated areas of the country, such an event would be more catastrophic than any other attack carried out on U.S. soil. It could result in hundreds of thousands of civilian deaths. Given those possibilities, this threat has the attention of everyone in this Department. It also has the attention of our President. I have personally briefed him on what we know at this time. He has asked that I continue to keep him apprised of additional intelligence as it becomes available. Are there any questions at this point?"

Again there were no questions, just lots of note taking.

"I'm going to turn to our plan of action going forward. We need to monitor this situation on two fronts. The first is to keep tabs on Al-Tabari. This will be done in two ways. We will continue to monitor his cell phone. We will locate him and surveil him to determine who he is working with on this plot. The second is to carefully watch the Simulation Scientific business, especially Will and James Woltzberg. Agent Peterson, I'm going to ask you to lead these crucial initiatives. You will report directly to me on this assignment. It crosses many functions within our Department. The technology is being researched by the Science and Technology branch, the nature of the health threat by the Health Affairs branch, and the Intelligence and Analysis branch are reviewing intelligence intercepted from Al-Tabari. I want to emphasize that we must work together in order to successfully protect our country from this plot."

"I don't think that I need to tell everyone in this room that this information should be treated with the highest level of confidentiality. If this story were to be leaked, it could spark panic, or force the terrorist cell to accelerate whatever plans that they have. Now, we all have a lot of work to do, so let's get out there and get it done."

With Leonard's final words, all of the individuals around the table began to gather their things and leave the conference room.

"Leah, could you hang around for a minute?" Leonard asked before she could rise to her feet. He waited until everyone else had left the room, and then closed the conference room door.

"Regarding Al-Tabari, we believe we've identified the apartment building where he's currently living. Once we have a positive ID on the ground, we need to not only keep track of him but also identify anyone that he comes in contact with. If we need additional field agents to trail other suspects, we'll give you those resources. We'll provide you with as many agents as you need to monitor all individuals involved."

"We haven't identified anyone else involved with this plot?" she asked. "When we intercept this chatter who is he talking to?"

"We haven't been able make a positive ID on the other person or people. They're using disposable cell phones. For the life of me, I cannot understand why Al-Tabari is not using one as well. We believe that he's speaking to the same person over and over. But we can't assume whoever is on the other end of those calls is the only one he's working with. We believe there are others on the ground, and by monitoring him he'll lead us to them." Leonard clicked the mouse and the images of Will and James reappeared. "You'll also be working with Will Woltzberg. At this point in time he knows only that people from his company are dying. He doesn't know anything about the chatter we've intercepted or what we believe to be the ultimate goal of the individuals carrying out the killings. I need you to explain what we're doing, and that the well-being of his company is now a matter of national security. Then you need to watch him and his family to ensure that they're kept safe. We'll provide you with resources to assist you with this task."

"Should I tell him exactly what we believe the terrorist plot to be?" Leah asked.

"Yes, you can share what we know with him," Leonard replied. "Do you have any other questions or concerns?"

"No sir," Leah replied.

"Good. Now let's get out there and keep the future of the United States secure."

CHAPTER 25

Will was nearly thrown from his barstool from the impact. He grabbed James' arm to maintain his balance, steadying himself. Beer spilled all over the bar and onto his pants, getting them wet.

"Oh shit, sorry, next round is on me," the kid sitting next to Will said once he saw what he had done. He'd been playfully wrestling with his friend.

"No problem," Will said, despite his facial expression saying something different. Beside him James was in hysterics.

"How come this sort of stuff always happens to me?" Will asked as he began to wipe his pants dry.

"Because you're not quick enough to get out of the way."

The two brothers were sitting at the bar at Fourth and One, taking in a Celtics game. Behind the bar a brunette in tight denim shorts was busy serving drinks. She had Chinese lettering tattooed on her neck, and as James sat at the bar, he wondered what the letters meant. The two brothers sat in silence for a moment as Will feverishly blotted his pants with napkins from the bar, and James focused on the television.

"So any word from Charles on the case file from Scott's murder?" James asked.

"I've been leaving him voicemails on a daily basis asking about the status. He finally called me back today. He still hasn't been able to get it. But he did have some news on his investigation into Vijay's murder. There was a significant finding."

"Oh yeah? Does he have a suspect?"

"Not quite. He said the crime scene was nearly spotless. There was almost nothing left to go on. But they did find a few pieces of hair that didn't belong to Vijay."

"So they have the DNA of the person who killed Vijay?"

"They sure do."

"So it should just be a matter of time before they find the guy, right?"

"I wish it were that easy. They've already run the DNA against all the records they have in their database and they didn't get a match. Apparently whoever has done this hasn't been arrested for a crime before."

"Wow, so even with the DNA they don't have any suspects?"

"I'm afraid so," Will replied.

Suddenly, James felt a hand on his shoulder. He turned, thinking the same patrons who had knocked Will's beer over were now bumping him. What he saw when he turned caused him to freeze in shock, like a deer in the headlights of an oncoming eighteen wheeler. Standing behind him was Nadir Massoud. Being so close to the man gave James a sense of impending doom.

"James Woltzberg, I thought that was you. It's really good to see you." Nadir said, his hand still on James' shoulder.

James wanted to jerk away from him. He wanted to stand up and tell him to never touch him again. But with Will sitting next to him watching the exchange, he told himself to keep cool.

"Likewise," James said.

"So how've you been? Gosh, it's been so long."

What kind of mind fuck is this guy trying to play? James wondered. Nadir had him cornered and he knew it. James could see in his eyes that he was enjoying it, thriving on it.

"I've been good, and you?"

"Oh, you know, work and the family, it takes up all of my time. I'm just glad I was able to get away tonight. Gotta love the green this year," Nadir said as he motioned toward the Celtics game.

"So have you spoken to Jon lately?"

"Jon?"

"You know, Jon Ferris,"

Finally, Nadir removed his hand. He switched to a different kind of mind game now, James thought.

"Ummm, no, I haven't seen him in years," James said. Out of the corner of his eye, he could see Will taking it all in. What if Nadir mentioned the money-laundering scheme? James hadn't gotten back to him about his offer. Would he tell Will about it? Is that why he came here? James couldn't let that happen.

"Will, could you excuse us for a moment?" James asked as he rose from his seat and headed over to an open table a safe distance away from his brother. The two men took seats facing one another.

"How did you know that I'd be here? Are you following me?"

"Let's say I have a vested interested in keeping tabs on you. What do you expect? I haven't heard from you since we spoke last week." Nadir said, his face emotionless.

"I've thought about your request. I can't give you control of SimSci. My brother owns half of the company."

"Well then, maybe it's time to discuss this issue with him. It just so happens he's over there at the bar. Let's take a walk back over there—"

Nadir had risen from his chair, and James grabbed Nadir's arm and pulled him back down into it.

"Wait!" James pleaded. "Please, I'll tell him, I just need some time."

"I've given you time, and you've done nothing with it. I can't wait any longer."

"Going over there now will only make things worse. Give me some more time!"

Nadir sat back in his chair and stared coldly at James. "You have twenty-four hours. This is your final chance. Don't make me sorry that I gave it to you."

Nadir rose from his chair and headed for the door. On the way he walked up to Will and placed his hand on his shoulder. Will turned and found himself staring into Nadir's icy eyes.

"Send Sarah and the two boys my best."

Before Will could respond, Nadir was halfway to the exit. Seconds later James settled nervously on his seat at the bar. He read the confusion on Will's face.

"Who the hell was that?" Will asked.

"Just an old friend who I hadn't seen in a while."

"How does he know who I am and how does he know Sarah?"

James was trying with all his might to look calm. "I've known him for years. I'm sure I've mentioned both your names before."

Will didn't look like he believed a word. "You didn't seem too thrilled to be running into him. What, was he a bookie you owed money to from your sports gambling days?"

"Something like that."

Will turned his attention back to the game. James asked himself the same question his brother had: How did Nadir know Sarah's name? What else did he know?

CHAPTER 26

As the plane touched down onto the runway, Leah Peterson unhitched her seat belt. She was the only person on the private flight besides the pilots and a single stewardess. All were employees of the federal government. She disembarked and immediately headed for a predetermined area where a black Ford Explorer would be waiting for her. Her first destination was Simulation Scientific's headquarters. No one at the organization knew that she was on her way, and she didn't have an appointment with the man that she was going to see.

Prior to her arrival in Boston, she had performed extensive research on both the company and Will Woltzberg. She knew everything that was publically available about the company, and some things that weren't. She had just finished reviewing her notes one final time as the SUV approached SimSci.

"We're here, Agent Peterson," her driver said as he pulled to the curb. Leah thanked him and got out of the car. Despite the vehicle being parked right in front of a fire hydrant, the driver turned the vehicle off. This was one parking violation that wasn't going to receive a citation.

Leah entered the building and walked over to the reception desk. The secretary at the desk greeted her with a warm smile, one that Leah didn't return. Instead she reached into the pocket of her suit jacket and showed her identification badge.

"My name is Agent Leah Peterson. I'm with the U.S. Department of Homeland Security. I'm here to see William Woltzberg. It's regarding a matter of national security."

Startled, the secretary dialed Will's extension. "There is someone here to see you. She says that she's from the U.S. Department of Homeland Security."

Inside Will's office, he wasn't sure if he was more shocked or confused with what the receptionist had just told him. Why would someone from the Department of Homeland Security come here to speak to me? he thought.

"Tell her I'll be right down," Will replied and hung up the phone.

In the foyer, he found a woman in her early thirties standing at the receptionist desk. She was dressed in a dark business suit, and had long brown hair and hazel eyes. Her mouth was a thin slit, her forehead large and protruding. He guessed that she was about five foot three, with a broad build. As soon as he emerged from the back offices, her eyes locked with his. He found it strange that she wasn't sitting down in one of the many chairs in the foyer for guests. She had remained standing at the receptionist's desk, as if she had no intention of waiting long.

"William Woltzberg," he said as he extended his hand.

"Leah Peterson, Field Agent with the U.S. Department of Homeland Security. I'd like to speak with you in regards to a matter of national security."

Her handshake was firm and her facial expression stoic. Will could hear the deep southern dialect in her voice.

"Please follow me. We can discuss this in my office."

On the way to his office, he stuck his head into James' office.

"I'd like you to meet Leah Peterson. She is with the Department of Homeland Security."

Will watched the change in his brother's expression. "A pleasure," James said.

"Do you have a few minutes to sit down with us?" Will asked.

"Sure," James replied, and followed Will to his office.

"So you'd said that you're here regarding a matter of national security?" Will asked once they all were seated.

"That's correct, Mr. Woltzberg."

"Please, call me Will." Without consciously realizing it, he picked up the Rubix Cube that he kept on his desk. He sat back in his large leather office chair and twisted the colorful cube as he listened to Leah.

"The following information is considered confidential. The reason that I'm here sharing it with you today is because it involves you and your company."

Will couldn't imagine how anything that his company was doing would impact the country's security, but he nodded and she continued.

"We've recently intercepted terrorist 'chatter' that's led us to your organization. We believe that a terrorist cell wants to use your software to discover how to create a particularly deadly strain of an existing virus. Then we believe that they'll use this knowledge to harm U.S. interests, both domestically and abroad."

Will looked at James, and the look of bewilderment on his face matched Will's own. "How are terrorists going to harm people using our software?"

"It appears that they've found a way to use your software that you never envisioned possible. You see Will, not everyone shares your altruistic ambitions. We believe that they want to use the software to create a particularly deadly strain of an existing virus.

Once they have this virus created in cyber space— I think the technical term is in silico— they'll create the right environment for the virus to mutate in nature. But they won't stop there."

Her discussion was interrupted by Will's phone ringing. He let it go to voicemail, and Leah continued. "Once the virus actually exists, the terrorist organization will infect some of its members to act as 'suicide bombers' and go into populated areas and spread the virus."

"They'd kill thousands of people." James cried.

"Thousands? I don't think so. If they found the right virus, they could kill millions," Will countered, shaking his head in disbelief. "Jesus Christ, we've created software that provides the blueprint to create a biological weapon."

"We believe that these individuals are responsible for the deaths of Scott Bredahl and Vijay Kalam. These people may be targeting you two next. Because of this risk, I've been assigned to keep both of you under surveillance so that you remain safe. We're doing this for two reasons. First, obviously, your personal safety is a concern. But should these individuals access this software, we would need your assistance in using the software to determine exactly what they're doing with it."

The Rubix Cube was no longer twisting in his hands. Will was at a loss for words. Instead, his mind sifted through the events of the past few weeks. If terrorists had killed Scott after trying to get access to ViroPredict, that would explain the piece of paper with the company's name and the name of their software in Scott's house. It would explain why Scott's computer was sitting on his bed turned on. It could also explain why their DNA wasn't in the criminal database. The pieces to the puzzle were starting to fit together. But the picture the puzzle was revealing made Will sick. He suddenly came to a realization about the capabilities of the software he'd created. In the wrong hands it could be cataclysmic.

"Do you have any questions about anything that I've told you so far?" she asked.

"We've already hired a private security company for the office. I don't think that it's necessary for you to be here as well," James informed her.

"You'll be canceling their services. You won't be needing them anymore. We'll be watching over you for the foreseeable future."

"What in the world makes you think that any of what you said is happening?" Will asked, his face pale.

"As I mentioned, we've intercepted terrorist 'chatter' in a series of telephone calls that led us to these conclusions. The calls were made by an individual that has ties to terrorist organizations that we've been monitoring. The caller made reference to a computer program on a number of the calls. At first we were unsure of what he was referring to. A team of intelligence agents began scouring the Internet to find it. We had it narrowed down to a small number of software packages when the news about Vijay Kalam caught our attention. Then the pieces began to come together. It all fit. The individual whose calls were intercepted was physically located in Cambridge, and your company is also in Cambridge. When Vijay was murdered, and we subsequently heard about Scott, it left little doubt in our minds. Your company's program is the program at the center of this plot."

"So what does this mean to me and my company?" Will asked.

"Beginning tomorrow you will be monitored twenty-four hours a day. Business should be conducted as if nothing out of the ordinary is taking place. However, we will be screening all potential clients and software licensees to ensure that they have no known links to terrorist organizations. Again, this step should take place without impacting your daily business activities."

Will understood what Leah was telling him. Two of his employees had been murdered because of the work that they'd done at SimSci. He and James could be next.

141

"I'll be following one of you, and the other will be under police surveillance. Again, this is for your own protection."

"I have a friend who is the Cambridge Police Department's lead investigator in Vijay's murder. He's made some progress in identifying the person who killed him. They've found his DNA, and they've made quite a bit of progress."

Leah shifted in her chair, frowning at the mention of local police. "We've already reviewed the evidence collected from the crime scene. While your friend and his team did a good job finding that DNA, it turns out upon closer inspection, there was another person in that room. We found a third set of DNA at that crime scene."

"So the murderer is not acting alone?" James asked.

"It appears not. Going forward, we will be working with your friend, Detective Madre, I believe, to gather evidence and determine exactly who committed this murder and what relation they have to the terrorist organization we are monitoring. Do either of you have any other questions?"

The brothers looked at each other in shock. James shook his head. I've got so many questions, Will thought, I don't even know where to begin.

CHAPTER 27

Radiant diamonds glistened on Sarah's wrist as she twisted it, admiring the beauty of the bracelet. Her gaze shifted back and forth between the jewelry and the mirror on the glass display case in front of her. She already knew what earrings and necklace she'd wear with it, and she had numerous outfits that the collection could be worn with. The saleswoman stood behind the counter obediently, no doubt calculating what the commission would be based on the five-figure price of the bracelet.

Out of nowhere, Sarah heard a deep voice from behind her.

"It's beautiful, we'll take it."

Suddenly Sarah felt two large, strong hands on her shoulders. She involuntarily shrugged upon feeling the strange hands and quickly turned around. She gently pushed Alan away and flashed a playful smile.

"No, please don't listen to him. He's off his meds," Sarah said to the woman behind the counter.

"But that's what friends are for, to lift each other's spirits."

"I'm sure that you can find a less expensive way to lift my spirits," Sarah said as she unfastened the bracelet and carefully handed it back to the saleswoman thanking her as she did so. "Come on, Alan. Let's find a place to talk."

The two left the store and stepped out onto the cobblestone walkway of Faneuil Hall Marketplace. The Marketplace, existing in downtown Boston since 1742, was now an outdoor mall for both tourists and locals to visit to shop and dine. Although Sarah had just completed the former, it was not the reason for her visit there today.

It was a dry and cloudless night. Sarah tugged at her jacket as a frigid breeze swept past them. A dusting of snow rolled by, its destination at the mercy of the wind.

"May I suggest we get a quick drink at Carmine's?" Alan asked.

"As long as it's not too far, I'm parked just over there," she said, pointing to a towering parking garage less than a block away.

"No, it's right there." Alan indicated a small sign posted on a building some fifty yards away.

"That store had so many beautiful pieces of jewelry," Sarah said as they made their way over to the bar.

"Well, if you didn't like the one you were trying on, you could've picked another one."

She glanced at him and smiled. "It must be nice to be able to buy something that expensive without having to think twice about it."

"The compensation that comes with being chairman of Sander has its benefits," Alan said, not bragging but stating a fact. "The watches and cars are nice, but that isn't what I really enjoy."

"So what then? What does a powerful man like you do with the money you've made?"

He cast his hand over the entire scene. "Being CEO has afforded me the opportunity to see the world. I've tasted its cuisine and drank its wine. My five senses have taken in a portfolio of experiences that I can't put a price on. It's something everyone should experience."

Sarah was captivated by Alan's words. How many times had she imagined traveling the world? How different would her life have been if Alan had the confidence he had now back when the two were in college? He'd been cute in a shy way back then. Would she have dated the man had he extended such an offer?

"Sarah?"

Sarah's eyes blinked and quickly focused on Alan as he spoke to her.

"Are you okay?" Alan asked.

"Sorry, I was just trying to remember what level I parked on in the garage."

"I was asking you if you thought this place looked all right."

"Oh, yes, this looks perfect."

The two entered the restaurant. The atmosphere stood in stark contrast to the bar they'd met at last time they were out. The bar encompassed the majority of the large room, with only a few small tables lining the perimeter. Multiple televisions hung on every wall, and there was a jukebox in the far corner. The bar was packed, but they managed to find two people leaving and quickly claimed the empty barstools. They were situated right next to a group of rowdy college kids. Sarah could hear them talking about a concert that they'd be leaving to go to shortly. Alan pulled out Sarah's chair and took her jacket from her. He then seated himself in the chair next to her. The woman behind the bar came over to take their drink order. Alan ordered a glass of top-shelf scotch, Sarah a cola.

"Sarah, please, one drink," Alan insisted as he called the bartender back and ordered her a dry martini.

"Ok, just one," she said as she flashed a sexy smile and a wink in his direction. She then reached into her purse and took out an envelope and handed it to Alan.

"This is what we talked about last week."

"Ah, we are getting right down to business, I see," Alan replied, impressed.

"We don't have to talk business. You know what I need. I think enough's been said."

"Then no business it is."

She remembered what he had said outside. "So what's the most interesting thing you've done in your travels around the world?"

Alan pondered the question before responding. "I'd have a hard time choosing between scuba diving in the Great Barrier Reef in Australia and a fourteen-day wildlife safari in South Africa."

"What's Australia like? I've always wanted to go there."

Alan loved sharing stores about his travels and provided Sarah with all the details about the trip. As he spoke, Sarah clung to his every word. "And you do all of this by yourself?"

"I've taken many companions with me on these excursions. You see, I've been in many relationships over the years, dated many beautiful women."

"But you haven't found 'the one' to settle down with?"

Alan blinked at the question. "I've dated many women from all parts of the world. Once I thought I was in love, that I'd found 'the one,' but things simply didn't work out as I would've liked."

"I'm sorry."

"Please, no need to apologize. But I do believe someday it may happen, this time for real. Like everything in life, falling in love is a risk, one where the reward is high, but so is the damage if it fails. Taking measured risks is how I've gotten to where I am today, I thrive on them."

She saw a look growing in his eyes, one that reminded her of when he touched her hand the other night. It energized her, as if his lust for life was contagious. She suddenly felt the urge to do something exciting, something exhilarating. She finished her drink and forcefully set the glass onto the bar.

"Let's do a shot!" she demanded as she grabbed Alan by the arm. Before Alan could even accept her offer she had ordered two shots of tequila from the bartender.

"Cheers!" she shouted as she held up her glass for a toast.

The pair tilted their heads back and downed the shot glasses. Sarah's face wrinkled like a prune after she was done.

"I honestly can't recall the last time that I took a shot of tequila!" Alan said.

Sarah wasn't sure if she was already feeling the effects of the shot or the adrenaline from taking it, but her heart was racing. She felt so alive she didn't want the rush to stop.

"Two more!" she shouted to the bartender over the voices of the college kids next to her.

As the bartender was filling their shot glasses, Sarah saw one of the college kids go over to the jukebox to fire up a song. Moments later, a classic Bruce Springsteen anthem was filling the air. The group of kids next to Sarah began to sing along with the lyrics.

"I love Bruce Springsteen!" Sarah shouted over the chorus beside her.

One of the boys turned to Sarah. "He's playing tonight at the Gahhhhhden!" he shouted in an exaggerated Boston accent fueled by the alcohol.

"We should go! I wonder if there are tickets still for sale!" Sarah said, turning to Alan.

"Lady, it's been sold out since the hour that they went on sale," the kid said.

A wave of disappointment came over Sarah, tempering her frenzy.

"Excuse me," Alan rose from his seat and excused himself from her presence. Sarah spent the next few minutes talking to the group of kids. She saw Alan come back in from outside the bar, a calm smile showing from ear to ear.

"Let's go," he said, grabbing her jacket off her seat.

"What? I don't want to leave yet."

"I just called my good friend Stu Markowitz. We've got front-row seats waiting for us, so we better get going!"

Ecstatic at hearing the news, Sarah jumped off of her seat, gave Alan a kiss and hugged him as she jumped up and down. Deep down a part of her brain was asking, "what did I just do?" but the rest of her was having no part in rational thinking.

Alan put his arm out. "Shall we?" he asked. Sarah took his arm and the two headed off to the rock concert.

* * *

The files on top of Colleen's desk were neatly organized, and the overhead light above her desk was off.

"Looks like she's gone for the day," Will said as he and James headed to his office.

"Well, it's six-thirty, what do you expect?"

Will looked down at his watch, stunned at how long the meeting had run. "Jesus, where does the time go?" Will asked as he sat down at his desk. James took one of the seats across from it.

A bright yellow paper stuck to his computer monitor immediately caught his attention. He peeled it off as he read it.

Nadir Massoud from Sage Pharma called, said "it was important"

"Hmmm, do you know a Nadir Massoud? I could be wrong, but I think he's CEO of Sage Pharmaceuticals. They're right up the street." Will said.

James' mouth hung open as he scrambled to find the right response.

"Jesus! Look, Will, there's something we need to talk about."

Will, who had already begun checking the messages on his voicemail, saw the concern on his brother's face and put the phone down.

"I'm listening."

"Nadir Massoud is the man who approached me at Fourth and One last night. He's calling you because of what he and I discussed. You see, I've gotten us into some trouble."

"What sort of trouble?"

"Do you remember years ago when the bank canceled our line of credit and we were struggling financially? When we were working twelve-hour days? We were small and the money wasn't coming in the door fast enough. Do you recall what a mess we were in?"

"Yes, I remember when we thought we weren't going to make it. God, I remember it like it was yesterday. We barely made payroll. You landed those big R&D contracts, like clockwork one after another. Without them we wouldn't have been able to pull through."

James sighed and shook his head. "Those big contracts you remember, they weren't real."

Will's face radiated confusion. "What do you mean? I remember seeing the invoices and sales orders! The money sure was real. It got us through that rough patch!"

James was starting to sweat. "Do you ever remember doing any of the work for those contracts? Any work at all?"

"So where did the money come from?"

"You have to understand, I was doing what I thought was best for us at the time! I had no idea.."

"Where did it come from?" Will shouted.

Despite his guilt, James would not stand for being shouted at. "It was dirty! It was all dirty money. I made the invoices and sales orders up!"

149

"What the fuck do you mean 'dirty'? What does that mean? Did you steal it? Was it drug money? What was it?"

"I had a college friend who got himself involved in some bad stuff. He was paid a lot of money for stealing hundreds of credit card numbers. He had to do something with the money, so he approached me. The timing was everything, he needed help, we needed cash to float the business."

Will instantly understood the implication. "So you made up fake invoices and laundered the money through our company! What is wrong with you!"

"At the time it seemed like the only choice that we had!"

Will wanted to reach across the desk and throttle his younger brother. But that wouldn't do any good. He took a couple of deep breaths, struggling for control.

"So this is all in the past, it's all behind us now, right? Don't tell me you're still doing this."

"No, it was just that one time— eight fake invoices."

Will was puzzled. "So what does all of this have to do with Nadir Massoud? Is it the same Nadir Massoud who is CEO of Sage?" Will asked as he tapped his computer back from sleep and began an Internet search for Sage Pharmaceuticals. He quickly found their homepage and looked at their management team. Staring back at him was the man he'd met the previous evening at Fourth and One.

"He was involved in the deal," James said miserably. "He knows everything. Worse, he has evidence that ties me and SimSci to the money. He's got it all tied up in a nice neat bow!"

"That's impossible to believe. I'm looking at his mug right here online. He's the CEO of Sage Pharmaceuticals. Why would he get involved in something so low?"

"For all you know, it was the same reason I got involved in something like that. It was a long time ago, and people were in very different places."

Will slammed his closed fist onto his desk. "Fine, say you are right about why he got himself involved in this quagmire. Why would he be coming after you now? He's CEO of a successful drug company. Why is he dredging this up?"

"Because I didn't have anything he wanted until now."

"What does he want?"

"Our company."

"What! What do you mean, our company?" Will shouted, as the veins in his neck bulged.

"He wants us to transfer control of SimSci to him."

"This arrogant son of a bitch thinks he's going blackmail us for this company!" Will jumped back to his feet and stormed around his desk and stood over his brother. "Let me get a piece of this prick!"

"What are you proposing we do?"

"*We* aren't going to do anything! You've already done enough. I'm going to have a talk with this son of a bitch!" Will shouted. He grabbed his phone and dialed Nadir's number before James could do anything.

Nadir's voicemail picked up and Will smashed the phone back into its receiver.

"First thing tomorrow I'm going down to his office to talk to him. If he thinks he's going to blackmail Will Woltzberg, he's out of his *fucking mind*!"

CHAPTER 28

"What we are looking at here are Himalayan whiskered bats. You can see that its dorsal fur is a blackish brown color. In case you were wondering, the term 'blackish brown' is a technical term that us scientists use when we don't know what color to call it," Nigel joked as he held the small bat in his hand up to the camera. "They have a typical body mass of three to five grams and measure between thirty and thirty-five millimeters. As you can see, they have very sharp teeth. Have a look at these."

He positioned the bat so Marcel could capture footage of the tiny, razors inside the bat's mouth. Once Marcel nodded his head, Nigel let go. The bat flew off into the darkness of the cave. Marcel pointed the camera in its direction and the bright spotlight on top of the camera helped film the bat for a few seconds longer.

"Now let's see what these bats look like as they come out of the cave at night," Nigel said.

Marcel knew that was his cue to stop filming the scene and he shut the camera off. He kept the camera on his shoulder as he looked down at his feet. He was ankle deep in bat guano and was struggling to keep his balance while holding the heavy camera in his hands.

"Are you two ready to go get some fresh air?" Jao asked.

"Sure am." Marcel handed his camera to the local guide. Once the camera was out of his hands, he was able to wipe the sweat from his face. The inside of the cave was over one hundred degrees, and all of the men were sweating. But the heat was just one of the reasons being in the cave was unbearable. The air quality was poor, and the group had to wear a device on their chest to ensure the levels of harmful gasses didn't reach dangerous levels. Worst of all was the constant pattering of bat droppings from the creatures huddled above them.

Jao said something to the local guide in Thai and the man responded in his native tongue. Then he began guiding the group outside. While the guide had no problem navigating the treacherous path back to the cave entrance, that wasn't the case for the other three. Although each man had a hard hat with a spotlight on it to help them see, the light only illuminated a small patch in the pitch-black darkness. Centuries of bat guano was built up on the floor of the cave, creating a foot of mud-like substance for the men to trudge through. Beneath the layer of bat guano the floor of the cave was rugged, with sharp rocks and uneven terrain that made it extremely difficult for the men to maintain their balance. Thirty long minutes later, they escaped the cave.

As they emerged, the bright sun caused them all to squint. Their faces were filthy from bat droppings and sweat. Nigel opened the backpack that Jao was holding for him and took out a clean cloth to wipe his face. Although he felt good about their shoots so far, he was growing tired of being away from home. They'd fallen two days behind schedule due to the rain, which meant that he would have stay in Thailand longer than he'd planned.

"I feel like I have bat shit all over me," Marcel said as he wiped himself off with a cloth that he kept in his backpack.

"Take a number," Nigel replied. "Can I take a look at the shots?"

Marcel took the plastic protective covering off his camera and began rewinding the last shoot to the beginning. As Marcel was working with the camera, Nigel looked over at Jao. He was lying on the ground with a cloth over his head.

"Here you go," Marcel said as he handed the camera over.

Nigel watched the shots that they had taken and then handed the camera back to Marcel.

"They came out pretty good. I think we can call it a day."

"Thank the Lord." Marcel took a bottle of water out of his backpack and poured it over his head, and then wiped it down with the cloth. "I can't recall the last time I felt this dirty on a shoot."

That comment drew a chuckle from Nigel whose gaze wandered to Jao. He was lying on his back with a towel over his face. He hadn't spoken since they'd gotten out of the cave. Nigel slapped him on the leg.

"Hey, Jao, are you ready to head back to the hotel?"

"I'm definitely ready. I'm not feeling good."

Jao didn't move as he responded to Nigel's question, the towel still over his head.

"What's wrong?" Nigel asked.

"I think I might be getting the flu or something. My head is hurting and I think I may be getting a fever."

"Okay, let's call it a day then. It's got to be from the heat in the cave. That and the smell of bat shit has probably gotten to you. I was thinking of calling it a day anyhow. So let's head back to the jeep and go back to the hotel."

With that suggestion, Jao sat up and Nigel helped him to his feet. The other men gathered up all of their belongings, and the foursome headed back to the Jeep for the ride back to the village.

CHAPTER 29

"I don't care what his calendar says. He's going to see me this morning as soon as he gets in!" Will said loudly enough to draw the stares of the people throughout the small executive wing of Sage Pharmaceuticals. Be cool, he cautioned himself. Being a hot head isn't going to get you anywhere. He took a seat a few feet away from the receptionist and waited for Nadir.

Fifteen minutes later, he saw Nadir turn the corner in the hallway, and as their eyes met, he extended his hand to Will.

"I didn't expect that my message would result in a face-to-face meeting, Mr. Woltzberg."

"Is there somewhere we can talk?" Will asked as he firmly squeezed Nadir's hand. Nadir's receptionist nervously tapped her pen as she watched the exchange.

"Let's step into this conference room. Danielle, will you please ensure that we aren't disturbed?"

Will followed Nadir into a windowless conference room. Nadir motioned for him to take a seat as he closed the door.

"I trust you got my message?" Nadir asked.

"My brother James happened to be in my office when I got it. He filled me in on why you were calling."

"Good, I'm glad to hear James is coming clean with you. I don't know how much detail he went into."

"I know what information you have and what you want from us in return for not turning it over to the police."

"Good, then our discussion here should be a short one."

Will nodded his head in agreement. "Yes, it will be a short one. I don't know exactly why you thought that trying to dig up dirt that's years old, and then trying to blackmail my brother and I with it was a good idea. I've got news for you, Mr. Massoud, it isn't going to work. I'm not going to be threatened into handing over my company to you or anyone else!"

"Well then, I will just share what I know with the police.."

"You won't share *shit* with the police," Will said emphatically. "Because when you do, they will begin an investigation. My brother said he's sure you were involved in this scheme just like he was. As you might know, aiding and abetting charges come with a penalty as well. So does the charge of an accessory to commit a crime. Which one of those applies to you, Mr. Massoud?"

No response.

"Well? Are you going to say something?" Will jumped out of his seat. Nadir's silence was like gasoline on a fire, fueling Will's rage.

"Fine, you don't have to talk to me. You can take your empty threats and shove them up your ass," Will informed him firmly. "If you come near anyone in my company again, I'll have my friends in the police department have you arrested. You picked the wrong person to fuck with, Mr. Massoud!"

Will grabbed his suit jacket and stormed out of the conference room.

* * *

Nadir waited for him to leave the executive wing, then rose from his chair and headed back toward his office.

"Cancel my next meeting," he said as he passed his receptionist. He closed his office door behind him and picked up the phone. He waited patiently for someone to pick up. Despite the encounter he'd just had, he remained calm. Getting angry would serve no purpose.

"We need to talk. Things haven't worked as we'd hoped," Nadir said once the phone was answered. He then listened patiently. He knew they couldn't discuss this matter on the phone, and he wanted to end their discussion as quickly as possible.

"It's time to pursue our other avenue."

CHAPTER 30

A cloudless, deep blue sky hung above Walter Jenkins Jr. Only the gentlest of breezes could be felt on the vast green expanse on which he stood. He watched in dismay as his tee shot sliced into the dense forest that lined the fairway. The faint sound of the ball speeding through leaves and then hitting a tree followed.

"God dammit," he muttered as he handed his Callaway driver to his caddy.

"There's a small pond back there. It's probably landed in there," Jesse Schilens said as he took the final drag from his cigarette, then stomped it out on the ground.

"I'm going to find that fucking thing and hit it out, if I can. I don't want the stroke penalty. I can't afford it if I want to shoot a sixty-five." Walter replied.

"Suit yourself, you stubborn prick," Jesse said.

Walter was walking over to the area his ball had landed when his phone rang.

"Could you excuse me for a moment? Go ahead with them," he said, gesturing to Jesse and his caddie. "Give me the three iron. I'll find my ball."

Walter's caddie nodded obediently and headed toward the others. Walter turned his attention to his phone.

"Tell me you've got good news for me," he said as he ran his fingers through brown hair that was beginning to lose its battle with gray.

"What did Mello bid?......That low?" Walter said, his voice rising.

"I don't care if we take a loss on the job. I want you to lower the bid. I didn't build the largest construction company south of the Carolinas by letting some upstart out bid me!"

He listened patiently as his general manager tried to explain all of the reasons they couldn't go lower.

"I don't care. Hire immigrants if we have to. I know that's what Mello is doing anyway. Forge their fucking papers. Put sand in the cement, buy the lower-quality steel. I don't give a fuck, just do what you have to to win the bid. If he wants to play hardball, let's play. This is the biggest highway project in all of Georgia in the past five years. We aren't letting Carlos Mello put his construction company's name on it! Just win the fucking bid!"

He disconnected the call just as he arrived at the spot where his ball entered the woods. He ducked under a large branch and began the daunting task of finding his ball.

After five minutes of searching unsuccessfully, he found himself near the pond that Jesse had mentioned. He turned as he heard the sound of footsteps behind him.

"Still haven't found the god damn—"

He was expecting to see Jesse, or his caddie. Instead he found another golfer, wearing freshly pressed gray pants and a dark blue windbreaker. Walter didn't recognize him as a member of the country club.

"Tough day for both of us, I guess," the man said as he approached.

"Yes, tough day. If you see a Titleist Pro V, let me know," Walter replied.

"I think mine went in the drink," the man replied. The two men searched for their balls, but the stranger soon called out, "Well

162

what do you know! I think this might be yours. It's in there good, but I think you can get it."

Walter stopped searching and headed over to where the man was standing. His eyes were focused on the spot at the edge of the pond that the man was pointing with this club. He was less than a foot away from the man when his feet were swept from under him.

Paul quickly smashed Walter across the spine with his golf club, slowing the man from getting to his feet. Paul mounted the man roughly and used all of his weight to force Walter's head into water. Paul felt the man thrash under him as he struggled to bring his head above the surface. After a measured amount of time Paul pulled Walter's head out of the water and turned it so he could look into his eyes.

Mud covered Walter's face, and his mouth was wide open as he sucked in air. Paul knew it would be just moments before he'd be able to call for help.

"Carlos Mello asked me to send you a message. He said he'll see you in hell."

Before he could respond, Paul quickly thrust Walter's head back under the water. It took less than a minute for the bubbles to come floating gently to the surface. Then Paul felt Walter's muscles weaken until they were faintly twitching. Paul waited another minute just to be sure he finished his job. He knew how much clients hated a job that wasn't done right. Comfortable that Walter had finished his last construction job, Paul quickly rose to his feet and began to head back the way he came, away from the fairway.

Thirty minutes later, he was safely back in his car. He'd left his phone on the seat of his car while he'd been dealing with Walter. It showed that he had one missed call. He recognized the number. It was a very loyal, well-paying client. He pulled out of the parking lot he was in and dialed the number.

"It's been a few weeks since we've spoke," he said.

"Well, I was hoping I wouldn't have to."

"I'm glad that we do."

"The men you're watching….I need them to go away. They've become a problem."

"The brothers?"

"Yes, I want you to do James Woltzberg first."

"You know the terms, payment up front and all cash," Paul said.

"I know how this works. We've been through this before. You know you'll get paid."

"I'm just giving you a friendly reminder."

Paul hung up the phone without waiting for a response. He smiled as he set his GPS to find Route 95 so that he could head back to New England. Business was booming.

CHAPTER 31

The wrapper from a fast food chain containing uneaten bits of a breakfast sandwich sat next to Omar's picture on top of the video equipment inside the black van. Leah held on tight to the warm coffee that she'd purchased, anything that would keep her warm. Outside the van, heavy wet snow had engulfed the region. New England in the winter wasn't her ideal choice for an assignment. In the past hour that she'd spent in the back of a black van, she found herself wondering how different her life would've been had she stayed in Nolensville, Tennessee, and became a local cop like her dad. The weather sure would be a lot warmer.

The van was parked down the street from an apartment building that, per GPS tracking, was where Omar Al-Tabari had made many of the phone calls that had been intercepted. She began monitoring the building before dawn, but hadn't seen Omar. Additionally, per the intelligence team back in Washington, no phone calls had been made.

The van was equipped with cameras on all sides so that Leah could see anyone approaching the van. It also had a camera pointed at the building. All of the cameras fed into screens inside the van that she was monitoring. The images were also sent via satellite back to the Department of Homeland Security's headquarters in Washington, D.C.

Her instructions had been clear. First, she would determine which apartment Omar was living in. Then she'd wire it with both video and audio equipment, allowing her to monitor his actions and discussions. She would also put a small device inside the modem on his computer so that she would be able to monitor any communication that Omar made via the Internet. It would also allow her to see what websites Omar was visiting. All of these activities were designed to find the other people involved in planning the attack.

Through the work she was doing, enough evidence might be obtained to apprehend Omar and bring him in for questioning. But having been involved in many of these operations in the past, she didn't think that bringing Omar into custody right away would be likely. The normal protocol was to identify as many individuals involved in the plot as possible and then round them up all at once. Unless intelligence indicated that a terrorist attack was imminent, they wouldn't settle for just one individual.

But this was also no ordinary operation. Leah had never been involved in a terrorist plot as elaborate as this one. Typically a terrorist cell would plan on planting bombs in highly populated areas. Their communication was usually sloppy and the evidence trail was plentiful. In cases like this, tracking down all of the bad guys could be done by the keystone cops. She was hoping that this was the case with the operation that she was currently involved in. But the level of sophistication that was discussed in the briefing with Leonard Webb had Leah concerned. Using computers to simulate a virus mutating, and then replicating it in real life, was something that Leah considered science fiction. The fact that this terrorist cell might have the resources to perform such an operation was chilling. If they were that sophisticated, she doubted that the individuals involved would be dumb enough to leave a long trail of communications for her to find.

Her thoughts were drawn back to the present when she saw a man walking toward the building on one of the monitors. He was tall and lanky, with a long gait and had a long dark beard. He was wearing a taqiyah, which Leah knew many Muslim men wore. She picked up the picture of Omar, and although the video feed was coming from a low-resolution camera, she was certain about what she saw. It was Omar Al-Tabari. He trudged through the wet slush on the apartment building stairs and went inside. No sooner than the door to the apartment building closed, the phone in the van rang. It was an agent from Washington who was monitoring the surveillance cameras remotely.

"Agent Peterson," Leah said.

"Leah, this is Agent Shapiro. Are you seeing what I'm seeing?"

She replied in the affirmative as she gazed out one of the windows in the van. She was watching to see which apartment lights would turn on. Windows in an apartment on the second floor were illuminated. Leah made note of the windows and passed the information along to the agent on the phone.

"Good work, now that we know what apartment he lives in, you can get it wired up. I know you know how dangerous this part of the job is, but I wouldn't be doing my job if I didn't remind you."

"This ain't my first assignment. I'm a big girl, I've got it under control." Her words were soaked with pride and independence.

"I'm not suggesting it is. But whether this is your first or thousandth, you don't know what you're walking into once that door swings open."

"When it does, I'll be ready."

CHAPTER 32

"Can you page James and have him come to my office? Tell him it's very important," Will called out to Colleen, from behind his desk.

Colleen nodded, and James quickly appeared.

"You called?"

"Yes, come in. Close that behind you," Will said.

"Did you get in touch with Nadir?" James asked.

"Yes, we spoke. He won't be bothering us again, and if he does, let me know."

"What did you say to him?" James persisted.

"I told him he was bluffing, plain and simple. He won't go to the police with what he knows. If he was as involved as you think he was, then he'd be as much in the crosshairs of the police as you would be."

"What did he say?"

"Nothing. I didn't give him a chance to say a thing before I stormed out of there."

Will could feel himself getting aggravated again. The combination of revisiting his discussion with Nadir and the papers that sat in front of him on his desk had put him on edge.

"I hope you're right, I hope this is the last time we hear from Nadir," James said, breathing a sigh of relief. "So what did you call me in here for?"

"This," Will said as he handed over the stack of papers. "Have a read through these. Take your time, it's very important."

"You want me to read through all this right now?" James asked.

"Yes, I've already held onto this information too long without acting on it."

James shook his head in disbelief and began to attack the daunting task in his lap.

* * *

Tanner placed the phone in its cradle after listening to his voicemail. Apprehension brewed on his face. It was the second message from Monica in as many days asking him to call her. Although she didn't say so, he knew she wanted to know if he was going to help her prove Will was responsible for the murders of Vijay and Scott. Could my boss be a cold-blooded murderer? He'd grappled with the question since speaking with her a few days earlier. I just can't believe Will could it, he thought.

His thinking was interrupted by the sound of his phone. He answered it before its second ring.

"Could you come into my office for a moment?" Will asked tersely.

"Sure," Tanner replied and hung up the phone.

What could he want? Could he want to question me about what else I know before he has me killed? Tanner suddenly felt sick to his stomach. Remember how quickly he changed that day I brought the data from ViroPredict to him? Calm one minute, furious the next, his voice filled with ire. You're being ridiculous, he kept telling himself, but in the back of his mind, Monica's suspicions lingered. He was relieved to see James in Will's office when he arrived. Relief was quickly replaced with apprehension. What if James was involved too?

"Please have a seat, and close the door behind you," Will said in his usual congenial manner. "James and I were just looking at the data you had shared with me a few days ago. Do you remember our discussion?"

Tanner's mind shifted to the conclusion reached by the data. Remember it? It's keeping me up at night, Tanner thought. "Yes, I remember the discussion. I know the data well."

"So you're sure that it's right?" Will asked.

Tanner nodded his head.

"Can you start at the beginning and explain to me exactly what variables you used to attain these results?" Will asked.

"We'd been doing work for some time with the strain of rabies most common in animals today. We had been using ViroPredict to understand how the virus would mutate under thousands of different environments. This testing had been ongoing for the past six months." Tanner checked to make sure Will was following. Will sat stone faced as he waited for Tanner to continue.

"The initial findings were insignificant. Under most environments, we saw evidence of minor viral mutations, but the DNA remained relatively unchanged. Of the mutations that we did see, none significantly altered the manner in which the virus infected animals, or the underlying symptoms seen once the animal is infected. As expected, when the density of the population increased, we saw an increase of mutations in the virus. While this is not unheard of, it did cause us to dig a little deeper to identify an environment where mutations can become dangerous and where existing vaccines had become ineffective. We began to examine the population trends in Asia in both human and disease-carrying animals, mainly bats."

"No need to go into all of the details, just give me the summary," Will said, shifting impatiently in his chair.

"Without getting too technical in describing our population modeling assumptions, simply put, as the population of bats and humans increased, so did the mutations. When we assumed that bats and humans were put into close contact with one another, we found that one of the probable mutations is the one that the data indicates."

"So once this mutation takes place, can you walk me through the changes that take place in the virus?"

"Under the right circumstances, when bats and humans cohabitate in the same geographic area, the rabies virus will eventually mutate in this manner. Once it does, the virus changes significantly. Right now the rabies virus is found in and is transmitted through saliva. It is typically spread when an infected animal or person bites an uninfected animal or person. When this specific change takes place within the DNA of the virus, the virus becomes able to survive in an aerosol mist. To put this in laymen's terms, once this mutation takes place, the virus becomes airborne, and people will be catching rabies like it's the flu. Once we were comfortable with the data, I shared it with you."

Tanner paused for a moment, carefully choosing his words.

"Shortly after that, I discovered the most troubling aspect of this mutation. The changes that had taken place in the new strain were so dramatic that no current vaccine would work on it. A new vaccine would need to be developed. That process could take months. Then the mass production of the vaccine would need to begin. Again, we're talking about another few months before enough would become available to contain an outbreak."

Tanner's conclusion confirmed Will's fears. While not an expert, Will knew what the rabies virus did to the people and animals it infected. It attacked their central nervous system. Once it reached the nervous system, the infection was fatal within days. The early symptoms were headache and fever, but as the virus progressed, the symptoms got much worse. In the later stage of the illness, anxiety, hallucinations, muscle spasms, and paralysis set in and respiratory failure ultimately caused death. Will thought about watching someone in his family die from the virus and quickly decided he'd rather euthanize them than let them suffer the way they would with rabies. The thought of something like this happening made the hair on the back of Will's neck stand up.

He walked over to the window in his office. Outside snow had begun to fall and the sky was a light gray. The flakes looked small and light as they gently fluttered down to the ground. The pavement in the parking lot could still be seen through a thin white cloak.

"Do you know what this could mean? I don't think that I'm overstating the gravity of the situation when I say that this could wipe out a huge chunk of the human population on this planet." Will said.

"I'm aware of the impact it could have. That's why I'm sharing this data with both of you."

"What was the time period that the simulation was run through?" James asked.

"If conditions were right, then this could take place in the next one to two years," Tanner replied.

This was the first piece of good news that Will had received. Given a twelve-month time frame, SimSci could work with some of the world's top pharmaceutical companies to create a vaccine for this new strain of rabies. Will felt much better about what he was hearing. ViroPredict was doing exactly what Will had created it to do, save the lives of millions of people around the world.

"I know that Lisa has left SimSci, but before she left, did she have a chance to review the algorithms in ViroPredict to ensure that they are working properly?"

"She started to, and when she left, I had to work with the rest of her team directly. They are still reviewing them all. I'd say they are nearly complete, and they haven't found anything that would lead them to believe the software is not working correctly."

"While they are finishing up, I want you to summarize your findings in a report. I don't want to waste any time in beginning negotiations with one of the big pharma companies," Will said.

"Got it," Tanner replied.

"Are there any other significant mutations that you found in these models?"

"No, but isn't this one big enough?" Tanner asked.

Will chuckled in response to Tanner's question. He had to concede that point to the young scientist.

"If you find anything else like this, I want to know as soon as you find it," Will said.

"I'll absolutely let you know if I find anything else like this."

Feeling it was the best time to warn him, he added, "We're still running some models on the source virus. There are many environmental variables that we still need to test."

"Well, so far it looks like you're doing an excellent job. Please keep it up," Will said.

With those words of encouragement, Tanner left Will's office.

"I don't think there is any doubt this is the most significant viral mutation we've found so far using ViroPredict," Will said.

James nodded his head, "A mutation like this could be as bad as the flu strain from 1918 or the polio virus."

"Jesus Christ, this could be our big opportunity. If this data is right, and we can get out ahead of this and produce the vaccine, we could save the world from a disease so crippling it could wipe out hundreds of millions of people."

"We need to stay on top of this. We need to begin work on the vaccine as soon as possible. Any ideas what pharma company we should reach out to?" James asked.

A small moue of distaste passed Will's lips. "I think Sander would be the most logical company to share this with. I know Monica Rowe, and if anyone can produce huge quantities of a vaccine in a short time frame, it would be Sander."

James nodded his head. "Well, take some time to think about it and let me know how you'd like to proceed."

Will couldn't believe all of this was happening at once. It was clear that the potential virus that Tanner had found needed to be his top priority. But so did managing SimSci, especially in light of so many positions in the company vacant. He also knew he needed to stay on top of Charles about getting information about the deaths of Scott and Vijay. Add on top of that Leah Peterson asking him questions. Will rubbed his temples as all of the events of the past ten days swirled in his head.

"Given how deadly this virus could be, I think this needs to be our highest priority. We need to get that vaccine created before our window of opportunity closes."

CHAPTER 33

For the second time in as many days, Leah held a warm coffee between chilled hands. Outside, it was colder than yesterday. As a result of an overnight snow coating, patches of ice littered the ground. She'd reviewed the plan in her head twice already this morning. Luckily, she'd installed all of the equipment that she would be using today many times before. She'd been sitting in the van for three hours waiting for Omar Al-Tabari to come out of his apartment so that she could go in to wire it for surveillance.

The doors to the apartment building finally swung open and Omar walked out. Leah quickly sat up to get close to the monitor. She wanted to ensure that the man leaving the building was actually Al-Tabari. Upon closer inspection, there was no doubt in her mind. She shifted to the front seat of the van to follow Omar making sure that wherever he was heading would allow enough time to wire the place. Based on her experience, Leah knew she would need about thirty minutes. She was just about to pull off of the curb and into traffic when she saw Omar hail a cab and ride off in it.

She quickly climbed back into the rear of the van and grabbed the equipment she needed. Crossing to the apartment building, she put a small handheld device up to the door, sending an electric frequency that allowed the front door to unlock. Once inside, she knew exactly which direction to head as she'd memorized the path to Omar's apartment from the building blueprints that she had in the van. She arrived at Omar's front door and took a deep breath. This was the riskiest part of the operation. No matter how sure she was that the apartment was empty, she could always find an unwelcome surprise. She quickly manipulated the lock, put one hand on her gun, and opened the apartment door. She pulled the gun out of the holster and held it up, ready to fire as she searched the apartment for occupants.

The apartment was small, consisting of a small kitchen and living area, a bathroom and bedroom. A large window in the living room provided enough sunlight to light the living room and kitchen area. The kitchen was spotless, not even a dirty dish from the morning's breakfast in it. The living room floors were hardwood. There was a Muslim prayer rung in the center of the room next to an old sofa that had a circa 1970 floral design. Missing from the room was a television or entertainment system of any kind. She went room by room, thoroughly searching each to ensure no one was hiding anywhere before moving onto the next. Once the entire apartment was secure, she breathed a sigh of relief, put her firearm away, and began going to work wiring the apartment.

* * *

Across the hall from Omar's apartment, a man stood at the door of his own apartment looking through the peephole. In his hand he held his own weapon, a Kel-Tec P32 semiautomatic handgun. If they chose to enter his apartment, he would be ready. But he didn't think they would. His role was now proving to be valuable. Without him, Omar wouldn't know what was happening. He would come home to a trap. It was clear that the Americans were now aware of what he was trying to do.

He stood at his door for over thirty minutes, waiting for Leah to come out. Finally he saw her exit the apartment. He immediately grabbed his cell phone and dialed the number that Omar had instructed him to use. He knew that no one would answer the phone. No one ever did. He closed his eyes and envisioned the empty trailer where the phone sat, a trailer that no one had physically visited in over four years. A trailer situated within a handful of others in a small trailer park deep in an Alabama town with a population of one thousand people. When the voicemail picked up, he left a message that only he and a handful of others would understand. He knew Omar would be checking the messages left on that phone. After Omar received the message, he would never return to the apartment across the hall again.

CHAPTER 34

The voice message on the answering machine simply said, "The cattle are in the ranch."

Omar hit the disconnect button on his cell phone and ended the call. He checked the messages on the answering machine many times a day, and now he was reaping the benefits of this disciplined routine. Based upon the message, he knew that he couldn't go back to the apartment. Arrangements had been previously made to allow Omar to have another place to stay if he needed it.

He approached a map of the subway routes throughout the city of Boston and surrounding cities. Once he'd made note of the series of trains that he would need to take, he proceeded into the entrance and down into the station.

The living arrangements had been thought out well in advance. He had no belongings in the apartment that he cared to retrieve. Material goods hadn't meant anything to him for many years. Suddenly he felt himself go back there, to the day when he'd lost everything.

Sand swirled around the boys as the torn soccer ball came to a stop inside the goal. In the one hundred ten degree sun, Omar watched his older brother raise his hands in celebration. His brother's shirt was filthy and torn, grime had stuck to his brow as perspiration gathered. The boys were playing soccer in their hometown of Al Saqrh in the Al Anbar province of Iraq. With no actual soccer fields to play in, the boys played in the arid purlieu where their goats grazed. Their goal was constructed with a few pieces of spare wood, the field lines drawn with a stick.

Omar's bare foot dug into the sand as he took a broad stride toward his sibling to congratulate him. Before he could go any further ground shook and all the boys tumbled to the ground as a deafening explosion reverberated in their eardrums.

"I saw it! It was a missile!" one of the boys shouted in Arabic.

Omar and the other boys immediately ran to see what had happened. As they ran, he could hear one of his friends shouting over and over, "The Americans are attacking!"

When they arrived at the site where the missile had landed he saw a sight a young child never forgets. The missile hadn't struck his home directly, as he could see the massive hole in the earth where the weapon had landed. However, his house had been completely destroyed by the percussive energy from the weapon.

"Ommy! Baba!" His brother called out for their parents. They had been home with their two sisters when the missile struck. He and his brother ran into the debris to see if they could find any of them. They found their two sisters and father first. His father's face was singed, his legs bent unnaturally in opposite directions. One of his sisters' legs had been torn off, shrapnel lodged in her chest. Her mouth hung open and her front teeth were gone. His brother dropped to his knees next to her and clutched her remains bellowing in horror. As Omar continued to search for their mother, any hopes that they'd find her alive were destroyed when he found her body just feet away from their house. She'd been thrown by the force of the impact. The image of his mother's body was one that he would never forget. Her jaw had been torn from her face, leaving the rest of her face intact. Her skin charred, her hair gone. But the one image that he remembered more than anything else about that day was the sight of her eyes open, fixed in a glassy, fey stare. A stare that would be set for eternity.

The sound from the blast left his hearing partially impaired, and the ringing in his ears had left him with a permanent reminder of what had become of his family. It was the day Omar lost everything he'd cared about. As he stood waiting for the train, all of the muscles in his body were tight, and his hands made two fists by his side.

The sound of the approaching train brought Omar's mind back to the present. After all of the passengers disembarked, Omar boarded the train and found an empty seat. The memories he'd just brought to the front of his mind elicited a rage so intense that he wanted to take the blade from his belt and slice the throats of everyone on the train. But he knew that he couldn't do that. He knew that thoughts like that would interfere with the mission. When they had successfully completed it, hundreds of thousands, if not millions of Americans would be dead. Then plenty of American children would experience what he and so many other children from his land had felt.

His thoughts turned to the U.S. official who had entered his old apartment while he was gone. The plan to be notified worked exactly as it should have. But my careful planning doesn't change the fact that someone had entered my apartment. They may know what I have planned. It's probably the Russians' fault. They can't be relied upon in such a high-precision operation. I need to turn up the pressure on them.

The public address speakers on the train clicked on and the driver announced they were at Omar's stop. He got off the train and took a look around to acclimate himself with where he was. His destination was just a block away.

Upon arriving at the donut shop, he saw Boris and Yuriy sitting at a familiar table. He nodded to the man working behind the counter, then sat down with the two Russians. He greeted them with a simple nod of his head.

"We need to target one of the brothers next," Omar said as he took out a picture of James Woltzberg and placed it on the table. "He will have the information we are trying to get."

Boris picked the creased picture up off the table. "Why this one and not the other?"

"They both could provide us access to the software. But this one is less stubborn. He's more impulsive and we believe he's more likely to wilt like a daisy in the equator's hot sun."

"We will get him," Boris said as he put the picture in his pocket and began to rise from his seat.

"Wait," Omar demanded. Boris sat back down. "The work you've done so far is sloppy. You're leaving a trail behind. This cannot happen again. If things don't work out with this man, you must dispose of him properly. Understand?"

Omar's icy glare bore down on Boris as he waited for an answer. "Yes."

Omar rose to his feet. "Good, I hope you will have good news in the next few days."

He turned, nodding to the man behind the counter serving coffee to a patron on the way out, and left the shop. A frigid breeze greeted Omar outside. He had a ten minute walk and shivered from the cold. He zippered his jacket up tight and made his way to the place he now called home.

CHAPTER 35

Nigel estimated that the spotlight on top of Marcel's helmet was nearly twenty feet above him. It shone like the lone headlight of a locomotive at the end of a dark tunnel. He winced in pain as he tried to move his right leg. He knew that he'd broken it in the fall.

"Stay calm!" Marcel shouted from the ledge above.

"I can't move my leg! I think it's broken. I don't know how stable this ledge is!" Nigel shouted back up to Marcel.

"I'm dropping down a rope to you," Marcel shouted.

Nigel felt the sweat dripping off him. To make matters worse, his sweat was mixing with the bat droppings falling on him from the thousands of bats that hung on the cave's ceiling high above. He writhed in pain and with each move he made, he could hear small rocks falling off the ledge and hitting the bottom of the hole below. Nigel thought that the drop to the bottom of the cave was another fifty to seventy-five feet, based on the amount of time between the time the rocks fell from the ledge and the time that he could hear them hitting the bottom.

"Can you see the rope?" Marcel asked as he shined the spotlight down to where Nigel had fallen.

"I can't see anything! You're flashing the light right in my face!" Nigel shouted.

He'd lost the spotlight on his helmet when he fell into the hole. Marcel shifted the light so that the light wasn't shining directly into Nigel's eyes. Then he could see the rope swinging back and forth. He tried to grab it as it swung past him. He missed, and the act of reaching for it caused his leg to move just enough to send a sharp pain up it.

"Just grab onto the rope and we will pull you up!" Marcel shouted down.

He doesn't understand just how hard that is, Nigel thought. As he lay in pain he watched the rope swing back and forth above him. He tried to grab the rope a second time as Marcel lowered it farther. The pain in his leg was excruciating as he stretched for it. He missed. As he opened his mouth to breathe, the sweat and bat droppings ran down his face and into his open mouth. A vile, salty taste filled his mouth and he felt like he was going to vomit. He tried again to grab the rope. This time he got it. He wrapped his hands around the rope as many times as he could.

"Okay, I'm ready!" he shouted.

The men began to pull him up. He could hear their grunts. He could feel his leg dangling, and with each rock that jutted out from the side of the cave and hit it, the pain got worse. He tried to ignore it, tried to concentrate on the rope. But he couldn't, the pain was short-circuiting his mind. He could feel himself getting lightheaded and his grip loosening on the rope.

His left hand was the first to give. The rope began to unwind from around it. He tried to stop it with his right hand, and as soon as he did, the rope began to unwind from that hand as well. His eyes widened and his heart raced as the last piece of rope slipped out of his hands and he began to fall farther into the hole toward the bottom. He took a deep breath and with it, the taste of sweat and bat droppings filled his mouth again. He knew he wasn't going to make it out of the cave. He hoped that when he hit the ground, the impact would kill him instantly. He tried to scream as he fell toward the ground, but he couldn't hear his voice, no sound came out. Suddenly he felt his hand wrap around something.

He thought he was grabbing the rope, and when he opened his eyes, he saw that it wasn't a rope, but the sheet that he'd been using as a covering. He looked around and saw that he wasn't in a cave falling to the bottom. He was safe in his room at the hotel in the village. The sweat was very real — he was covered with it when he awoke — but the bat droppings were absent. He wiped his face on the sheet and looked out the window. He tried to guess what time it was based on the light that was shining in from the outside, but then grabbed his watch from the table next to his bed. It was almost ten in the morning. He was supposed to meet Marcel, Jao, and the local guide at nine-thirty at Jao's jeep. He still had to shower and shave. I've got to let them know I'm going to be late, he thought.

He left his room and took a look around the parking lot. He saw the Jeep that the men had been traveling in, but none of the men were near it. Maybe Marcel's in his room, he thought. He went over and knocked on his door. He waited for a moment, but Marcel didn't answer. Where the hell is everyone? he thought. Suddenly, a large van with flashing red and white lights on top of it pulled into the hotel parking lot. The vehicle was smaller than an ambulance that Nigel was used to seeing in the U.S., but the flashing lights on top of the vehicle combined with his previous international travel experience helped him recognize it. He turned back toward Jao's room to see if the men were there. As he got closer to the room, he realized that the door to the room was open. Then he saw the two medics from the ambulance heading toward him, and he suddenly realized that they were heading toward Jao's room. He broke into a sprint toward the open door. When he turned to enter the room, what he saw made him stop short.

Marcel and the local guide were in opposite corners of the room, their eyes filled with terror. Jao was on his bed in nothing but his underwear. His eyes were open wide staring at the ceiling. The expression on his face was one that Nigel had only seen in horror movies. It was the look of a man whose mind was wrestling with something in his body. Something so horrible that he'd shut out everything else, because he knew if he lost the internal battle, then nothing else would matter. His mouth hung open and saliva poured out of it. His wrists were tied to the bed posts on opposite ends of the bed frame with a torn bed sheet. Nigel watched as his body jerked violently on the bed, contorting into positions that weren't natural. Without the restraints around his wrists he would be writhing around uncontrollably.

Nigel knew from his training that Jao was demonstrating symptoms of rabies. Once symptoms began to show, the effects of the virus were irreversible, and it was always fatal. That headache he had a few days ago must've been an early symptom. Why didn't I realize it? He turned to Marcel.

"Did you find him like this?" Nigel asked.

"Yes. Neither one of you were outside this morning, so I began going door to door to find you two. I came to his door and it sounded like two people wrestling inside. I thought he may be in some kind of trouble, so I kicked in the door and found him on the floor like this. Just as I was going to get you, our friend came out of his room and we tied him to the bed to keep him from hurting himself or anyone else."

"Did he bite or scratch either of you?"

"No, we were both very careful to make sure that didn't happen."

The men were interrupted by the two medics that had arrived in the ambulance. They took one look Jao and began asking questions in Thai. The only person in the room that understood them was the local guide, and the three native men had an animated discussion, arms waving, fingers pointing. One of the medics motioned to the door and the local guide left the room. Nigel and Marcel followed.

Once outside the room, Nigel asked, shaken, "Did you see a scratch or a bite on him?"

"He was scratched up pretty good, but I think most of those were from him writhing in the room all night," Marcel replied.

"Did either of you see him yesterday?"

"No, I haven't seen him since Tuesday, the last time that we shot footage in the cave," he stopped short. "He could've been in that room for two whole days."

Nigel looked at the local guide waiting for his response when he remembered that the man didn't speak English. "Jesus Christ, I can't believe this," Nigel said in disbelief. "Didn't he get inoculated?"

Marcel shrugged his shoulders.

"How could someone going into a cave full of bats not get a rabies vaccine?"

Anyone who knew that they would be in frequent contact with wild animals, particularly those considered common carriers of the virus, would be crazy not to receive a dose of the rabies vaccine. An experienced guide like Jao should have known as soon as he was bitten by a bat that he would need to get a series of "booster doses" of the vaccine. All people in his line of work were aware of the risks of rabies and the need to not only get the initial vaccination but to get additional booster shots if exposed. Both Marcel and Nigel kept vials of booster doses with them, just in case.

The medics exited the room with Jao on a stretcher, his legs and arms tied down. The three men watched the medics carry him to the ambulance and put him in the back. Just before the medics got into the van and drove off, Nigel ran over to them.

"What hospital are you taking him to?"

The two Thai men shrugged their shoulders and said something in Thai. Clearly they didn't speak English. Nigel scowled as the medics got into the van and drove off. He walked back over to Marcel, who still had a look of shock on his face.

"We need to find out where they just took him. I hope he'll be okay, but I think his chances are grim."

CHAPTER 36

Nick tried to focus on the different financial scenarios being presented to him by Peter Hammill, his Director of Financial Planning and Analysis. But with his head throbbing, he couldn't focus on the numbers. His eyes kept wandering up to the second hand on the small blue clock on the wall. Tick...tick...tick.... Finally, he interrupted Peter in mid-sentence.

"I understand what you're saying. All of this work looks really good. I'll tell you what, leave these documents with me and I'll bring them home with me tonight and we can regroup in the morning."

"Okay, no problem," Peter replied. "If you have any questions, just shoot me an email or give me a call."

"Will do. Thanks, Peter. Could you please close the door behind you?" Nick asked.

He waited for the snap of his door. He then opened the top drawer of his desk. Half of a small white pill was nestled in a small plastic bag inside the drawer. It was all that Nick had left, and half of a ten milligram OC would barely get him high. He knew he needed more. He'd been to Raff's the past two nights and Fletch hadn't shown up. He knew that there was a chance that he wouldn't be there tonight either.

Despite being only three-thirty, he began shutting his computer down. Then he grabbed his suit jacket off of the back of his seat, and his overcoat from the hook on the back of his office door.

"If anyone comes looking for me, tell them that I'm not feeling well. I'll be working from home for the rest of the day," he said to his executive assistant as he walked out the door.

Outside the sun was shining, unimpeded by clouds, making the day one of the warmest in the past few weeks. He headed to his Lexus and once inside, began driving to the ATM. At each red light along the way, he subconsciously tapped his fingers against the steering wheel, and his foot on the carpeted car floor. He drove up to the ATM and inserted his card into the machine. When prompted for the amount he entered one thousand dollars, then waited for the machine to process his request. Suddenly, an unfamiliar message appeared on the screen.

We're sorry, we couldn't process your request at this time due to insufficient funds in your account.

Nick slammed his hands on the steering wheel. Over the past few weeks his checking account had been brought down to less than twenty-five dollars because he was buying Oxycontin from Fletch. Since then he'd been dipping into his savings account to get the two hundred dollars a day he needed for the pills. Even with his salary as chief financial officer of SimSci, he knew that the cost of his habit was becoming unsustainable.

He slid his card back into the machine and repeated the steps to get to the screen where he was prompted to enter the amount of money that he wanted to withdraw. This time he tried five hundred. He held his breath in anticipation, and sweat began to form on his brow. As the machine processed his request, the driver in the car waiting behind him beeped his horn. Nick looked at the man in the car in his rearview mirror and fought the urge to get out of the car and confront him. The ATM screen flashed, and then the words "Transaction Approved" appeared on the screen. It began dispensing the cash from a slot below. Nick anxiously grasped the crisp bills and his card from the machine. As he drove away, he looked back and shouted:

"The machine's not going anywhere, so just relax, asshole!"

Raff's was only five minutes away. As he opened the door, his persistence was rewarded, as there in their regular seats were Fletch and LeSean.

Nick took a seat next to Fletch and the two engaged in idle chatter for a few minutes as Nick ordered a beer. Then Nick got to the reason that he'd come.

"So what's up with the orange carrots?"

"All that I have are eighties." Fletch replied.

"A half dozen will do."

"Let's go have a cigarette."

The two men got off their barstools and headed outside for a smoke. Nick knew that "eighties" were eighty milligram pills and would cost Nick eighty dollars each. He would be able to get six of them with the five hundred dollars that he had in his pocket. The transaction was quick and simple, and Nick was back in his car before he'd finished the cigarette.

The ride from the bar to his condo was filled with anticipation. Once inside, he took off his jacket and headed straight for the kitchen table. A spoon and small mirror were on the table, items left behind from the previous nights' activities. It took just minutes to crush up the pills and snort them. He stood up and as he did he began to feel the initial effects of the drug. He grabbed a beer from the refrigerator and went to sit in the recliner. He sat down, pulled the lever on the side of the seat to allow the chair to recline, took his shoes off one at a time with the help of the other foot, and waited for the drug to run its course.

Twenty minutes later, Nick lay in his chair with one leg hanging off the side. His arm also hung off the recliner with the remote still in it. All lights were off and the hue from the television shone on everything in the room. His eyelids were half shut, his eyes rolled back in their sockets. He breathed heavily through his open mouth. Slowly the remote control slipped out of his hand and bounced on the hardwood floor. The impact caused the battery casing to come unlatched and the batteries rolled out. The sound of the impact caused Nick's eyes to open wide, and for just a second the room came into focus. Without lifting his head from the back of the recliner, he looked around for a moment to see what had happened. Must have been the TV, he thought. It didn't matter what had happened. Everything in the world was just fine. His eyes rolled back into his head and he fell back into his torpor.

* * *

Will turned up the car radio as popular Boston talk show hosts Dennis and Callahan were debating whether or not it was time for a new baseball stadium in the City. Traffic in and around Boston was always a drag during rush hour, but the wet snow that was steadily falling today multiplied the problem. For the past few days he'd been working with James and Tanner to study the data that Tanner had shown them in his office. He was very concerned that a flaw in the software had caused the results. If news of this potential virus got out and it was later found that a glitch in Viro-Predict caused it, the uproar could destroy the software's credibility. He had stopped all other software upgrades and development, directing all of the remaining software developers to review the existing source code and algorithms. But still no one could come up with anything that showed that the results of the simulation were inaccurate.

The epic battle with the rush-hour traffic finally ended, and Will emerged unbroken as he arrived at SimSci. He knew that Leah wouldn't be far behind. He'd seen her outside his house in the morning, but had lost her in the traffic. As he entered the lobby, he saw Tanner Fitzgerald waiting for him in it. He knew based on the look on Tanner's face that something was wrong.

"Good morning, Tanner. Is everything all right? You don't look so good."

"I need to talk to you. It's very important," Tanner replied.

"Does it concern the ViroPredict data? If so, grab James."

Will went directly to his office, Tanner to find James. They arrived in Will's office moments later.

"So what's troubling you?" Will asked.

"It's the rabies modeling that I've been performing. We found a problem with ViroPredict."

"Well, what's the problem?" James asked.

"Remember when I told you nearly all of the algorithms had been checked? One that hadn't at that point in time was reviewed yesterday. This particular algorithm helps ViroPredict calculate the time that lapses between viral mutations. To sum it up in the most basic of terms, the time scale table in the software wasn't accurate."

The brothers sat motionless in their chairs. Will hadn't thought that such a fundamental flaw in the software at this late stage of development was possible.

"So what does that mean to our rabies simulation?"

"Because the time scale was wrong, the results that the model produced weren't accurate. But we've fixed the problem and rerun the model with the right time scale," Tanner said.

"And?"

"When we run the simulation with the new time scale, the model shows the mutation happening much sooner. In fact, the model suggests that the earliest that the mutation could occur is not in a few years; rather, the earliest it could've occurred was *a year ago*. In the right environment, this could happen any day now. Worse, it could have already happened."

"You're saying that the rabies virus might have already mutated and could be airborne and infecting humans today?" Will asked.

"Yes."

"But you don't think it's happened yet. Correct?" James asked.

"No, I don't think it has. Or if it has, it's in a location so remote that no civilized society has become aware of it. I mean, if something like this was occurring, it'd be a matter of days, maybe weeks, before every major news outlet in the world was reporting on it on a daily basis. Think about the avian flu and the H1N1 flu strains. When they began infecting people, a day wouldn't go by where you didn't see a story about them in the news."

Will nodded his head in agreement. This mutation couldn't have taken place yet. But that didn't make him feel any better about the situation. The fact that it could happen any day made the situation much more severe.

"I'm going to need the new data supporting what you're telling me. I need to think about what I need to do," Will said.

"Okay, no problem." Tanner said as all three men rose to their feet.

"What does your gut tell you on this one?" Will asked just before Tanner opened the door.

"My gut tells me we need to begin work on a vaccine immediately."

Will nodded as Tanner opened the door and left.

"Do you think we could've gone this long without discovering an error in the time scale?" Will asked.

James shrugged his shoulders. "I guess anything is possible."

"Jesus, I wish Vijay were still here."

* * *

In his office, Tanner sat with his door closed. He replayed the discussion he'd just had. Will's tone was very different than the first time that he'd brought the problems with ViroPredict to his attention. In fact, his tone had been that way in their past two meetings. It was calm, and curious. He seemed determined to get to the bottom of the issue, not simply cover it up. He also seemed genuinely concerned with the potential pandemic the software had uncovered. But was it just an act? Had he realized how he sounded in their first meeting? Maybe he didn't want to alarm me, Tanner thought. Could the calm, determined demeanor just be a facade so that I don't start to put the pieces together?

Tanner nearly jumped out of his seat when his phone rang. He looked at the caller ID and recognized the number as Monica's. He let it go through to his voicemail. He still wasn't sure what he was going do. He did know one thing, though. If what she said was true and Will was acting, he belonged in Hollywood, not Cambridge.

* * *

Will was running late. The discussion he'd had first thing in the morning with James and Tanner had backed up his entire day's schedule, and he hadn't yet caught up. But he knew that this was one meeting he needed to attend.

"Just make yourself at home," Will said as he walked into his office to find Charles reading the *Wall Street Journal.* "How the hell did you get in here?"

"Receptionist let me right in. She recognized me from a few days ago. I told her you'd be expecting me."

"Let me see if Leah's around."

"Right here," Leah replied from Will's doorway.

Upon seeing Leah, Charles rose from his seat and extended his hand. "Detective Charles Madre, Cambridge PD."

"Agent Leah Peterson, nice to meet you," she replied as the two shook hands.

James briskly entered Will's office. "Looks like the party started without me," he said as he took a seat at the large mahogany table in Will's office.

"Well, now that everyone is here, I guess we can get started. I asked you all to meet here because we're all working toward the same goal, finding the monsters who have murdered two of my best employees. I want to meet as often as we need to so we can share information."

"I thought you were a homicide detective," Leah asked, looking at Charles.

"I am, and I've been assigned to Vijay's case. Even if I wasn't, I'd help Will as a friend to find these bastards."

"I have something that I think you'll find interesting," Leah began as she opened her laptop. After a few mouse clicks she turned the computer around so that everyone could see the screen. A grainy black-and-white video began to play.

"This surveillance camera was monitoring Bredahl's apartment complex. Now watch." Two men came into the picture, got into a black car and drove out of the lot.

"These two men are persons of interest."

"How did you get that? I spoke to the cop on the Bredahl case, and he said they didn't save any video footage."

"Let's just say the Department of Homeland Security doesn't take no for an answer."

Will could see the frustration on his friend's face. Charles was beginning to realize that his work on the case was about to take a back seat to Leah's.

"Why are these two 'persons of interest'?" James asked.

"Recall that after the local authorities found one set of DNA at Vijay's crime scene, we reviewed their evidence and found a second set. Well, we reviewed the surveillance video from Mr. Bredahl's apartment complex looking for two people, not just one. The time that these two men arrived, as well as the time that they left the complex, are consistent with the time of the murder. Further, they are the only two men to arrive at the apartment complex together within four hours of the time of death."

The skepticism Will felt showed plainly on his face. Leah saw it and paused. "How do you know you're looking for two men? What if it was a man and a woman responsible for Vijay's death?" Will asked.

"The work we've done with the DNA has shown us that the murderers were male."

"How do you know that from the DNA?" It was James' turn to ask the question.

"Without getting too technical, and frankly I don't know enough to get technical, we sent the DNA off to the lab for single nucleotide polymorphism analysis."

"We've done some work with SNP's," James said. "You can't tell whether a person is male or female from SNP analysis."

"It's common knowledge that you can identify traits such as eye and hair color, as well as ethnicity from SNP analysis. But the FBI and Department of Homeland Security have made a number of significant advancements in this field. One of them is the ability to identify the sex of a person whose DNA is found at a crime scene."

Will could see how surprised his brother was with Leah's news. If a private company developed that technology, they'd be able to sell it for millions of dollars. "So what about the rest of the information you got from the DNA? You know, hair color, et cetera."

"All of that information also points to these two," Leah said, gesturing toward her laptop screen. "The DNA tells us the murderers' hair color is black, and both have brown eyes. You can see that one of these men appears to have dark-colored hair, while its impossible to tell about the second, because he's shaved his head. The most interesting thing that we discovered was their ethnicity. We'd expected the murderers to be of Middle Eastern descent. But the DNA indicates that the men are Eastern European."

"But when we had spoken earlier, you said that we were looking for people with ties to the Middle East and Muslim extremist organizations," Charles said.

"We still are. I've shared the profile of the man we believe is leading this plot, Omar Al-Tabari. These two men are likely working for him."

"Do we know who they are? What are their names?" Will asked.

"We've identified one of them by running their DNA through a criminal database. His name is Boris Kozlov."

"So these two could lead us to Al-Tabari," Charles said.

"Yes. That's why I wanted to share this video with you, Charles. But I also think it's important that you both see it as well," Leah said, turning her attention to Will and James.

"And why is that?" Will asked.

She became dead serious as she included the two in her gaze. "You both need to know what these two men look like, because there's a good chance that they could be coming after you next."

CHAPTER 37

The Boston skyline was visible past the waters of Marina Bay. The waters were calm, assisted by the breakwater that sat yards away, and the few boats that were in the water were at peace. At the edge of land, a few men were lowering a boat into the water. With hundreds of slips still vacant, they'd no doubt have lots of work in the coming months.

As Sarah sat at a table on the veranda of one of the restaurants on the boardwalk, she watched a seagull glide gracefully down to a rock on the breakwater, then ruffle its feathers. The unseasonably warm weather of the past few days was a clear sign that spring was on its way. It had given Sarah the urge to get outside, even if it was for just a drink before the sun went down and the temperature along with it. She'd met her friend Jackie Aaron for a night out. The two women had been friends for nearly ten years after meeting at one of Sarah's previous jobs.

"I can't believe he didn't notice the difference. I can even tell out here in this poor lighting," Jackie said.

"No kidding. And I thought he was going to love it. I swear all that he cares about is that company," Sarah said as she sipped her chocolate martini. Both her and Jackie were on their second drink.

"So what's next in your little make over?" Jackie asked. "Maybe a little lip augmentation?"

Sarah flashed a sarcastic look of shock toward her old friend. "What are you saying? That my lips aren't luscious red and just begging to be kissed?"

"If I was a man, I'd kiss your lips all night long!" Jackie said as the two laughed. "Seriously, I think you look great," she added as she raised her glass for a toast. "Here's to you looking better than ever."

The two women touched their glasses and sipped their drinks.

"Look at this one," Jackie said as she motioned with her head toward a man walking past them on the boardwalk. Sarah turned to have a look at what her friend was fixated on. Between an older couple taking a romantic stroll, and a younger one looking at the menu for one of the restaurants, was a man walking by himself. He was dressed in a long-sleeved windbreaker, jeans and boat shoes. A large bag was draped over one shoulder. He looked to be in his mid forties, slightly over six feet tall with an athletic build and dark skin.

"He must be getting his boat ready to put in the water. I'd sure like to fly my flag on his mast."

"He is a cutie," Sarah agreed. "I'll call him over."

"Don't you —"

"Hey you! My friend wants a ride on your boat!" Sarah said as the man walked by them.

Jackie turned red with embarrassment as the man turned back to them. "Maybe another time. I don't think you two have your sea legs tonight," he said as he kept walking.

Jackie slapped Sarah's arm, laughing with embarrassment. The man was right. Sarah didn't have her sea legs under her. She hadn't eaten dinner, and the two martinis had gone right to her head.

As Sarah watched the man walk away, another one came toward them. At first Sarah could only make out his dark pants and light colored jacket. As he came closer, Sarah's jaw slowly dropped. He was looking out onto the water, not toward the table at which they sat. Just let him walk by, she thought to herself. Let him go.

"Alan!"

He turned toward the two women. Upon recognizing Sarah, a broad smile filled his face as he approached.

"This is a truly remarkable surprise," Alan said, his eyes locked with Sarah's.

"What in the world are you doing out here?" Sarah asked.

"I'm sure I've told you about my boat. I keep it at this marina. I started getting it ready yesterday, and I wanted to work on it today. Besides, I needed some fresh air and the sights around the bay are quite astonishing at this time of the evening. I see that you two are enjoying yourselves."

"We just came out to have a few drinks. Just a quiet girls' afternoon out," Sarah said.

Jackie shifted uncomfortably in her seat, until finally Sarah realized her faux pas.

"Goodness, pardon my manners. Alan, this is Jackie."

"It's lovely to make your acquaintance," Alan said.

Even as Sarah introduced Jackie, Alan's eyes remained on Sarah. "It's such a magnificent afternoon. The clear skies allow all of the beauty of the setting sun to show itself." Alan motioned toward the water, eyes still locked with Sarah's. "Why don't the two of you join me for a drink on the boat? I'd like nothing more than the company of two beautiful women."

Sarah looked at Jackie. "Alan, could you give the two of us a moment?"

"Of course."

Alan walked over to the railing on the boardwalk to look out onto the water.

"That's him!" Sarah said, giving no other description, but Jackie didn't need one. She knew exactly who "he" was.

"Did you know he was coming out here? Are you using me as an excuse to see him here tonight?" Jackie asked, sounding annoyed.

"Of course not! I had no clue his boat was out here, or that he'd decide to come out to it alone on a Friday night!" Sarah said.

Jackie nodded her head, accepting Sarah's explanation. "So let me guess. You want to go out on his boat with him and make me be the third wheel so that nothing happens." Jackie said.

Sarah looked hopeful. "What's the harm of going out to see his boat?"

"There's no harm at all, but I'm not coming along," Jackie said.

The two sat in silence for a moment as Sarah considered her options.

"Are you going to be mad if I go with him?" Sarah asked.

Jackie cracked a mischievous smile. "No, I think you should. Why not? Go have some fun."

"Okay."

Sarah called Alan back over and finished her drink. Jackie did the same and in the course of less than a minute Sarah was saying her farewells to Jackie, abruptly ending their night out.

"Shall we?" Alan asked as they left Jackie with the bar tab.

"Lead the way."

The two strolled two hundred yards down the boardwalk to a black gate. Alan used a key pad to gain entry to the stairs that led down to the dock below. He then led Sarah to his eighty-three foot Viking yacht, bobbing quietly in the calm waters of the bay.

"Here it is," Alan said.

"Wow, this thing is huge," Sarah said as she sized up the boat.

Alan stepped into the boat first and extended his hand to help her keep her balance as she embarked. Despite Alan's assistance, Sarah's footwork was unsteady, her balance impaired by the alcohol she'd consumed.

"Let me show you around," Alan said with Sarah safely aboard.

He entered the code on a key pad and entered the cabin. Once inside, he turned a dial on the wall and recessed lights illuminated the vast cabin. The walls were lined with hand finished teak, the floor covered with plush carpet. Leather seats protruded from the right side of the cabin and Alan gestured toward them as he made his way to a bar at the front of the cabin.

"This is quite a boat," Sarah said as she absorbed her surroundings.

Alan reached into the fridge and pulled out a bottle of wine. He then took two glasses from a shelf and poured two drinks.

"Shall we sit outside and enjoy the weather before it gets too cold?" Alan asked.

"Certainly," Sarah replied and headed out.

The stern was facing the west, allowing a perfect view of the setting sun and the Boston skyline off to the right. Sarah sat down first, and Alan followed, pulling his chair to Sarah's until the two were touching.

"I can't believe I saw you out here today. If I were to allow myself to consider the possibility that our destiny is predetermined for us, then I would swear that it was fate that brought us together tonight," Alan said.

Sarah didn't cast aside Alan's notion. She did believe that at some level fate played a role in everyone's life.

"Here's a toast to fate, because if such a thing exists, I think I should thank it for allowing me to be out here with the most beautiful woman in the world." Alan said as he raised his glass.

"Oh, stop it."

The two sat in silence for a few moments as they drank their wine and listened to the sound of the gentle waves and the faint cries of the seagulls above. The sun was setting, and all the warmth that it provided went with it.

"We should go back to the bar for the next round. It's getting cold." Sarah said as she zippered the thick leather jacket that she was wearing.

"Let's go inside for a moment. I want to refresh my glass anyhow," Alan said, ignoring Sarah's request to head back to shore.

The two got up and headed inside.

"Why don't you take your jacket off for a moment?"

Sarah took her jacket off and handed it to him. Beneath it she was wearing a tight black sweater with the letters DKNY stitched into it in silver thread. The sweater hung over the top of her jeans, but clung to her hips.

"I guess I'll have one more glass as well," Sarah said as she went over to the granite counter to pour herself another glass of wine. She suddenly felt his strong hands on her shoulders.

"You're so tense. There's no need to be. The waves are meant to relax you." He began to message her shoulders. Slowly she began to relax as his hands made her muscles melt.

"That feels good," Sarah said as her breathing shifted from her nose to her open mouth.

"You really are the most beautiful woman in the world," he whispered into her ear.

She felt his breath on her neck, and it sent waves of warmth through her. She could feel him press up against her, pinning her between him and the counter. Then she felt one of his hands leave her shoulder and run down her side, over her waist and to her buttock. Normally Sarah would've jumped and pulled away from an advance like that from a man. But with his powerful but gentle touch, it only served to make her temperature rise. She couldn't remember the last time she felt a man's hands want her so badly. He wasn't rough or hurting her in any way, but she could sense the deep hunger. Like he wanted more, and was using every last ounce of self-restraint to hold back until she was ready to give it.

She turned to face him and looked him in the eye. No words were said, nor did there need to be. Alan leaned forward until his slightly parted lips touched hers. The sensation of feeling her bottom lip rubbed between his sent a lightning charge through her. All inhibition was lost, as he grabbed the bottom of her sweater with both hands and lifted it over her head.

Sarah distantly heard the sound of her cell phone ringing in her purse. She ignored it as his lips moved down her neck toward her breasts. Her breathing had turned to panting as she let him do as he pleased. His hands worked feverishly to unbutton her jeans, then his own.

Her phone began ringing again, and this time she tried to push him away, but he wouldn't relent.

"I should really see who that is," she said but he didn't respond. Instead he slid one of her bra straps off her shoulders. His hands proceeded to remove the other one. As he began to unsnap it, she came to her senses.

"I've got to get that. It's probably my son, Logan." Sarah said as she squirmed away from Alan and covered her chest with one hand as she adjusted her bra with the other.

"Missed it," she said as she pulled out her phone and tried to answer it. She looked at the caller ID and saw that it was Will's cell phone.

She remembered that the two of them were supposed to be having dinner with James and Cindy. Will knew that she had gone out with Jackie. Visions of Will calling her suddenly filled her head. What would Jackie say when Will asked her where she was? If she lied and said they were still out having drinks, Will would ask Jackie to hand the phone to her. If she said that they had just left the bar, then Will would be expecting her at James' shortly. Sarah's mind was racing as she played out possible scenarios that could occur.

"I've got to go," Sarah said firmly, her eyes filled with frustration, cheeks still pink from a few moments ago.

Alan advanced, his hands back to work trying to remove her bra. She slid out of reach and began to dress.

"Wait, why don't you stay for one more drink?" Alan offered.

But Sarah knew she had to call Will back before he discovered her whereabouts. She raced toward the door, putting on her jacket as she went. As she left, she caught a glimpse of herself in a mirror. She was shocked at her appearance. Her lipstick was smeared across her face, and her hair was sticking out at every imaginable angle. My God, Sarah, she thought, you look like a cheap tramp.

CHAPTER 38

All this work is about to pay off, Charles thought as he sat inside his unmarked patrol car. Through heavy snowfall he spotted Al-Tabari walking down the street and then entering a small ethnic grocery store. His adrenaline immediately began pumping. He'd spent every spare moment he had outside one of the largest Muslim mosques in the greater Boston area in hopes of coming across Omar. The grocery store stood across the street and two buildings down from an Islamic school. With the car stopped, he pulled out his phone and frantically began dialing.

* * *

Long days of sifting through intelligence data was beginning to get to Leah. She was about to get up and go for a walk to stretch when her phone rang.

"Agent Peterson, I hope you've got some good news for me."

"I was about to say the same thing to you, Andrew," Leah said calling Agent Shapiro by his first name. "I've got no new news to share. All of the work I'd done wiring the apartment appears to be a waste, because Al-Tabari hasn't gone back there."

"Has there been any credit card activity or email account usage?" Andrew asked.

"None, he doesn't appear to have a credit card or an ATM card, and there's been no other signs of him."

"What about the cell phone?"

"There was a call made from it the other day."

"What? Well we could've got back on him from that!"

"We found the person making the call. It was a bum outside a methadone clinic. He'd found the phone on the subway."

"Jesus Christ," Andrew said, pausing for a moment. "People over here are getting nervous, you know. They think that his disappearance may indicate the plot is going into the execution stage."

"I share their concern. I'm doing everything that I can to find him."

"What about the two men whose DNA was at the crime scene? Any new information on them?"

"We've got the license plate from some surveillance video and are trying to track him down but nothing yet." Leah heard her phone beep, indicating she had another call.

"Someone's trying to reach me, I've got to go, but if I come across anything solid you'll be the first to know."

Leah clicked over to the other call, unsure of who it was after looking at the number.

"Leah! I've got him!" Charles shouted into the phone.

"Who is this?"

"It's Detective Madre, I've got Al-Tabari!"

Leah jumped to her feet. "You've got him in custody?"

"No, I've got a positive ID on him. I'm going to apprehend him now! I wanted to let you know so you can get down here!"

"Where are you?"

"I'm on the corner of Grove and Pleasant!"

"I'm on my way!"

* * *

Charles got out of his car and approached the store with his gun drawn. Through the barred grocery store window he could see the clerk behind the counter, but not Al-Tabari. He reached the door and stormed through it, arms out in front of him, his gun ready to fire.

"What do you want?" the frail Indian man behind the counter cried as Charles stormed through the door.

"Just get down!"

The man behind the counter obediently dropped out of sight. Based on his immediate response, Charles didn't view him as a threat. His eyes scanned the rest of the small store but didn't see Omar. He methodically checked each aisle in the store, but the only other person he uncovered was an elderly woman who retreated, clutching her purse to her chest, absolutely petrified.

On the back wall Charles saw a door slightly ajar. He slowly approached and once he was within a foot of it, he kicked it open, gun ready to fire. Nothing. He found himself in a storeroom lined with shelves on all sides except for the wall facing out toward the rest of the store, which had doors allowing access to the refrigerator unit inside the store. The room was the size of a small bathroom. It was lit by a sole light bulb hanging from the ceiling. There was simply no room for a person to hide anywhere in the room.

On the far wall next to a stack of cases full of canned vegetables, a seven-foot beam of daylight breached the back wall. His muscles, tense with the stress from a potential encounter, relaxed. He dropped his gun to his side. Charles opened the door to look around, but he knew he wouldn't find anyone. All he saw were footprints in the freshly fallen snow leading away from the building.

He followed them down an alley, where they reached the sidewalk belonging to a street that ran parallel with the one he'd parked. The footprint he was following blended with those of hundreds of others on the busy sidewalk.

Out in front of the store, Leah stopped her car in the middle of the street and sprinted into the store, unaware of the lost chance.

* * *

Two blocks away, the doors to a Red Line train opened and Omar boarded. The need to eat had almost led to his capture. But the American's weak mind stood in his way like they so often do. Despite a simple black car and being in civilian clothes, it was plain to see that the man was part of law enforcement. As obvious was the fact that he'd recognized me, Omar thought. Had I run, I surely would have been caught, as the man would've given chase. It was much easier to calmly walk away. Omar chucked to himself. It was no wonder so many criminals run free in this land, as most of them were smarter than the men pursuing them.

His stomach growled as he sat on the train. He had still not eaten. But Omar knew that a meal would need to wait. Had he stayed where he was, his next meal would have been behind bars.

CHAPTER 39

The train stopped at the station, and an arctic wind greeted Omar as he disembarked. A radiant sun shone proudly in the sky, but it did little to warm the temperature on this cold, dry morning. He had a four-block walk to the Cambridge Public Library. He was headed there to meet a trusted associate. As he traversed the icy sidewalks, men and women in business attire hurried past him in both directions. He ignored their glares and before long reached his destination.

As he entered the building, he looked around the area near the front desk, where the two had agreed to meet. Two rows of wooden tables occupied the middle of the room, and he saw a few teenagers sitting at one of them. The group appeared to be doing more socializing than learning. Typical American youth, Omar thought. Next to the stairs were short bookshelves lined with magazines and newspapers. Nadir Massoud was sitting in a chair reading a newspaper with large Arabic print.

"Brother Nadir, it is good to see you."

"You as well. Shall we find a place to talk?" Nadir asked.

Omar led them to a secluded section where there were just two small tables and chairs nestled in a corner surrounded by elephantine shelves full of books. The two men took seats on opposite sides of one of the tables. Omar stared at the table as he began to speak. "I've asked the Russians to work on the younger brother after your attempts failed. Fucking Russians haven't gotten him yet. They are useless."

"So what now then? Do we simply wait?" Nadir asked.

"I think that we move forward in a new direction. I do have another possible means to get us what we desire."

"Does this option involve me?"

"Yes, it does. The enterprise that you control is in the pharmaceutical industry. It's the perfect guise to use to approach the company about an outright purchase of the source code."

"But I'm quite sure others have tried to acquire this technology previously," Nadir said.

"They have. But I want you to approach them in a different way. You see, the leader of the company, I believe you call it CEO, will not sell the software. We want to offer someone inside the company a substantial amount of money to give us access to the source code without anyone else at the organization knowing. This way, the CEO will not have knowledge that the software has been sold. Do you understand?"

Nadir nodded. "What makes you think that someone will sell this type of trade secret to us? What if they refuse?"

"Americans love money. They love the dollar bill and all that it stands for." A look of disgust filled his face. "Their knees buckle at the sight. When they hear about how much money we will give them, they won't say no. They never do."

"The CEO did," Nadir countered.

"The CEO didn't need to take our money. He owns the company. His pockets are already lined with money. But others aren't so fortunate."

"So who do you propose I approach with this offer?"

"The man's name is Nick Waters. He's the CFO."

Nadir smiled broadly at this irony. "So you think that the man who counts the money will be the one most easily tempted?"

"Yes, we do."

"How much money are you prepared to offer him?"

"We'll offer as much as it takes. We just need him to agree to help us."

Omar handed the piece of paper in his hand to Nadir. "That has all of Nick's contact information on it. I trust that you will know how to speak to him."

"Yes, I'll know what to say. I've had much experience dealing with money-hungry Americans."

"I've left a number where you can reach me as well. I ask that you not mention specifics over the phone. The authorities have become aware of my presence in their country. Instead, we shall meet back here in person to discuss. Just leave me a message with the time and date, and I'll be here waiting for you," Omar said, making reference to his new disposable cell phone.

"Very good. I'll be in touch."

CHAPTER 40

James was engulfed in darkness and sweat as he lay on his bed. He reconfigured his pillows, moving the one containing down feathers to the top and the foam to the bottom. He shifted to his back, then his side, then his stomach. The red light from the alarm clock on his nightstand emitted a blood red hue. He'd dozed off twice only to be awoken by the stray sounds in the house. Bumps and creaks that aging houses only seemed to make at night, while their inhabitants slept. James realized sleep was not going to come easy. His mind couldn't relax, couldn't rest. He rose from his bed and decided to go out to the living room to find some mindless entertainment on television.

On his way to the living room he went over to a window that overlooked the street. He stuck two fingers in between the dusty blinds to part them. Four houses down he could see them. Parked in an unmarked police car was a police officer assigned to watch him and ensure he remained safe, per the order of Leah Peterson.

He turned the television on and began to flip through the channels, looking for something to watch. Once he'd found a hockey game, he pulled the lever on the side of his recliner so that his seat could put his feet up. He tried to focus on the game and not the events of the past week. After watching the game for a little over half an hour, the sleep that James was hunting for came to find him.

* * *

The black Lexus SUV had been parked on the busy Cambridge side street for the past three hours. Paul Francis passed the time by going over the plan over and over again. He thought through all possible scenarios, and rehearsed what he'd do under each set of circumstances. There was never room for failure in any of his jobs. Since the police were nearby watching the house, he knew he'd have no time to escape if anything went wrong. He checked his watch and saw that it was one in the morning. It was time to get to work. He left his car and approached the house. After going through three adjacent yards, he arrived at James'. The only lights were coming from the living room.

He walked around to the side of the house where no one on the street could see him and began methodically checking each window. From a previous surveillance, he knew that the house wasn't alarmed. He steadily worked his way to the back. He checked the sliding door that led from the porch to the kitchen. Upon applying a little pressure to the door, he felt it give slightly. He couldn't help but smile.

Now that he'd found an entry point, he wanted to look around a bit more before going inside. Through the glass slider he saw no one in the kitchen or dining area. He saw the light from the television flicker in the darkness. The possibility of someone awake and watching television made him pause. He decided to walk the perimeter of the house to see if he could see through any of the other windows. He found one window with the blinds open a crack. He looked in and saw James Woltzberg fast asleep on his recliner.

He quickly returned to the sliding door. As he slid it open, he saw that the lock was broken. Why were so many supposedly smart people so stupid? He had one foot inside the house when he was startled by the high-pitched bark from a dog in another room. Seconds later he saw the tiny animal race around the corner from the hallway into the kitchen. How could there be a dog in the house? During his surveillance he noted that the couple had no kids or pets living with them. But he only had seconds to think about the dog before another noise captured his attention.

* * *

James was jolted awake from his recliner when he heard the dog barking in the kitchen. Sill disoriented from being abruptly woken, he turned and saw a stranger by the door. He ran toward his bedroom to get the firearm that he had in his nightstand drawer. He could hear Paul giving chase behind him.

"Cindy, get my gun! There's someone in the house!" he shouted as he entered the bedroom.

James whipped around and saw Paul as he came toward him. He had a familiar limp. Where have I seen him before? It hit him. He was the man in the park watching me play hockey, he thought. That realization froze James just long enough for Paul to close in on him.

He reached into his jacket pocket and James knew that he would not be able to make it to the nightstand to get his own fire-arm. He shouted at Cindy to get the gun again. He could hear her in a panic trying to locate the firearm. Fully awake, fury gripped James as he wrestled the man down to the carpet. He clamped both of his hands on Paul's wrists to keep his hands out of his pockets. This initial surge had left him winded. Suddenly he felt Paul's strength as he tried to free his arms. He just needed to hold on until Cindy found the gun.

"Cindy, get the fucking gun!"

"I'm trying to find it!" she shouted. He could hear the hysteria in her voice as she pulled the middle drawer completely out of the nightstand and dumped its contents onto the bed. But the gun wasn't there.

James was tiring quickly as the man struggled to free his hands from James' grip. His fury was quickly turning to panic. James, on top of Paul, tried to slide his knee to Paul's crotch to hit him in the groin. The maneuver put James off balance. Paul seized the opportunity to pull James over and before James could counter, he was the one who was underneath. With James' grip weakening, Paul tore his hands away from him.

The assassin yanked out a sweet-smelling cloth and shoved it over James' mouth and nose. James raised his arms to wrest the cloth away, but the man was too strong. Terror engulfed him he felt himself going under. Thoughts raced around in his head. Could this be how I die? Is this it? What about Cindy? I need to protect her.

Cindy opened the bottom drawer of the nightstand and saw the gun lying all by itself in the drawer. As his vision became glassy, James saw her panic and confusion as she lifted the gun in her hands. It was the last thing he saw before he was overcome by the fumes.

* * *

With the husband unconscious, Paul quickly turned toward the wife. He found himself staring down the barrel of a .22-caliber handgun. Cindy had the handgun out in front of her in a two-handed policemen's grip. Panic filled him — because he knew he would not reach her in time.

As Paul rose to his feet, Cindy closed her eyes and pulled the trigger. But the trigger was locked in its place. Paul realized the safety was still on. He could see by her confusion that she had no idea how to take the safety off, or even what a safety was.

He advanced confidently toward her, and when he was just inches away, she swung the gun at him in desperation. He put his arm up to block her swing and put the cloth full of ether up to her mouth. Like James, she struggled for a few moments then her body went limp in his arms. His job nearly finished, he threw her carelessly down onto the bed.

He took a moment to wipe the sweat from his brow. He stared at the woman unconscious on the bed in nothing but a silk night-gown and briefly thought about what he would do to her if he was fifteen years younger. Yet he knew how stupid he'd been back then. Giving into such urges on jobs like this only meant someone might discover his DNA. Instead, he rolled her over to the side of the bed where the covers had been pulled back and tucked her in as if she was sound asleep and nothing out of the ordinary had happened.

He then proceeded to strip James down to his underwear and tucked him on the other side of the bed. Once tucked under the covers, James looked sound asleep, like it was just another ordi-nary night in the Woltzberg home. Methodically, Paul pulled a copy of the *Boston Globe* out of his jacket pocket, then pulled a small bedroom trash barrel over to the side of the bed. He put the newspaper into the trash barrel section by section. He then took a package of cigarettes out of his pocket, lit one, and put the lit end up to the newspaper until it caught fire.

He quickly went to the other side of the bed and used a lighter to set fire to the bed sheets. He worked carefully to ensure that the entire side of the bed was burning brightly before he left. He didn't want to leave anything to chance. Slowly the flames began engulfing the bed, and before long, the pungent aroma of burning flesh filled the room.

As he turned to leave the house, he saw the small dog that had nearly caused the whole plan to unravel. It was staring at him and growling. For the first time that night he got a good look at the dog and realized that it was the animal he'd left for dead at the park. I should have never taken this dog from the shelter, Paul thought as he looked at the tiny beagle. James must have saved it from freezing to death the night they were all in the park together. The little puppy had survived one brush with death, but it wouldn't be so lucky this time.

Paul hurried past the dog, leaving it to burn alive in the house. In the kitchen, he slid back out through the slider. He limped back to his car, as fast as he could. Breathing heavily as he got in, he drove off into the darkness of the cold winter evening.

* * *

In nothing but his boxer shorts and a white tee shirt, Will opened his front door. Outside, the sun had just risen above the tree line, and its bright rays blinded Will. He crossed his arms in front of his chest as the cold air slapped him in the face. Charles Madre was standing at his front door in a black baseball cap with the letters CPD on it. Leah Peterson was standing behind him.

"What are you doing here?" Will asked, barely awake.

"Will, I regret to inform you that your brother and sister in law, James and Cindy Woltzberg, passed away last night."

Suddenly everything around Will felt twisted and slow, as if the fabric of time had been flipped out of balance. His vision slowed, he felt his legs turn to jelly. He staggered backward, and Sarah, wearing her purple satin pajamas, ran from her room and took his arm.

"What happened? What happened!" Sarah shouted.

Charles explained again, and upon hearing the news, Sarah burst into tears. Will's son Logan came barreling down the stairs but stopped short, alarmed by the sight of his stricken parents.

"How?" Will asked.

"The two were in their bed last night when their home burned to the ground. The scene is still under investigation, but nothing at this time leads us to believe that this was anything but an accident. An unmarked police car was parked down the street when it happened. They rushed in, but couldn't reach the master bedroom, where the fire originated."

"James would've gotten out. He couldn't have slept through a fire. He—" Will's voice gave out.

"I'm sorry for your loss." Leah said compassionately.

Will took a few tottering steps before he found himself in his wife's embrace. Will and Sarah cried helplessly in each other's arms. He felt her body cling to him, her arms squeezing him tightly as she whispered in his ear:

"I'm so, so sorry. I love you and I'm right here for you."

CHAPTER 41

For the third time this morning, Nick filled his large coffee mug full of black coffee. A good night's sleep had been replaced with a hazy opiate induced high. The restless night he'd had was taking its toll. He'd heard the news directly from Will, who'd called him when he first arrived at the office. The shock of the news was dulled by the throbbing between his temples. After the euphoria came the crash. Nick could only describe it as a feeling that his brain was swelling inside his head, pressing against every square inch of his skull. It made James' death seem distant and surreal.

He walked back from the cafeteria, and as he approached his desk, he saw that the red message light on his phone was flashing. When he didn't recognize the name of the person on the recording, he nearly deleted the message. But by the time he was through listening to it, he found himself pressing the replay button and taking notes.

The man in the message said that he had an interesting proposition for Nick. Nick wondered if the two men's idea of "interesting" were the same. He quickly dialed the number left on the recording.

"Nadir Massoud."

"Nadir, good morning, this is Nick Waters from Simulation Scientific returning your call."

"Ah, Nick, good to hear from you. Could you hold on one minute?"

Nick could hear a deep Middle Eastern accent in Nadir's voice as he spoke. It sounded as though Nadir was on a cell phone. Through the phone he could hear the sound of footsteps and then a door closing before Nadir resumed the discussion.

"Sorry about that. Let me take a moment to introduce myself. My name is Nadir Massoud and I'm CEO of Sage Pharmaceuticals."

"I know who you are, and I'm somewhat familiar with your company."

"Ah, good. We here at Sage are also quite familiar with the work that your team at Simulation Scientific is doing. We're very impressed with what you've accomplished."

"Thank you. I'd like to take credit for that, but really it's the hard work of the virologists and software developers that make all of it happen."

"I'm sure that you've got quite a team over there. The software that you've created has caught our attention. We're very interested in it."

Nick began to think that the call might be better handled by the sales department. Those people had the patience to deal with potential clients. "Over the past months we've had a lot of interest in the software. We've seen a nice uptick in our first-time licenses. If you'd like, I can have one of our sales reps give you a call and they can go over the various modules within the software and help you determine which ones might be right for your organization."

"We're not interested in licensing the software. We're actually interested in discussing a more robust use of it. I've heard that your CEO Will Woltzberg hasn't been interested in hearing any offers regarding the software unless they're the standard licensing."

Nick didn't think twice about Nadir's knowledge of Will's unwillingness to sell the company. People in the industry spoke to one another, and the word could travel fast.

"Well, you've heard right. Will is committed to the keeping the development of this software within the company."

"I can understand that. He wants to do what he thinks is best for your company. But that doesn't lessen my interest in the software and what I may be able to use it for." Nadir paused before his next statement. "I've learned over the years that making the right offer to the right person is how business gets done. Now, I've got a lot of money allocated to gain access to this software. I don't need a formal agreement or software license. I just need access to the source code for the software. Do you understand what I'm saying?"

Nick's eyes lit up for the first time that morning. "Yes, I think I get what you mean. Maybe we should get together for lunch to discuss this further."

"That would be great. But I'd like to do it soon. Time is money and the sooner we can talk, the more money we'll be talking about."

Nick couldn't believe his good luck. "How does tomorrow afternoon sound?"

"That would be perfect." Nadir replied.

"Do you know where the Pub 77 is on Tremont Street in Cambridge?" Nick asked.

"Sure do."

"Well, I don't know if I'll have time for a full meal, but I think I could spare a few minutes for a quick drink and a conversation. Are you free at two?" Nick asked.

"Two it is," Nadir replied.

"I'll be at the bar drinking a rum and coke."

The two ended their discussion and Nick spun around in his chair and faced the window in his office. This could be my ticket out of here, he thought. Suddenly his headache didn't seem all that bad.

CHAPTER 42

The sun was just starting to rise as Will headed into SimSci. The temperature was mild, and the roads were covered with water from the snow that had begun to melt. He hadn't slept well since he'd learned of his brother's death. His disbelief and sadness had turned into anger and acceptance. The anger kept simmering every second of the day. Charles had told him that the official cause of death was an accidental fire set inside James' house. But Will didn't believe that for a moment. He knew that Charles and Leah didn't either. Charles had admitted as much to him. He was operating under the assumption that James' death was linked to the others, and that one person was responsible for them all. If I could just go back in time, he thought. God, if I could just go back and warn him. He felt the muscles in his body tightening. He took a deep breath, then another. You're going back to work, he thought. You've got to hold it together.

This was his first day back to the office since James' death, and he knew it wouldn't be easy. He'd decided that the first thing he would do was to get into James' office and try to get his hands around everything that he'd been working on. Am I emotionally ready to go into James' office? Do I really want to try to go through his stuff? He stood outside for a moment fidgeting before heading in.

Once inside, he was engulfed in an eerie silence. An uneasy feeling roiled in the pit of his stomach. He somehow felt like he was snooping, and that any minute James would come down the hall with a perplexed look on his face and ask him what he was doing in his office. James wasn't walking through that door, though. He had to begin to move forward without his brother, his companion for all those years together.

Wiping away a tide that filled his eyes, he decided that email would be the most logical place to start. Upon logging in, Will was overwhelmed by the sheer volume of emails he'd need to go through. There were literally hundreds of them. He took them one by one, making notes on each as he read.

After twenty minutes of reading through emails, he came across a unique one. It was an electronic greeting card with an animated man dressed in a white coat. Entirely bald, he had glasses with thick frames and lenses. He had a test tube in his hand, and on the table next to him sat other animated lab equipment. Next to the equipment sat a big birthday cake with multiple candles with animated flames. Clearly the animated man was supposed to be a scientist of some sort. The contents of the test tube in his hand were bubbling, and all of the bubbles were in the shape of hearts. Will looked down at the words below the animation:

To a mad scientist,

I hope your birthday is test tubetacular! I wanted to send you a quick birthday card to let you know that you are in my mind and in my heart today. I feel so lucky to be married to such a wonderful man. You will always be a wonderful, loving husband first, and a mad scientist second in my mind. Happy thirty-eighth birthday!

Love always,

Cindy

Will's eyes filled with tears again. The card had been sent less than thirty-six hours before the two had died. Overwhelmed with sadness, he sat back in the chair and stared out of the window.

Suddenly, inexplicable anger filled him. With his hands, he swept nearly everything on James's desk onto the floor. His coffee cup smashed and his keyboard hung off the desk from its cord. He began to cry uncontrollably as he leaned his elbows on James' desk. Everything that had happened over the past few days was slowly sinking in. The man who had helped Will build SimSci from the ground up was gone. His brother was gone forever. There wasn't anything that he, or anyone else, could do to change that.

"I'm here if you want to talk,"

Will nearly jumped out of his seat at the sound of another person's voice. He looked up and saw Leah in the doorway, laptop bag strapped around her shoulder.

"I'm sorry for the scene in here, but—"

"Please, don't apologize," Leah said. "This'll probably be one of the hardest things that you have to do, you know, cleaning your brother's office out. I can't even imagine. I have a little sister at home and...."

Leah's voice cut out. Her brow wrinkled and she closed her eyes for a moment. Will saw a rush of emotion in Leah's face that he didn't think she was capable of showing. For just a moment, her veil was pierced and her human emotions had burst through.

As quickly as she let her guard down, years of training kicked in, and Leah field agent for the Department of Homeland Security was back.

"Well, I just wanted to let you know that I am here and if there's anything that you want to tell me that you think might help us in our investigation, I'm only two doors down."

Her words instantly sparked his interest. "I want to be part of this effort. Whatever I can do to help, I'm willing to do, even if that means contributing support financially. I want whoever did this to my brother found."

"Trust me, I won't hesitate to ask you if I think you can assist the investigation."

Neither of them spoke for a moment as they both thought about all that was happening. Outside, the low pitched sound of a big-rig's horn rang out.

"This all hasn't sunk in yet, with James, I mean," Will said as he felt his anger ebb to sadness once again. "I really want these guys caught. Are there any other leads that you're following?"

"We did come across something interesting the other day. But it's too early to say whether or not this is good information or just another dead end."

"I'm interested in hearing about it either way."

"The other day an agent from the Intelligence and Analysis branch told me he found a new email address had been created on a website that offers them. On the surface, not a big deal because hundreds of thousands of email address are created around the world each day. But two data points caused this one to be flagged. The first was the name of the person opening the email account. It was an alias Boris Kozlov had used in the past. You see, after days of digging we found some intelligence on Boris, including a list of aliases he's used in the past."

"But it could be someone's real name."

"That's where the second piece of data came into play. We obtained the IP address of the computer that the email address was created on."

"And?"

"The computer was located in an internet café in Boston."

"Did you check to see if anyone in this area has that name?"

"Are you trying to find a spot in the agency?"

For the second time that morning, Leah showed a side of her Will hadn't seen yet, this time her sense of humor.

"I considered law enforcement as a career growing up," Will replied.

"That is in fact what we did, and no one with that name owns property within a fifty-mile radius, or has a vehicle registered in the state of Massachusetts."

"So you think it might have been Boris?"

"Yes, we think that there's a very good chance. We're now monitoring that email address for future activity. As soon as we have some, we will get the location of the IP address from the ISP, send some folks to it and see what we find."

"This sounds like a huge break, no?"

"Only if it's Kovlov who's sending emails from the account. More often than not things like this are just another dead end," Leah said.

"Please keep me posted. I want these guys found."

He wanted more than that, though he didn't say it to Leah. He wanted to strangle this Boris Kozlov with his bare hands.

CHAPTER 43

The tropical sun beat down on the village, to the point that the sweat was dripping off Nigel's nose. For March, it was an exceptionally hot day in Thailand, and the temperature combined with the humidity made him feel like he was deep inside one of the dark caves that he'd come to explore. The electricity had been shut off three days ago and as a result, no building had air conditioning to assist in escaping the heat. But the lack of air conditioning paled in comparison to the other problems that Nigel had encountered. Over the past few days, the town had descended into a state of chaos. Last night, someone had tried to climb into the house through one of the windows. If they remained, their lives were in grave danger.

"We have to go today. It's only going to get worse," Marcel said, his forehead wrinkled with tension.

Nigel knew he was right. He'd spent the past twenty-four hours in denial. He'd hoped that they would hear a message over the radio that help would be coming, that somehow the U.S. was sending someone to rescue them. He was now realizing that there was no hope of that happening. If it did happen, they'd likely be dead by then.

So much had transpired in the past four days. After Jao had been taken out of the hotel, Nigel and Marcel had gotten directions to the hospital that Jao was taken to from an English-speaking hotel employee. When they arrived at the hospital, they were told that the doctors had diagnosed him with rabies, confirming Nigel's suspicions. They knew that they couldn't continue the shoot until they had gotten another translator, so they headed back to the hotel to work with people back in the U.S. to try to find another local. They were told that it would take a few days. While they waited, the nightmare began to unfold.

The next morning, Nigel was awoken by the sounds of sirens. He looked outside to see another ambulance pulling into the hotel parking lot, only this time it was being followed by a second one. When he went outside to find out what was going on, he saw another person being taken out of a hotel room.

As Nigel searched for the English speaking man that he'd found the previous day to find out what was happening, he saw a second person being taken out of a separate room. He watched the medics load them into the second ambulance. Later, he finally saw the hotel employee coming out of one of the other hotel rooms. The man told Nigel that he was told that the two people who were taken away had contracted the same disease as Jao had.

The statement caused Nigel's jaw to drop. Three cases of rabies in three individuals that had virtually no contact with one another, with no reports of rabid animals being caught or at least seen in the past few days, was virtually impossible. There had to be some mistake. Surely there was a misdiagnosis on the part of the medics. Not until a few days later had Nigel discovered the true scope of the predicament.

After finally getting someone to replace Jao, they began filming again. They were gathering in the morning for what was to be the second to last day of shooting when their guide came out of his hotel room and told them what he'd just seen on the local news. They had run a story about the hospital approximately ten miles away. The hospital had been overrun with cases of what appeared to be rabies. There were so many patients that the hospital had begun putting the patients in the halls, cafeteria, and any other room that had available space. But that wasn't the end of the story. Next they showed footage of a busy street in the town. On the streets people were walking around aimlessly. The men looked confused and the news anchorman had said that they were showing signs of dementia, a symptom of the disease. The town was so overwhelmed that the sick were now walking the streets and no one was doing anything about it. Local health officials were baffled by the extreme outbreak, as no ill wild animals were reported anywhere in the vicinity.

Nigel decided to suspend the shoot so that he and Marcel could go and see exactly what was happening. Using Jao's Jeep, they made the drive into the town where the virus was spreading. When they arrived, the situation was much worse than what their guide had described. There weren't just a few people in the streets like the footage had shown, there were bodies everywhere. Most were lying on the ground, their muscles twitching, their mouths foaming, running down their face and onto the ground.

Some were still experiencing the early-stage symptoms of the virus. Those people, still able to control most of their motor skills, were able to walk around. But they weren't going anywhere particular. Some looked disoriented, some terrified, some just confused. They weren't all so apathetic. Some were savagely attacking random people they met, hitting, biting, and scratching them until they ceased to breathe.

Nigel knew that the way the virus affected the mind caused victims to feel anxiety, confusion, paranoia, and terror, eventually resulting in hallucinations and delirium, and that's exactly what he was seeing as he drove through the streets.

Before long they realized the mistake they'd made by coming into town. They decided to head back to the hotel, but as they were proceeding toward the outskirts of town, a large military truck drove past them heading in the opposite direction. On top of the truck were four soldiers, each manning a machine gun. At that point, Nigel realized that they needed to leave as fast as they could. Minutes later, off in the distance they could see two large military SUV's parked in the road ahead. As they came closer, they saw the soldiers moving the SUV to block half of the road. Soldiers were putting up a wooden blockade to block the other half. Yellow flags were draped on all four sides of the vehicle. Nigel's stomach dropped as he realized that the military was setting up a quarantine.

The car in front of them tried to get through the blockade, only to be turned away by the soldiers. Nagel watched as the driver got out of the car. He was pleading with the soldiers to let him leave. The soldiers began to demand that the man get back into the car, but he refused to do so. Then without warning, one of the soldiers raised his gun and shot him once in the head. Nigel saw the man's knees buckle, and he dropped to the ground.

Nigel turned his own car around and headed back. They stopped at one of the first houses that they saw that looked both relatively secure and vacant, then forced their way in. He and Marcel had been holding up there since.

Two days had passed since then, and the mayhem in the town had only gotten worse.

"There has to be another way out of this town, one that isn't blocked by the military," Marcel insisted.

"I agree. Surely somewhere there must be a road out of the town that's not being guarded. But how will we manage to find it? There isn't much fuel in the Jeep. Running out of gas is too dangerous," Nigel replied.

They'd ventured out the previous day and drove around to see if the military were going house to house rescuing people, but all that they'd found were streets that would've been empty if not for the dead and dying people that they were littered with. It was a sight that Nigel only thought he'd see in the movies. The violence displayed by those infected was extraordinary. One was running around stabbing others with a large knife. Another was dragging people down by their hair and kicking them over and over again until they stopped moving. The violence was so severe that Nigel wondered if this was even rabies, or something else. Maybe it was another disease with similar symptoms. One that makes the people act out in a much more violent manner. He knew that he and Marcel had to find a way out to escape before they were attacked. "Let's at least try to find a phone that works," Marcel said. The two had left the hotel in such a rush that they'd left most of their belongings there, including both of their cell phones.

Nigel thought about trying to go outside to find a phone. But who would they call? Their production company? Their families? The U.S. government? Nigel wasn't sure that anyone could help them. The Thai government had quarantined the entire town. They weren't letting anyone in or out until they figured out how the virus was spreading so quickly. The only group that might have a chance of getting into the town to rescue them would be the U.S. military. Suddenly, Nigel jumped to his feet.

"I have an idea."

Nigel reached into the back pocket of his pants and removed a small leather pouch. It wasn't his wallet, which was kept in the opposite pocket, but when he unzipped the pouch, the wad of U.S. currency inside far outweighed what he kept in his wallet.

Although he knew how much money was there, he counted it to confirm the amount. When he was done, he'd counted one hundred one hundred dollar bills, or ten thousand dollars. Whenever he traveled outside the U.S., he carried the cash because he knew that ten thousand U.S. dollars could get a person out of a lot of bad situations in many parts of the world.

"I forgot about that stash of money that you carry around," Marcel said.

Nigel responded by simply nodding his head.

"Do you think that can get us out of this mess?"

"We should find out. What do you think?" Nigel asked.

"Let's try."

"Gather up everything that we need. I'm going to take a look outside to see what's going on out there. We've got to be very careful even getting to our Jeep."

He drew the dark blue curtains on the window to one side and squinted as the bright sun shined in his eyes. The house was on a main road in the village, a road that would normally have at least some traffic on it. But today there were no cars. A handful of dead bodies littered the ground, with a few that were still writhing. But none appeared to be a threat.

"I think the coast is clear. You ready?"

"Yes, let's go. Here, take this," Marcel handed him one of the handguns that they had with them.

Nigel went over to the door, opened it just a crack, and peeked out. Their Jeep was less than ten feet from the door and he didn't see anyone around it.

"Okay, I'm going out," Nigel said as he swung the door open all the way and ran outside.

The two men were halfway to the Jeep when they saw someone charge from around the side of the house. His greasy black hair was nearly down to his shoulders. He had a filthy white tee shirt soiled with a large blood stain. His denim shorts were ripped in numerous places and his feet were bare.

"Look at him! He's been infected!" Nigel shouted to Marcel.

When the man saw Nigel, he let out a loud scream and began running toward them. Nigel reached into his pockets for the Jeep keys so the two could jump into it.

"The keys are in the house!" Nigel shouted as he realized his mistake.

He tried the door handle to the Jeep, but the door wouldn't open, it was locked. As the man came closer, Nigel could see the sun glistening off the saliva running from his mouth down to his chin. My God, he's coming for me, Nigel thought. He tried to yank his handgun out of its holster, but the gun got caught on his belt and it fell from his hands. His eyes widened in terror. The man would be on top of him before he had a chance to retrieve his gun. He involuntarily let out a groan as he bent over.

The manic was just a few feet away when one side of the man's head exploded outward. Nigel simultaneously registered the sound of a gun blast. The man's limp body fell forward and nearly landed on top of Nigel. Nigel's glassy eyes were gripped by the sight of the blood that had begun to pool on the ground below the corpse.

"What the fuck are you waiting for? Get in the car!" Marcel yelled.

Nigel saw him holding his gun out in front of him, the smoke curling from the muzzle. Nigel got to his feet and ran back toward the house.

Once inside, he spotted his keys on the table that he'd counted his money on. He grabbed them and ran back outside. Marcel was still standing next to the car, spinning around in circles with his gun extended ready to fire at anyone that approached him from any direction. Nigel unlocked the Jeep and both men dove in. He turned onto the road and began to navigate through the bodies sprawled on the dirt road. As he drove, he wiped the sweat off his forehead with the back of his hand and looked over at Marcel.

"That was a close one."

Marcel's mouth was set in a grim line. "Let's just keep our eyes peeled so we don't have another encounter like that."

CHAPTER 44

Will flipped the switch, shutting off the lights in his office.

"Shit, I forgot to start my car," he muttered as he fished his remote starter out of his pocket. He turned back into his office, approached the window and pushed the button on the starter. He watched his brake lights flash, then began to head back out. He slowed as he passed Leah's office. She needed to know that he was leaving so that she could follow him.

"I'm heading out. Are you ready?" he asked.

"Ready for anything."

* * *

Boris had been circling the block for the past ninety minutes. The last thirty had been under a dark sky, as the sun had disappeared in the west. He watched the smoke slowly rise from a manhole in the middle of the road in between the cars that passed over it. Despite his insulated jacket, stocking hat, and Thinsulate lined boots, he was freezing. The cold had chilled him to the bone. Yet he knew he wouldn't be able to get into a warm car until he saw Will leave the SimSci offices.

He and Yuriy had been tailing Will for the past forty-eight hours. They'd learned about James' death before nearly anyone else. They'd planned on kidnapping him the very night of the fire, but when they arrived at his house they found it engulfed in flames. When they met with Omar to give him the news, he told them to go after Will, that he would surely know how to gain access to the source code.

As Boris approached the SimSci parking lot, his pulse thumped with excitement. He finally saw exhaust coming from the tailpipe of Will's car. He stopped and casually lit a cigarette. He knew from their surveillance over the past few days that Will used a remote starter to start his car. That meant he would be coming out of the office building to his car any minute. He took out his cell phone and resumed walking. Yuriy answered before the phone completed its first ring.

"Our friend should be leaving any minute. I'm fifty feet past the entrance to the lot," Boris said.

"Okay, I'm coming."

Less than a minute later, his black Mercedes appeared up ahead. Boris got in the driver's seat as Yuriy hurried around to the other side of the car. As soon as Yuriy had closed the door, the car peeled around the corner and double-parked outside the SimSci offices.

The car was facing the direction that they knew Will would turn when he left to head home. Soon enough they saw Will's Ford Explorer turn out of the lot. They were about to follow when another car barreled out of the SimSci lot right behind Will's. Inside the dark Dodge Charger, the two men saw that a woman was driving. Although both men had seen the car before, neither recognized it.

"Looks like these two are leaving together."

"Must be a coincidence," Yuriy replied.

Once the two cars were a safe distance ahead, Boris began to follow them. He knew that they didn't need to worry about losing Will in traffic. It was more than likely that Will was heading home. The worst-case scenario Boris could envision would be losing Will in traffic combined with him not heading home right away. He didn't think either of those things would happen, but even if they did, he knew they would simply wait near Will's house until he did arrive home.

The two trailed Will for nearly twenty minutes when they approached a busy intersection. As Will's SUV went through, the traffic light at the intersection turned yellow.

"Oh shit," Boris said.

He quickly put his left blinker on and cut off a car in the left lane that was attempting to speed up to make it through the intersection before the traffic light turned red. The car behind blared his horn as Boris sped through the intersection seconds after the light turned red. He looked back in his rearview mirror at the car he'd cut off. It was stopped in the left lane at the intersection behind him. He didn't notice the Dodge Charger stopped in the right lane. After the light, the road immediately merged the two lanes into one, and as a result, Boris found himself directly behind Will's SUV. Although better than being stuck at the light, being directly behind Will wasn't ideal due to the risk of being noticed. He took his foot off of the accelerator and allowed the gap between his car and Will's to widen. A few minutes later, a car took a right turn out of a parking lot and occupied the space between the two cars. Boris relaxed a bit as now he had room between him and Will.

"Close one," Yuriy said as Boris drove.

"Yes, it was. Do you have the duct tape?"

"Right here," Yuriy replied as he held it up.

"Just make sure you're ready."

"I'm ready."

"We'll be at his house in five minutes. Oh shit."

Boris saw that Yuriy appeared troubled as he looked in his rearview mirror. "Something wrong?"

"That car. I think it's following us."

Yuriy began to turn around in his seat, and Boris shoved him back down into it.

"Fuck's wrong with you? Sit down! Do you want them to see you turning around looking at them?" Boris shouted.

Yuriy sat back in his seat and didn't say a word. As expected, Will's SUV turned down a road leading to his house. They followed, and seconds later the car behind them did the same. The road Will lived on ended in a cul de sac. If the car behind them turned down that road, it was more than just a coincidence that they'd been heading in the same direction. He saw the sign for Will's street in the distance and knew that he'd have to make a decision quickly.

Will put his blinker on and turned down his road. But Boris didn't put his on. Instead, he passed Will's street completely. He kept his eyes glued to his rearview mirror to see what the car behind him would do. Seconds later, the Dodge Charger turned down Will's street as well. Boris slammed his palms against the steering wheel.

"Fuck! Someone else is going to his house. We need to wait."

He tried to regroup and organize his thoughts. He realized he needed to see who was going to Will's house. He saw a gas station and quickly turned into it, wheels screeching. He turned the car around to complete his surveil route. As he approached Will's house, he didn't see any cars in the driveway except the two that were parked there every night, which he knew to be Will's and his wife's.

He passed the house and continued to the ending cul de sac. The Dodge Charger was parked in the turnaround with its lights still on. Boris could see the outline of the figure driving.

"It's a cop," Boris said, pointing to the car. "That was a cop that left the office with Will. He's being followed by a cop everywhere he goes. We can't get him now."

"So what are we going to do?" Yuriy asked.

Boris cursed under his breath. "I don't know, but right now we can't do anything. We need to figure out another way to get at him."

Boris turned into the last driveway before the cul de sac and turned his car around. As he passed Will's house for the second time, he saw him walking up his driveway with the mail from his mailbox in his hand. Boris mashed the accelerator and sped away.

CHAPTER 45

Omar waited with increasing impatience for Boris and Yuriy to arrive for their meeting. They were over ten minutes late, and their tardiness only confirmed what Omar already knew. Hiring these men had been a mistake. He watched with a sharp eye as a red Lexus pulled up to the drive-thru window. He could hear the rock music blaring from the car's stereo as the Middle Eastern man behind the counter handed the driver a large coffee. Finally he saw Boris' car turn into the snow covered parking lot. He watched Boris get out and look around to see if anyone was tailing him.

The two men came into the donut shop and stepped up to the counter to purchase coffees. With white Styrofoam cups in hand, the two walked over to the table where Omar was sitting. Beside Omar's table, a yellow sign on the floor said "Caution – Wet Floor." Next to the sign was a mop bucket on wheels with a mop inside it. Behind the sign was a clear plastic tarp under a large portion of the tile floor, including under the table where Omar was sitting.

Boris turned back to the man behind the counter. "What the fuck is going on here?"

"Our roof is leaking. I'm sorry for the appearance," he replied as he began making a fresh pot of coffee.

* * *

Leah Peterson was in her office when her phone rang.

"We've got activity on the potential Kozlov email account. Working to get the physical location the IP address was assigned to."

Agent Shapiro's news caused her to bolt forward in her seat. Her hands gripped the edges of her desk as she held the phone on her shoulder. "How long will it take? We need this information now!"

"Just hold on, it should only take a second."

Seconds felt like hours as Leah waited.

"Got it!"

Leah grabbed the pen on her desk, ready for the address.

"It's 60 Commercial Street, Bits and Bytes Internet café. I'm pulling up a map now…"

Leah was out of her chair, and running down the hallway to her car as she listened for further information.

"It's right at the corner of Commercial and Tremont. There's another little coffee shop across the street from it on one side and a Seven-Eleven on the other side."

"Ok, I'm on my way down there with the cops now!"

"On your way to what?"

Leah turned and saw Will's head poking out of his office doorway.

"Not now, Will. There's been activity on Kozlov's email. We're combing the area for him."

Will quickly grabbed his jacket from the hook on the back of his office door. "I'm coming with you."

"This doesn't concern you. This is related to our investigation," Leah said as she raced down the stairs two at a time.

Will gave chase and caught up to her in the lobby. "Doesn't involve me? These animals killed my brother! I'm coming with you!"

Leah frowned, but she didn't fight it. "I don't have time to argue," she said as she ran to her car. "Just stay out of the way."

The two raced out of the office, jumped into Leah's car and headed toward Commercial Street.

* * *

"I hope you've brought good news," Omar said.

"No, I'm afraid that we didn't," Boris replied as he slouched in his seat, his eyes averting Omar's.

Even though he'd expected little progress from the two, he was still disappointed when they told him nothing had been done. "When do you think you'll have good news for me?"

"We're working hard to get our target and then extract the knowledge from him." Boris responded.

"You understand that I'm not happy with the progress that you've made. We are running out of time."

"We went to make our move yesterday. We followed him from the office to his home. Just as we were about to grab him, we saw someone watching us. A car had left his office the same time that he did. We thought it was a coincidence, but the car followed him all the way home. Then it parked just a short distance away from his house. Clearly, they were looking out for the well-being of our target."

"What did the security look like?" Omar asked as concern began to creep onto his face.

"It was night when we followed him. They were in a Dodge Charger. We couldn't see the driver. Like I said, it was parked outside his office and followed him home."

"But there was only one person in the car?"

"Yes," Boris replied.

"During the time that you've been watching Will, has anything else come to your attention that I should know about? Anything at all?" Omar asked as he fumed inside about how useless the two men had become.

"No, the man continues to work and go home. Nothing out of the ordinary. No strange visitors, no strange trips anywhere. A very predictable man."

Omar realized that the two men had no other information that would be helpful to him. From the table that he'd chosen, he could see the entire donut shop, and he quickly confirmed there was no one else in the shop. He then made eye contact with the man behind the counter, who'd been watching the three men since Boris and Yuriy had sat down.

"Do you remember when I told you that we needed to be very careful as we carried out this operation?" Omar asked, beginning to raise his voice. He could feel the muscles in his neck begin to tighten as he spoke.

"Of course, we have not used our credit card once. Not even for a burger. Also we have not touched a mobile phone. We have been very careful."

"I have friends in very high places. My organization has people inside the U.S.'s security forces. They have seen your emails!"

A fine spray of mist came from Omar's mouth as he began to shout. He took the taqiyah from his head and put in down onto the table.

Ten feet away the man behind the counter saw his signal. Like a well trained solider, he began carrying out the tasks as he'd been instructed. He stepped out from around the counter and turned the "Open" sign on the entrance around. Then he checked to make sure Boris and Yuriy still had their backs to him.

He went back behind the counter, took out a Glock 18 handgun, and silently approached the men. He crept within inches of Yuriy's head and pulled the trigger.

Boris reacted instantly to the gunshot. He jerked around to reach for the gun in the small of his back. But he couldn't react fast enough. The counter man turned the weapon and fired it at Boris. With Boris partially turned around, the bullet entered his temple instead of the back of his head. Blood and chunks of brain tissue sprayed the window on impact. Both bodies slumped lifelessly down in their seats, and then Boris slid to the floor into the blood that was beginning to pool on top of the clear plastic tarp. That's what it was there for.

Omar stood up and examined his clothes to see how much of the blood had sprayed on him. He'd felt droplets cover his face and hands. He rushed behind the counter and changed into the spare clothes that were underneath it. With his hands cupped, he scooped water from the faucet and splashed his face, cleaning the blood from it.

"I trust you can handle this clean-up, Tabish," Omar said to as he walked over to the entrance, still drying his face with napkins from the dispenser on the counter. Tabish nodded in agreement as he began to clean the blood spatter off the windows.

As Omar left the shop, he looked over at the black Mercedes nearby. They wouldn't need that anymore. As he reached the sidewalk, his skin prickled with alarm. Three uniformed police cars were parked in the coffee shop across the street. He briskly walked to a narrow alley and turned down it so he could watch them from the shadows. In no time he saw a black Dodge Charger race down the street.

* * *

Inside her car, Leah wasn't focusing on the Internet café, where three state troopers were interrogating everyone inside. She and four other unmarked cars were searching the perimeter, looking for any sign of Boris Kozlov. When she saw his black Mercedes right across the street from the café, she brought the car to a screeching halt.

"Jesus Christ, there it is!" she pointed at the vehicle.

"Is that Kozlov's car?" Will asked.

"Stay here!" Leah shouted as she put her car into park and jumped out. "I've found Kozlov!" she shouted to the dispatcher as she ran toward the shop. Leah ignored the closed sign and barged inside. The gruesome scene froze her momentarily, giving Tabish enough time to race behind the counter. As he reached for the Glock, Leah instinctively reached for her own weapon. Before he could pull the gun from behind the counter, Leah fired hers four times, hitting Tabish twice. The second bullet took his head off, and Tabish's body crumpled to the ground, leaving the wall behind him covered with blood.

From behind Leah, Will stood in motionless horror, struggling to comprehend the scene.

"The building's clear,"

Leah put her weapon away and crisply walked over to the bodies on the floor. She shook her head dolefully.

"This was our one good connection to Omar," she said as she squatted near Boris' remains to get a better look, "and it looks like this lead has just gone cold."

CHAPTER 46

Tanner unwrapped the grilled chicken grinder he'd just gotten from the sandwich shop across the street and took a giant bite. The mayonnaise from the sandwich dripped from one end of the sandwich onto his keyboard. He swore under his breath as he quickly put his lunch down and grabbed a few napkins from the thick wad the deli had given him. He used them to sop up the white mess between the keys on his keyboard. Finally, he resumed his daily ritual of browsing the Internet while eating lunch. Having just finished an article on the upcoming baseball season, he moved on to browsing world news on the website that he considered the best for current world news and events, INN.com.

As the main page loaded, he browsed various headlines from news around the world on it. With invisible hands, the headline grabbed him.

Small Thailand Town Quarantined Due to Rabies Pandemic

He clicked on the link and began reading the article. Halfway through, he put his sandwich down. He'd lost his appetite. He read through the article three times, then headed to his office door. Take a deep breath, he thought as he was about to leave.

What the hell do I do first? He turned back to his computer to print the story, and took it to Will's office.

When he got there, his office door was closed. Normally Tanner wouldn't interrupt Will in the middle of a closed door meeting, but this situation was anything but ordinary. He knocked on the door as he looked through the glass beside it. Both Will and Nick Waters looked up from the papers they were perusing, and then Will waved him in.

"I'm sorry to interrupt, guys, but Will, I need to talk to you. It's extremely important," Tanner said as he opened the door.

"Umm, okay, Nick, can we finish this a bit later?" Will asked.

Nick, moving none too quickly, rose to his feet.

"What's up?" Will asked.

"You've got to see this," Tanner said as he closed the door behind Nick and passed the story to Will with anxious hands.

Seconds passed with tortoise-like speed as Tanner stood over Will waiting for him to finish. When Will was done, he curled his lips inside his mouth and shook his head. "Jesus Christ, I can't believe this."

"The story is saying that representatives from the World Health Organization and the U.S. Center for Disease Control are on their way out to the location to independently verify the claims. But—"

"We don't need them to," Will said, completing Tanner's last thought.

"They think it's a few wild animals spreading the disease."

"The model was right. *The model was right,*" Will said in wonder.

"You don't think there's any chance this truly is being spread by wild animals, do you?"

Will shared Tanner's skeptical look. "Absolutely not. It's impossible. Look at the number of people that they think might be infected. How could that many people be exposed to an infected wild animal — not just exposed but either bitten or scratched?"

"So what do we do? Who do we contact? The CDC?" Tanner asked.

"The story said that the CDC is already on its way to the scene. We need to begin vaccine creation and production. If we spend time going over the data with the CDC," he explained, "our resources will be spent cutting through red tape instead of creating the vaccine."

Tanner nodded at the logic of this statement.

"Okay. Let me hold onto this article in case I need it. This story speeds up a lot of things, but I think that we still need to keep this between us. Understand?"

"Yes," Tanner replied as he rose from his seat and headed to the door.

"Okay, good. I've got some calls to make," Will said.

Once back in his office, Tanner closed the door and sat down at his desk. He considered his past discussions with Monica. With the exception of a small problem with the time scale, ViroPredict had worked exactly as it should have. The in silico modeling predicted that the rabies virus would mutate, and then it did so in the real world. If the software was working, then there were no flaws to hide. Tanner thought back to the meeting he'd just had with Will. He didn't look or sound like a man who was trying to hide something. He seemed as surprised as I was after reading that article. When he put all the pieces of the puzzle together one thing became clear. Monica's suspicions were wrong. But why would she think he was trying to hide something?

Suddenly the truth hit him. Monica didn't think Will was trying to hide something at all. She made the whole thing up, Tanner thought, so that I'd help her get her hands on ViroPredict's source code. Because if she had that, she'd be able to create her own software, giving her access to the multi-million dollar market opportunity SimSci currently had all to itself.

Tanner felt goose bumps on his neck as he recognized how close he'd come to being fooled. He realized he had to tell someone what Monica was trying to do. But who could he tell? What proof do I have? There were no emails, texts, or voice messages to support these accusations. Just his memory of the phone calls he'd had with her. He'd need more proof before he told anyone what he suspected. He just wasn't sure how he'd get it.

* * *

"I'll have a rum and coke, please."

The waitress began making the drink while Nick admired how her black pants fit snug around her slim waist and wide hips. He was at the Pub 77 waiting for Nadir to arrive. The bar was one of a franchise of hundreds, well lit and family friendly. Dozens of televisions hung above the bar. Black and white photos of times past lined the walls. Nick was replaying the meeting with Will in his mind. The two men had been reviewing financial projections for the year when they were interrupted by Tanner Fitzgerald. Why did he barge into Will's office like that? He had the look of a man who had seen a ghost. Something about Tanner's interruption didn't make sense, but Nick wasn't sure what it was. He rubbed his temples as he replayed the day. His head throbbed. He needed a fix.

He heard the door to the bar open. Nick was certain that it was Nadir from the moment he entered. He was no more than five feet nine inches with a thick head of hair and dark Middle Eastern features. The navy blue Armani business suit that he was dressed in, with a silk handkerchief in the breast pocket, showed that he wasn't living paycheck to paycheck. He immediately made eye contact with Nick, walked over to him and extended his hand with a wide smile.

"Nick Waters, I presume. Nadir Massoud, pleasure to meet you."

"Likewise," Nick responded as the two shook hands.

Nadir took a seat at the bar and ordered a cola. "I appreciate you meeting me like this. I'm sure it isn't easy to get away. I trust that you're quite busy in your role as CFO."

"I am. But I'm also able to prioritize. You sounded like you've got something very important to discuss with me," Nick responded.

The waitress retuned with Nadir's drink. He took a sip then placed the glass neatly on a white napkin on the bar. Then Nadir leaned up against the bar, breaking eye contact, choosing his words carefully before he spoke.

"We're both very busy men, so I won't waste your time. As I mentioned to you on the phone, I'm very interested in what your organization does. Its work is unmatched in quality and in its end product, the ViroPredict software."

Nick nodded to confirm that he was listening. Nadir's gaze zeroed in on Nick.

"As we previously discussed, I've heard through the grapevine that your CEO has no interest in selling his company. That's fine with me. Frankly, I find that most of the time formal business agreements and the paperwork and regulations that come with them only serve to slow down what is fundamental to business. That is, making deals."

Nick chimed right in, "I've never been a big fan of paperwork."

"So then it sounds as though we're in agreement. All that I need is access to the source code to ViroPredict. Do you have access to this?"

"I don't directly, but I can get it if I need to. Of course, I couldn't tell you what any of it meant. I don't know C++ from Java. Hell, I'm lucky if I can fix my printer when it gets jammed."

Nadir didn't join in sympathy, choosing to ignore the comment. "I recognize that disclosing such proprietary information cannot be done without the proper incentive," he said. "In your opinion, what is access to the source code for ViroPredict worth?"

This was the point in the discussion that Nick had been waiting for. He knew Sage Pharmaceuticals wasn't a huge company, but having the source code for ViroPredict would quickly change that. This was his big chance to cash in on all of his hard work at SimSci. He was going to aim high with his first price.

"I'm sure you understand the risks that I'd be taking allowing you access to this data. I'd be risking my career if I were to be caught. That really puts the monetary value of this proposal in the millions."

Nadir seemed unfazed. "How many million?"

"Eight million," Nick replied.

"That's a lot of money, Mr. Waters."

"Again, what you're asking of me is quite substantial as well."

Nadir finished his soda and then smiled at Nick.

"You have a deal. But to be clear, the terms are payment only after I've had the ability to obtain the source code."

Nick didn't like the sound of that. "I want half of the money before I show you anything. How do I know you'll pay me?"

The question quickly wiped the smile off Nadir's face. "Who do you think you're dealing with, some sort of Colombian drug lord?" he said outraged. "I'm CEO of a well-known pharmaceutical company. Our shares are publicly traded."

"Look, ummm, I didn't mean to-"

"I've been burned on deals like this before. For me to offer half of the money up front is too risky. You must understand, for all of the benefits of deals without all of the messy, time-consuming paperwork, they also have their drawbacks. One particularly large one is that there's no guarantee that services will be performed. I could hand you four million dollars and never see you again. On the other hand, you know where to find me, and my fortune is bought and sold on Wall Street each day. You tell me, Mr. Waters, who's the bigger flight risk?"

Nick had to concede the point. He suddenly felt like he was bargaining from a position of weakness. Despite the fact that he held the keys to the technology that Nadir needed, Nadir was holding eight million dollars. Whether Nick made the deal or not, Nadir would remain CEO of Sage Pharmaceuticals, with a net worth of tens of millions, if not hundreds of millions, of dollars. Nick would leave the bar the holder of several bank accounts with a combined value of fifty dollars, and a mortgage bill that was nearing forty-five days past due. Nick didn't have the means to even buy another couple OC's to get him through the week.

"Twenty-five percent up front," Nick demanded. He tried to look and sound strong, but Nadir saw right through him.

"Nick, the terms of the offer are payment after services are rendered." He tried to take out some of the sting. "It'll all be cold, hard cash, all tax free. Surely a financial mind like yours recognizes the value of an all-cash transition from an income tax perspective."

Nick really didn't have a choice. "Well, you're making this a difficult decision, but I do understand your concern. You've got a deal."

"Excellent. This is going to be a mutually beneficial relationship that the two of us are forming. You'll see," Nadir said. "How do you propose you give me access to the data? I'm going to need it via a desktop with a USB port for a removable storage device."

Nick had given this question careful consideration prior to his arrival. He wanted to have an answer ready so that Nadir knew that he was serious about the deal. "I'm going to have you come to SimSci in a few days. We'll need to get you in when Will Woltz-berg is out of the office. I don't know what time or day that'll be, so you'll have to be ready at a moment's notice. Will this be a problem?"

"No, I'll be available when you call. This is my top priority."

"Good. When you arrive, ask for me. I'll sit you down and have one of the newbies in the software engineering department give us access to the source code. We'll say that you're from the CDC, and that your visit to SimSci is highly confidential, so they keep the information to themselves. Then you'll get what you need and we'll get you the fuck out of there."

"I can see you've already thought this out," Nadir said, nodding his head. "The planning sounds good."

"As you're getting what you need from the system, I'll be count-ing the cash in the briefcase that you'll be bringing to me. You won't be getting access to the data until I see the money," Nick said as he watched the expression on Nadir's face. The slight wince was almost undetectable, but Nick saw it. With that subtle reaction, doubt began to creep into Nick's mind.

"Sure, no problem," Nadir responded.

The two men discussed other small details concerning their agreement before Nadir rose from his bar stool and explained to Nick that he had a meeting to attend. "I'll be waiting for your phone call."

Nick watched Nadir leave the bar while he remained seated to finish his drink. As he did, he tried to fight back his headache. He didn't have any pills either on his person or back at his condo. Worse, he didn't even have enough money to get a single eighty milligram pill. As he thought about the multiple millions of dol-lars that he'd have shortly, it dawned on him how he could solve his problem. A simple cash advance from one of his credit cards would serve perfectly. Despite the fact he didn't have the cash now, he knew that by this time in two weeks he'd be able to resign from his position as CFO of SimSci and never have to worry about money again. These thoughts brought a broad smile to his face.

CHAPTER 47

"I have Will Woltzberg on line three," Monica's secretary said.

"Good afternoon, Will, to what do I owe this pleasant surprise?" Monica asked.

"Well, I'll speak frankly and tell you that nothing about this surprise is pleasant," Will said tersely. "What's your email address? I have a story that I'd like you to see."

Monica gave him the address and listened to Will typing furiously.

"There, I just sent something to you. I need you to read this. Take your time. I can wait while you do."

"Okay, I just got your email, clicking on the link, okay, got the story......oh my," Monica said.

As Monica read the article, Will looked around his office. It was a mess. The large conference table had papers scattered across it. The same was true for his own desk. The only spot that was absent any clutter was soiled with a dried ring of coffee. He realized the office's disarray resembled what his life had become.

"Well, isn't this a scary story?" Monica said, pulling Will's attention back to their conversation. "What does this have to do with us?"

Although he found her lack of empathy repulsive, he brushed those feelings aside. He knew that the need for the vaccine took precedence. "The story says that the virus is being spread by wild animals that have been infected."

"Yes, I read that," Monica replied.

"But I know the virus isn't being spread by one or two infected wild animals, like the traditional rabies virus."

"What are you talking about? What leads you to this conclusion?"

"The virus has mutated. It's no longer being spread by contact with the infected animals' saliva. It's become airborne."

"Will, what on earth are you talking about? I don't think I understand where you're going with this," Monica said bluntly.

"We've done in silico modeling of the rabies vaccine using ViroPredict in our labs. The results of the simulations demonstrated that eventually there would be a region of the world where the human and animal population would produce an environment where the rabies virus would mutate and become able to be transmitted like the flu virus, through the aerosols created when an infected person coughs or sneezes. Based on the population growth and other assumptions that we used, the results showed that a mutation of this nature could happen any day now. The story I sent you is evidence that it already has."

Will waited for a response but got none.

"Are you still there?"

"I'm reading this article again," she replied, her voice muffled.

Another moment went by while Monica finished reading the article.

"ViroPredict was able to model this in the lab?" she asked.

"Yes."

"So then you must have the DNA makeup of the strain. If you give us that, we can begin working on the vaccine."

Will was glad she grasped the solution so fast. "You're the only person outside SimSci that I'm sharing this with. I'm sharing it with you because of Sander's production capabilities."

"This vaccine could be worth billions." Monica was able to identify the profit potential in the bleakest of situations. "We should draft up a memorandum of understanding right away. A revenue and profit sharing agreement that would allow us to split everything we make from this. How does fifty-fifty sound?"

"That's fine," Will agreed. "But more importantly we need to get to work on this right away. If this truly is an airborne virus, then it could spread outside the quarantined region very easily. The military guarding the perimeter of the town could contract rabies, not realize it, and spread it to their families, then eventually all of Thailand. After that it'll quickly spread around the world."

Monica was struck by the implications. "This could be more deadly than the 1918 flu."

"Yes, and the deaths will be much more traumatic for everyone. Dying from rabies is a painful way to die for both the person infected and the family who must watch them. This could create a worldwide panic as the stories circulate through the media across the globe. People could be afraid to leave their homes, world economies would come to a screeching halt, and in places where the virus was the worst, the vaccinations would need to be administered by the military to keep the public from rioting in the streets."

"Jesus Christ. Have you alerted the CDC or NIH?" Monica muttered.

"No, not yet."

"But surely we'll need to let my employees developing the vaccine know."

"Yes. But we need to keep that group of people as small as possible while not sacrificing development time. I have a man here who will lead the work from our end. His name is Tanner Fitzgerald."

Silence filled the line again.

"Monica, are you there?"

"Umm, yes, I'm here. Based upon what I'm reading, this sounds like you'll want your best people on this project. Are you sure Tanner is the right person?"

"I've worked closely with Tanner for some time now. He's one of my most trusted employees. In fact, he's the one who discovered this virus using ViroPredict. He's definitely the right person for this project."

"I'll need to give some thought to who will be working on this here. Why don't you and Tanner come out here tomorrow? By then I'll have identified a project team and we can begin discussing the next steps."

"That sounds good."

No sooner had Will hung up the phone than he saw Nick walk by his office. "Nick!" he called. "Come on in." Will looked him up and down. He had his winter jacket and hat on, as if he'd just come back from a late lunch. His face looked more worn than it normally did. He hadn't shaved that morning. Dark bags hung below drooped eyelids. He didn't know what was wrong with Nick, but he was beginning to become concerned about his CFO.

"Look, Nick, I wanted to let you know that I'll be out of the office for most of tomorrow afternoon. We'll have to finish our discussion the following day. You don't anticipate needing me for anything else, do you?"

"Umm, no, that's fine. I won't need you for anything."

"Okay, good. Let's catch up at some point next week."

"Sounds good," Nick said. He had turned to leave when Will called back to him.

"Hey, Nick."

"Yes?"

"You look exhausted. Why don't you go home for the day and get some rest, come back tomorrow refreshed?"

"Hey, thanks," Nick replied wearily. "I just can't shake this cold."

* * *

As Nick walked back to his office, he tried to suppress the animosity he felt toward Will. He had to keep his cool. Pretty soon he'd be getting back at Will for taking advantage of him for all of these years.

He walked into his office and closed the door behind him. He dialed the number that he'd received less than an hour ago. Nadir picked up almost immediately.

"Didn't think I'd be calling you so soon, did you?" Nick asked.

"No, frankly I didn't."

"An opportunity just opened up for you to come here and take a look at what we discussed. How does tomorrow afternoon sound?"

* * *

Monica sat in her office replaying the discussion with Will over in her head. He had said Tanner was one of his most trusted employees. It would explain why he hadn't been returning my phone calls, she surmised. Tanner has no intention of helping me get the source code, Monica thought. But what about what I told him about the murders of Scott and Vijay? What if he shares what I told him with Will or the police? No, she thought, I can't let that happen.

CHAPTER 48

"I never thought that wad of cash that you carried around would come in handy. Boy, was I wrong," Marcel said as he finished his beer. "Still, we were lucky we found a checkpoint with just one guard. It made it so easy for him to take the money. If there had been others with him like we saw at the other checkpoints, I'm not sure they would have taken the bribe. You know how it goes, the more people involved the greater the fear one might rat the whole group out."

Nigel, who had been resting his head on the table in front of him, finally picked it up. "You're right we're so lucky to be here right now waiting for a flight back to the states instead of fighting for our lives in that hell-hole."

Their waitress came over with two plates with curly fries hanging off the sides and placed one in front of both of the men. "Can I get you anything else right now?"

"No, everything is perfect," Nigel replied as he and Marcel sat staring at the two quarter pound burgers and fries.

They were sitting in one of the restaurants inside the Suvarnabhumi International Airport in Bangkok, Thailand. Their journey from the village to Thailand's capital city had taken over a day, despite being only a four and a half hour drive, due to numerous wrong turns and bad direction translations. They'd used their credit cards to purchase plane tickets back to the U.S. They were devouring their first hot meal in over a day while they waited for their flight to depart.

"I wonder what the reaction has been to the story." Nigel said after consuming the last French fry on his plate. The two had reached out to Marcel's friend at the International News Network, or INN, as soon as they were a safe distance from the town. Their experiences served as the basis for a report that now captured the attention of health experts around the globe.

"Don't know, but I'll bet it's getting a lot of play nationally, maybe even around the world."

"We should try to find a newspaper written in English. Surely there's one in the airport," Nigel said.

"Don't know if the story would be in the papers yet. I mean, we just passed it along twenty-four hours ago. It may not have fully circulated yet," Marcel replied.

"But it can't hurt to have a look."

Marcel waved that idea away. "We won't have much time to check before our flight. It's supposed to leave within the hour."

"I can't wait to get back to the U.S.," Nigel said as he rubbed the back of his neck.

"Yeah, this will be my last journey to this place," Marcel agreed. "Why don't you wait here for the check? I'll go to try and find a newspaper."

Once Marcel left, Nigel rubbed his temples and the back of his neck again. His head was pounding and his muscles were stiff. He knew he had a fever as well, making the other ailments worse. Although these symptoms were consistent with the early stages of rabies, he couldn't have contracted it. He replayed the past few days over and over in his head, and at no point did he ever even come within a few feet of a carrier, either animal or human. The closest I'd been was when I'd left my keys in the house and the ill man had come charging at me, he thought. Possibly he might have gotten some of the man's blood on his clothes when he was shot. But even if he had, the virus couldn't be transmitted through blood.

"All set?" Nigel looked up and saw his waitress in front of him.

Nigel nodded his head and the waitress left the check with him. He whipped out his Amex card, then closed his eyes and rested his head on the table as he waited for Marcel to return.

Ten minutes later, Marcel came back, but with no paper in hand. He put his hand on Nigel's shoulder as he returned to the table.

"Are you okay?"

"Yes, fine, I'm just resting." Nigel replied. "No luck finding a paper?"

"No, I couldn't find one. I'm sure that there must be some around somewhere, but I wanted to get back here so we didn't miss the plane. I don't know about you, but this is one flight that I don't want to miss."

The words drew a chuckle from Nigel as he rose from his seat.

Forty minutes later, Nigel was looking for an empty seat on a flight bound for the U.S. He found one, and immediately sat down, rested his head on the back of the seat, and closed his eyes. God, he thought, I can't get back to the U.S. soon enough.

CHAPTER 49

Monica was waiting in the bar of a hotel in downtown Boston. As she waited, she swirled her martini glass and watched the small, thin chocolate shavings stick to the side of the glass and slowly slide back into the drink. The windowless bar was sparsely lit. The bartender looked like he'd had a few during his shift, his gait awkward and ugly. From across the bar, she could feel the lustful gaze of a man bearing down on her. She'd arrived a few minutes early, as traffic was light. She knew that she wouldn't need to wait long. The man she was meeting was never late for an appointment.

As he entered the hotel bar, Monica could see him clearly favoring his right leg. She briefly wondered how a man with such a pronounced limp could perform his job as a contract killer so efficiently. I need not worry about it, she thought to herself. He's never let me down.

"Glad you could make it, Paul."

"When one of my biggest clients tells me they need to see me right away, I listen."

"I have some new information about our friend Will. I'd like you to finish this assignment tomorrow."

"Tomorrow?"

"He's coming to my offices tomorrow afternoon. He'll be with another person, one of his lead scientists. You'll have a clean shot at both of them in the parking lot of my office building. I need you to take care of this problem then." Monica knew she had to rid herself of Tanner as well. She was sure he wasn't going to cooperate with her, and she had told him too much. "It's important that you are able to take out the pair. It's the only chance we'll have to kill them both at once."

Paul shifted uncomfortably in his chair. Monica read his body language. "Something wrong with this plan?"

"Your offices are in the heart of Boston. I'd prefer to carry this task out in a more private setting. But to be clear, I don't make it a habit of disappointing clients. It's bad for business," he replied calmly.

The man's cold, robotic stare gave her the chills. This was a man who had no regard for human life and no guilt in ending one. But at the same time she found him familiar. He was going to do whatever it took to get the job done. She broke eye contact with him and her lips formed a sly smile.

"Is that it? Just take him out at your office tomorrow afternoon?" Paul asked.

"Yes."

"Okay. You won't even know I was there," Paul said as he stood up and limped out of the bar.

The bartender hurried over to Monica. "That was quick. I didn't even get a chance to get him a drink."

"I wouldn't worry about it. He wasn't planning on staying long.

CHAPTER 50

He opened his eyes when he heard the footsteps approaching from the other end of the large room. Although large racks of books blocked his view, he was quite certain that it was Nadir Masoud. He hadn't heard any footsteps in the past ten minutes in this secluded section of the library.

"I see that you got my message. I'm glad to see you were able to make it, brother Omar," Nadir said as he took a seat.

Omar nodded his head. "I wanted to provide you with an update regarding how I've been progressing. Things are moving quite quickly. Frankly, they're moving quicker than I expected," Nadir said.

"This news is good," Omar replied, stone faced. As he spoke, he ran his fingers across the letters "MGO", initials carved into the wooden table at which they sat.

"You were right. The one who counts the money folded like a house of straw. He's weak, as you predicted. He told me he'd let me in to get the source code to the software that you need. I'm heading there tomorrow."

"This is wonderful to hear," Omar said brightening up. "I knew you'd be able to help our cause."

"I've run into one problem that I must make you aware of. Our friend requested eight million dollars in return for letting me have access to the software. I trust this amount is fair, based upon our last conversation."

"That's fine. He will get what he has coming to him. That isn't a problem," Omar replied.

"No, the problem is that he wants it when he delivers the access to the source code. He wants me to bring it with me to his offices tomorrow."

For the first time in the discussion, Omar became concerned. This would pose a problem. With Boris and Yuriy gone, and Nadir going to retrieve the information so soon, there was no time to find anyone else to take care of any problems that the CFO may create. What concerned him more was the law enforcement agent that he'd seen with Will Woltzberg the day Boris and Yuriy were killed. If she was at SimSci the day Nadir went in, there would be risks. But they were so close now to getting the code. He weighed the risks and rewards carefully. This may be our only shot, he thought. We must grasp it.

"This is not a concern to me. I'll handle our friend. What time are you going to meet him tomorrow?" Omar asked.

"I'm meeting him at two in the afternoon."

"I'll be coming with you. Not into the offices but I'll remain outside. When it comes time to pay him, I'll see to it that he gets his reward for what he's done."

A look of surprise appeared on Nadir's face. "Are you sure you want to do this yourself? Do you want to reconsider? Maybe I'll ask the man for more time."

"No, please, time is very important. I'll be there tomorrow. We can't let this opportunity slip through our fingers."

CHAPTER 51

"Sir, are you all right? Sir?"

The sound of the stewardess's voice echoed in Nigel's head as his leg twitched uncontrollably. He felt like his leg was asleep. He was slowly losing sensitivity in his toes. How will I stand up when it was time to disembark? He knew he wouldn't be able to get off the plane under his own strength. It took all of his energy to open his eyes and focus on the woman speaking to him.

"Please fasten your seat belt. We're preparing to land."

Nigel's arms slowly complied with what his mind was telling them to do, and the stewardess thanked him. The discomfort in his legs was just the beginning. He felt like his brain was swelling, pressing against his skull, and the pain was nearly unbearable. His dry throat made him feel even worse. This must be what a person stranded on a remote island must go through as they die from dehydration, he thought. To be so thirsty that you consume salt water from the ocean that only makes you thirstier and thirstier. As he felt the plane descend, he accepted what was happening to him. The fifth stage in the Kulber-Ross model – Acceptance. It was his time, he could already feel his mind becoming discon-nected from his body. From this point forward he would need to go it alone. If you were lucky, a loved one could hold your hand.

But they can't come with you. Everyone has to take this last journey alone.

He felt the wheels touch down on the tarmac and the rapid deceleration as the plane came safely to a halt. After nearly twenty minutes, he could hear the other people on the plane begin to talk. He could hear the questions that they were asking each other. Why aren't we heading to the terminal? Why is it taking so long to let us off? Why are the stewardesses in the cockpit?

Yet for all of the questions, he didn't hear a single definitive answer.

Soon he heard more questions. Why are military Jeeps surrounding the plane? Is that man putting on a biohazard suit? Why do those soldiers have guns? With this second stream of questions, the crying and shouting began. He heard one man pounding on the cockpit door, shouting at the crew to tell him what was happening. Finally the crackle of the loudspeakers silenced the passengers.

"Folks, this is your captain. We've been instructed at this time to park the jet in this location. The U.S. Center for Disease Control has worked in conjunction with the FAA to quarantine all jets traveling from the Far East due to a regional pandemic in that part of the world."

As the pilot spoke, a lady in the back of the plane screamed at the top of her lungs.

"I don't have any idea when this quarantine will be lifted. There will be a few people boarding shortly to perform a visual inspection as well as hand out questionnaires in order to obtain some basic information about each of you and your travels abroad. As soon as I have additional information, I will let you know. The stewardesses will be coming out shortly to provide everyone beverages. I'd like to advise you to conduct yourselves in an organized and civilized manner. If you don't, the soldiers outside the plane will do what is necessary to maintain order. Remember, we are all in this together."

Within his mind Nigel laughed at the pilot's final comment. No, he thought, I'm going this one alone.

CHAPTER 52

A calendar reminder popped up on Tanner's computer screen, reminding him that he had to be in Will's office in five minutes. He jotted down some notes so that he could remember where he left off in his work when he resumed it later that afternoon. He wasn't sure how long the meeting would last. Given the magnitude of the subject matter it could be a long one. When he arrived at Will's office, he found Will standing up looking out of the windows in his corner office. The sun was shining brightly, filling the office with its rays. He knocked on the door to get Will's attention.

"Are you ready to go or do you need a few minutes?" Tanner asked.

"I'm ready."

On his way out Will stopped at Leah's office. He was surprised to find a man in there with her. He was sharing the desk with Leah, but was working independently from her, with his own laptop computer and files in front of him.

"Are you ready to head out?" Will asked.

"Yes, I'm ready. Before we leave, I'd like to introduce you to Andrew Shapiro. Andrew, this is Will Woltzberg, CEO of Simulation Scientific," Leah said.

Andrew rose to his feet and extended his hand. He was well over six feet, with the build of an NFL linebacker. His skin was pale, his face littered with freckles. His huge hand swallowed Will's in a vigorous embrace.

"Pleased to meet you, Andrew," Will said.

"Andrew is also from the Department of Homeland Security. He was in the area performing some related work and will be spending the day here while the two of us visit Sander. We'd like to maintain a presence here in your office while you and I are gone," Leah said.

"Well, welcome to our offices. Make yourself comfortable," Will said.

Leah reached for the suit jacket that was resting on her office chair. Without her jacket on, Will could see the handgun that she'd attached to the belt on her waist. He hadn't noticed her carrying it previously.

"Are you ready?" she asked.

"Sure am," Will replied.

The threesome walked out of the office. On the way out they passed Nick's office. Will took note of Nick's appearance. He was clean shaven and in a Black pin-stripe suit with a maroon tie. The dark circles were still obvious, but above them were eyes that were alert.

"I'm heading out to an off site meeting. I should be back by the end of the day."

"Sounds good," Nick said as his gaze shifted from his computer screen over to Will.

As they stepped outside, they walked into a blast of cold air. The temperature flashed on a neon sign belonging to a bank across the street— twenty-one degrees. The strong rays that had illuminated Will's office reflected strongly off of the snow on the ground. Will squinted in response to the bright white landscape.

"I'll be following the two of you in my car," Leah said as she reached into her jacket pocket and took out a set of keys. Will and Tanner headed toward his car.

"Let's go over a few things before we get there," Will said his vehicle roared to life. "Like I mentioned yesterday, we're meeting with Monica Rowe, CEO of Sander Pharmaceuticals. We're in the process of negotiating an agreement between the two companies to begin development of a vaccine for the new strain of rabies that we've identified using ViroPredict. I've shared the story you'd found about the virus spreading in Thailand with her. She basically knows as much as we know right now. Are you with me so far?" Will asked.

Tanner nodded his head, his mouth set tightly.

"The goal of the meeting today is for you to meet the people on her team that you'll be working with to create the vaccine. Once we've all had a brief introduction and review of the issues, you'll likely go off with her folks to begin to review the DNA makeup of the strain that ViroPredict has generated. We should only be sharing information relevant to vaccine creation. I don't want her team having access to any of the inner workings of ViroPredict. Understand?"

"Yes, I've got it," Tanner replied.

"While you meet with them, Monica and I will be going over an initial draft of the documents that will outline the agreement between the two companies."

"This all sounds good. It's exactly what I was expecting based upon our discussions yesterday. I'm ready."

Will was reassured from the confidence that Tanner had. He was glad that Tanner was the one who was working on this project with him. The two rode in silence for a few minutes before Tanner spoke.

"Did you see the latest news this morning regarding the situation in Thailand?"

"No, I didn't. What happened?" Will asked apprehensively.

"A couple of things have happened. Apparently, representatives from the CDC and WHO have arrived in the town. No one would speak on record, but word leaked that both groups are baffled by how the virus is spreading so quickly. There are also reports that soldiers from the Thailand military who were sent to quarantine the town are contracting the disease. Then another report stated that the CDC has requested thousands of biohazard suits be sent to the area. That's led to speculation that they don't know how the illness is being transmitted."

"Jesus Christ. I can't believe this," Will said.

"It gets worse, much worse," Tanner continued. "One of the soldiers who had contracted the virus was taken to the hospital, where they found a large sum of U.S currency in his pocket. They fear that a group of Americans paid the soldier off to escape the area under quarantine. The soldier has already fallen into a state of delirium. The story said that when he was questioned about the money, his answers weren't intelligible. So of course it's led to massive speculation that these people may be heading to the U.S., or possibly are already in the U.S. This is going to be the lead story on every news report in the country within twenty-four hours."

For the rest of the drive, the two rode in complete silence as Will's mind worked to grasp the gravity of the situation.

Twenty minutes later, the men were getting out of their car at Sander Pharmaceuticals with Leah behind them. As he walked through the parking lot, Will didn't give the area surrounding Sander's office a second glance. He didn't notice a man in a long dark overcoat walking among the other pedestrians across the street from the parking lot.

Walking with a pronounced limp, the man was looking directly at Will. He spied a bench to sit on and proceeded to take a mobile phone from his pocket. He began working diligently on the hand-held device despite the frigid temperature.

Monica came out to the reception area to welcome them.

"Will, Tanner, so good to see both of you again," she said as she extended her hand.

Will shook it and introduced her to Tanner. The two shook hands, and Monica led them to her office and closed the door.

* * *

Once Leah left, Andrew moved downstairs to the SimSci reception area to watch the people coming in and out of the building. He was checking emails on his laptop when Nadir entered. Andrew looked briefly at the man. He noted his Middle Eastern attributes, and wondered what he was doing at SimSci. But when he overheard him at the front desk ask for Nick Waters, any concern he had about the man was alleviated.

Nadir glanced out the wall-length windows that sheathed the reception area. Across the street was a man with a black hooded sweatshirt with a large green shamrock in the middle and the word "Celtics" above it. Baggy blue jeans and nubuck work boots completed the man's outfit. He was leaning against a silver Nissan facing the SimSci offices. The hood on the sweatshirt was up, and from where Nadir was standing he couldn't see the man's face. But he didn't need to.

"Nadir, good to see you again," Nick said.

Nadir smiled warmly, trying to put his prey at ease.

"I'm glad that you were able to find some time in your schedule to meet me today."

Nick led him into the hallway behind the receptionist and the two went into a room that was painted in all white. Scientific instruments were placed on several tables on one side, rows of computers on the floor, each with multiple flat-screen computer monitors attached to them, on the other.

"I thought you were just a software company," Nadir asked.

"We are, but the virologists frequently examine real world viruses, genes of animals, and God knows what else as they evaluate how close the simulations run inside the computer come to real life."

"Ahh, I see. Very interesting."

Nick led him to another room and motioned for Nadir to sit at one of the four chairs that surrounded a large table with multiple computer monitors on it. Nick picked up the telephone and punched in a number.

"Hi, Greg, this is Nick Waters. Could you come to the lab conference room?"

Nick hung up the phone and took a seat next to Nadir.

"It should be just a minute. Our first-year computer programmer is on his way to get us what you're looking for."

Less than a minute later, a thin, tall man with a short-sleeve shirt and tie walked into the room. He had thick glasses and a receding hairline.

"Greg, I'd like you to meet Frank Jones. Frank is with the CDC. He's here today to inspect our ViroPredict software. Specifically, he's interested in the source code for the software, for all modules. I'm hoping that you can assist us with this today."

Greg was cautious as he extended his hand. Nick could read the uncertainty on Greg's face.

"Will is aware that Frank was coming today, but had to step out unexpectedly for an important client meeting. He asked me to work with Frank and get him everything that he needs. As you can imagine, the work that the CDC is performing is quite confidential. Therefore, I'd ask that you keep what we're doing today to yourself. The only people in this company that know about this are you, me, and Will. So again, I'd ask that you not mention this to anyone, not your direct supervisor, not your lunch buddies, no one. Understood?"

Greg nodded his head in response and obediently sat down in front of one of the monitors. Five minutes later, Greg looked up and motioned to Nick.

"This is all set. The code is written in Java and each module is in a different window. You can toggle between them all at the bottom of the screen."

"Perfect. Thanks, Greg. I think that's all that we need. No, wait, there's one more thing. Can we simply close these windows and shut this computer down when we are done? I don't want to damage the software. This isn't in the production environment, is it?"

"No, you'll be fine. This is the test environment. Just close the windows and turn the computer off."

"Very good. Thanks, Greg. Could you please close that door on the way out?"

Greg responded in the affirmative and closed the door behind him. As soon as he did, Nadir reached into his pocket and pulled out a portable USB flash drive. He dropped into the chair in front of the computer monitors.

"Hold on, Mr. Massoud," Nick said, scowling. "Part of the agreement was payment upon services rendered. Where's the money?"

"It's in my car," Nadir responded. "Did you really expect me to bring three briefcases full of cash inside this building? Don't you think that would look a bit suspicious?"

"No more suspicious than me taking three briefcases full of cash out of your car and putting them into mine."

"Look, a deal's a deal," Nadir said easily. "Let me get what I need onto this flash drive. Then you can hold onto it until we get to the car. We can make the exchange at the car."

Nick thought the offer through for a moment, and then agreed. "Okay, that sounds good. How much time are you going to need?"

"Just a few minutes."

"Okay, I'm going to wait here while you do what you need to do."

Nadir didn't respond, but went to work extracting the information Omar had asked for from the computer. Ten minutes later, he took the flash drive out and handed it to Nick.

"Here you go. Now let's finish our work here so that we can begin to enjoy the fruits of our labor."

Nick took the drive from him and led Nadir out to the reception area. As the two exited the office building, Nick immediately felt the frigid cold outside. He was so anxious to receive the money that he hadn't bothered to bring his jacket.

* * *

Andrew was fully immersed in his work when Nick and Nadir walked through the reception area. He looked up briefly and saw that Nick was headed out in the middle of a New England winter with nothing but a thin dress shirt on. Andrew's forehead wrinkled as he wondered why Nick would to do such a thing. He suspected that Nick was simply walking his guest out to bid farewell and would turn right around. But when he walked past the visitor spaces and continued out to the street, Andrew put his laptop down and watched with increased curiosity.

"My car's over there," Nadir said, pointing.

"Why'd you park on the street?" Nick asked, annoyed. "We have visitor spaces in our lot."

Nadir didn't respond. He was too preoccupied with the man wearing the black hooded sweatshirt. Nadir pressed the unlock button on his car not once, not twice, but three times. Each time he did so, the car's headlights flickered.

As soon as the headlights flashed for the third time, Omar got into his car and waited. Nadir brought Nick to the back of his car and opened the trunk. Then Omar shifted his car into drive.

Inside Nadir's trunk Nick spied three large black leather briefcases. His eyes widened as he reached to open one of them. Nadir reached out to block him.

"The flash drive," he said in a calm, confident tome.

Preoccupied with the briefcases, Nick handed him the flash drive and leaned into the trunk to open one. It was locked. He was about to ask Nadir for the key when he heard a car door open behind him. He was grabbed by the back of his shirt and the waist of his pants and pushed into the backseat of a car. As he began to regain his balance, he saw the silhouette of a man towering over him. The man quickly came into focus. His eyes were bulging from his head, his jaw clenched tightly. Omar pulled a Desert Eagle Magnum pistol from his black sweatshirt and quickly fired two shots. The first bullet missed Nick, going through the back seat cushion. The second found its mark, and buried itself deep inside Nick's brain. Omar watched Nick's body slump back on to the seat. Blood began to pour from the bullet hole just above Nick's left eye onto the tan leather seats of the Nissan. Omar stared blankly at Nick's lifeless body, his gold shirt damp with blood. Suddenly, his mind left the cold Boston street and took him back in time. He saw the body of his mother as he had years ago when she'd been killed. He stood frozen outside the car as his mind's eye relived that day.

"Get the fuck down on the ground!"

Omar was jolted back into the present by a voice shouting somewhere behind him. He turned to see a man sprinting from the doors of the SimSci offices toward him with his gun drawn. Omar quickly ducked and ran around his Nissan to the driver's side. As Andrew fired his weapon, Omar dove into the front seat of the car and pulled into traffic. An oncoming vehicle couldn't stop in time. It struck the back of Omar's Nissan, causing it to go into a tailspin in the middle of the street.

* * *

Andrew stopped on the sidewalk after firing the first shot from his gun. Pedestrians who just a few moments ago couldn't wait to reach their destination now paused, in awe of what was unfolding in front of them. Andrew couldn't continue to discharge his weapon on the crowded Cambridge street. Too many innocent lives were at risk. As the Nissan spun out of control, he thought he'd be able to apprehend the driver when the car came to a stop. Yet the driver regained control of the vehicle and roared off down the street.

Once Andrew realized he couldn't catch whoever was driving the car, his attention turned to Nadir.

"Get down on the ground!" Andrew shouted.

"Officer, I don't know—"

"I don't give a fuck what you don't know. Get down now!"

Andrew closed on Nadir with his weapon pointed at him the entire time. Nadir was so dazed by what had just happened, he didn't comprehend Andrew's instructions. Once Andrew was close enough, he tackled Nadir. He didn't struggle, and was brought down easily. Moments after Andrew had Nadir pinned on the ground, police arrived. Andrew indentified himself and told the police what he'd saw. Then he instructed them to have all cars begin searching for the Nissan that had driven away from SimSci.

"What did I do? I didn't have anything to do with that!" Nadir shouted.

"You're not under arrest. You're just being detained for questioning. Those cuffs are for everyone's protection," Andrew said. He tried to gather his thoughts. He quickly realized that he had to let Leah know what had just happened. He reached into his pocket and quickly dialed Leah's cell phone number.

She answered it on its second ring.

"Leah, it's Andrew. Look, we've got trouble over at SimSci."

"What's going on?"

"A man came in with Nick Waters. They were inside for less than half an hour. When the two came out, they seemed to be in a hurry." Andrew paused to catch his breath. "They went out to the guy's car, and out of nowhere another car came and the driver pushed Nick into it. The driver had a gun and shot him."

"Did you catch the driver?"

"No."

"Did you get a look at him?"

"No."

"What about the man who went into SimSci with Nick? Is he involved?" Leah was firing questions at Andrew as fast as he could answer them.

"Don't know. We've got him in custody. He claims he knows nothing, but I haven't had a chance to really question him." As he spoke, Andrew watched a large bald man wave his arms wildly as he described the sequence of events that just unfolded to a late-arriving bystander.

"Is the situation under control?"

"Yes, local cops are here and some state police just arrived. I've instructed the cops to tell all cars in the area to be looking for the Nissan that got away. I've got the situation under control."

"Okay, if something else happens call me immediately. I have to watch what's happening here," Leah said, and hung up the phone.

* * *

Inside Sander, Will couldn't believe how smoothly the meeting with Monica had gone. He was leaving with drafts of the agreements between the two companies in hand. He was pleased that the people at Sander whom Tanner would be working with appeared to be quite intelligent.

"So you have everyone's contact information? I expect as soon as Will and I can put the finishing touches on this agreement, you can begin working with the Sander team," Monica said to Tanner as they were walking to the exit.

"I do. As soon as Will lets me know we're ready to start, I'll give your team a call," Tanner replied.

The reception area of Sander's office was similar to SimSci in that large panes of glass accounted for much of the wall space. As Will and Tanner put their jackets on, Monica looked outside, her eyes scanning the area. To Will she commented, "It still looks very cold out there. Watch out for any ice."

"We will. I'll be in touch after I have a chance to review the agreement. Frankly, I expect that it'll be done later today, given the time-sensitive nature of the issue we're dealing with," Will said as he shook Monica's hand.

With farewells complete, Will and Tanner headed for the door. Instead of heading back to her office, Monica remained in the reception area.

Outside of her car, Leah saw Will and Tanner walk out of the office, and she put one hand on the firearm attached to her belt.

"Is something wrong?" Will asked as he walked toward her.

* * *

"I'll explain on our way back to your office," she said, continuing to monitor their surroundings. She was focused on the passing cars, recalling Andrew's mention that the attack at SimSci came from a vehicle in motion. She was so focused on the passing traffic that she didn't notice when the man in the long overcoat got up from the bench and crossed the street.

"Is everyone okay?" Will asked again with a sense of urgency.

"Let's all get back to the offices and I'll explain the—"

Leah's response was cut off by the sound of a gunshot. Leah saw Will twitch spasmodically, then blood spray from his midsection, spraying the car beside him. She pushed him to the ground in between two cars as two more shots rang out. Tanner instinctively ducked as well. A windshield right behind where he was standing exploded in a hail of glass fragments. Out of the corner of her eye, Leah saw the flash of the gun firing. Leaving the two civilians, she crawled in between the cars. She returned three shots of her own in the direction the attack was coming from. A man she'd seen sitting across the street moments earlier was standing at the entrance of the Sander parking lot firing a high-powered gun at the three of them.

"Are you okay?" Leah asked.

Tanner nodded feebly, but Will didn't respond, his eyes wild and afraid like a bear trapped in a cage. The side of his shirt was soaked with blood. Leah shifted her attention to the gunman a hundred feet away as he fired another few shots at them. She returned fire, and her second shot smashed the window of a car parked directly adjacent to him. She saw the man shield himself from the breaking window, nearly losing his footing as he did so. Once he'd regained his balance, he seemed to recognize that he wasn't going to get another crack at killing them and began to hobble away from the parking lot.

"Stay here! Don't leave Will alone!" Leah shouted to Tanner.

When she emerged from her crouch, she saw the man nearly one hundred yards ahead of her. She wasn't sure she'd be able to catch up to him. She began jogging at a measured stride, gun ready to fire. She saw the man turn back once to see if she was still behind him. Those seconds were just enough for a pedestrian diligently texting on his Iphone to walk right into his path. The two collided, and the man nearly fell, but remained on his feet and continued on. Dodging others on the street, Leah was gaining steadily when without warning she felt her feet come out from under her. She landed on her back with a bone-bruising thud, and felt her head crack against the ice. She remained on the ground stunned, and then sat up. She looked down at the patch of black ice that she slipped on and slowly rose to her feet. She felt her head spinning as she desperately searched for the man she'd been chasing. She spotted a group of men at a bus stop and a few people walking briskly to their destination, but the gunman was gone.

"Are you okay? You're bleeding pretty bad."

Leah turned around and saw a look of concern on a young man's face. He looked to be barely out of college, peach fuzz where facial hair should be, but still old enough to recognize a serious injury. She put her hand up to the back of her head and felt the cold, thick blood in her matted hair.

"There's an ambulance over there," the man said pointing to Sander's offices where an ambulance was pulling in, siren blaring.

Leah looked one final time for the man who tried to kill Will, but he was gone. As she ran, with much more caution, back to where Will was, guilt and anger filled her mind. The man might have just killed Will and she'd let him get away.

When she arrived in the parking lot, the paramedics were applying a compress to Will's side. In no time, he was placed onto a stretcher, and loaded into the back of the ambulance. Tanner was standing next to the paramedics trying to convince them to allow him to come with them. Will's blood was spattered all over his suede overcoat.

"Is he going to be okay?" she asked after identifying herself to the paramedics.

"Don't know. He was shot in the midsection, looks to be internal bleeding. We've got to get him out of here. He's lost consciousness."

"I'm coming with you," she said. She and Tanner hopped into the back of the ambulance once Will was loaded in. During the ride to the hospital, Leah replayed the events to Andrew, telling him to mount a task force. Tanner was in shock from what had happened. The paramedics worked feverishly throughout the ride. When they arrived at the hospital, they took Will out of the ambulance and wheeled him into the hospital's emergency room.

"I'm sorry, the two of you will need to wait out here. I'd suggest that you contact any family members that he has," the paramedics said and then disappeared through two swinging doors into the emergency room, leaving Tanner staring blankly at Leah, hair disheveled and coat unbuttoned, still trying to comprehend what had just happened.

"Is he going to be okay?" Tanner asked Leah quietly.

Leah answered the question the best that she could:

"I don't know."

CHAPTER 53

"The doctor told you that you really need to stay on your back. I'm going to call him in here if you don't listen to his directions," Sarah said as she sat by Will's bedside.

Will's hospital room was filled with beeps and clicks of the various machines that he was hooked up to. Sarah sat beside him, her eyes red and swollen from a steady stream of tears. Her face was noticeably absent of makeup, and she was wearing an old sweater and slacks. Since Will had been shot, she'd given her undivided attention to being at his side.

"I've been on my back long enough," Will complained. "I'm well enough to sit up. I've got guests coming,"

"Suit yourself."

Will struggled to adjust the pillows in his hospital bed so that they were propped behind his back. Although Sarah didn't want to help because he was being so stubborn, she gave in when she saw him wince. The couple was startled by a voice coming from the doorway.

"You know I told you not to sit up. You need time to heal. Your body doesn't heal as quickly as it did when you were twenty-one."

Will and Sarah turned toward the door and saw Will's doctor.

"I think you've got me confused with an old man down the hall! I'm ready to play eighteen holes without a cart!"

"Then you're the oldest looking twenty-year-old I've ever seen," the doctor replied as he picked up the chart clipped to Will's bed. He reached for the glasses hanging from his neck and put them on the end of his nose. After reading the latest notes from the nurse, he pulled the johnny to one side to examine Will's lower torso. Then he pulled back the bandages to examine his wound and the stitches that were helping it heal.

"How do you feel?" the doctor asked as he removed his glasses and allowed them to once again hang around his neck.

"Kidding aside, I feel great. To be honest, I'm ready to go home," Will said.

"You were lucky the bullet was lodged in your spleen. A few inches in another direction and it could have hit your lungs, or worse, your heart. You are a lucky man."

The doctor paused as his gaze went back and forth from Will to Sarah. "Even though it was just a mild wound, you still need a few days to heal before you go anywhere."

"Not if I decide to just get up and leave first," Will said.

"I'm not sure you'd get too far with him outside," the doctor said, motioning to the uniformed police officer standing outside Will's hospital room.

"Since he's there for my protection, I'm not sure he'd physically keep me in the room now would he?" Will said jokingly.

"But it is in your best interests to stay here for a few more days, and he knows that."

He gave in at last. He hadn't thought he would get permission anyway. "Okay, fine doc, I'm not going anywhere."

The doctor continued giving Will instructions on what to do to ensure that his gunshot wound healed properly. Will listened half heartedly while Sarah sat by his bedside, listening much more attentively.

Just as the doctor was winding down, Tanner knocked on the door. "Should I come back at another time?"

"No, certainly not. Come in, we were just finishing up," Will said, waving Tanner in.

"I'll let you see your visitor, but listen, you need your rest," the doctor warned, patting Will on the knee. "I'll be checking back in with you tomorrow."

As the doctor left, Tanner came in and took a seat on one of the two naugahyde chairs.

"So, how you feeling?" he asked. His foot tapped nervously on the tan and white tiles, and Will wondered if he disliked hospitals.

"I'm fine. I was just telling the doctor that I'm ready to go, let me out already. But he said that I need to stay here a few more days."

"Well, that's good to hear. When I mentioned that I was coming to see you, everyone at the office told me to send you their best. Everyone is looking forward to your return."

The mention of the office instantly made Will concerned. "What's the morale like over there? How's everyone holding up after what happened?"

"I don't want to upset you in your current state—" Tanner began.

"I'm fine. I'm going to be leaving this place in a few days. Don't sugar-coat it."

"Well, it's been better. We've had four more people leave since Nick was shot." Tanner saw the alarm on Will's face and hastily added, "The increased security Leah has provided has helped, though. It's very visible and has reassured many people. But you can't blame them for being scared."

It was what Will feared. Nick had been killed and Will knew that he'd almost ended up on the growing list of those who had been murdered. Naturally people are going to be afraid after all that happened, Will thought.

"How about the vaccine?"

Tanner brightened at the change in topics. "We've been making good progress."

Will spotted Leah as she appeared at his hospital door. She was wearing a baseball cap to cover her head, a pair of casual jeans, and a bulky gray sweatshirt with the DHS emblem on the front.

"Would you like me to get you a seat?" Tanner asked as Leah came into the room.

"No, I'm fine," she replied.

"How's that head gash?" Will asked.

"Not so great. It turns out I needed eight stitches. But worse than the stitches is the little bit of hair that they had to shave off. I can't go anywhere without this," Leah said, pointing to her baseball hat.

"At least you're walking around. You could be bedridden like me," Will replied. Uncomfortable laughter was shared by the group, as they all remembered how close death had come.

Leah quickly got down to business. "The reason that I'm here is to share some information, both about Nick's murder and the man that tried to kill you."

Tanner uncertainly rose from his seat.

"No, Tanner, stay, you need to hear this," Will said.

Leah was about to protest but relented. "Mr. Fitzgerald, the discussions that we're having in this room must remain between us. What we're discussing is a matter of national security."

"Nothing will leave this room," Tanner confirmed.

"Let's start with Nick. When he was killed, we took the man that had come to see him at your offices into custody. His name was Nadir Massoud. He is CEO of a company called Sage Pharmaceuticals."

"Nadir Massoud!" Will shouted, jerking up, stopped only by the sharp pain that thrust him back down into bed.

"Do you know Mr. Massoud?" Leah asked.

"Know him? That son of a bitch tried to blackmail us! He wanted us to give him the source code to ViroPredict so he could sell it through his own company! What the hell was he doing in our offices with Nick Waters?"

"He was doing the same with Nick, trying to get ViroPredict. But I'm not so sure Nadir was doing this for his company," Leah remarked sternly. "Given the intelligence we already had that indicated that a terrorist group was also trying to obtain this very information, we began to investigate Mr. Massoud's background. We found numerous donations to the Foundation for Middle Eastern Unity, a not for profit organization based in Pakistan that has ties to Muslim terrorist organizations. We then put Mr. Massoud through a series of intense interrogations, and he admitted that he was working with a man who I will simply call Omar, the man we know is leading the cell planning the terrorist plot involving ViroPredict."

"My God, how did Nick get himself involved with terrorists?" Tanner asked.

Leah's expression turned sour. "Well, it turns out your CFO had become a heavy opiate abuser in recent months and had burned through what little savings he had on them. We believe he was trying to obtain more money to spend on the drugs."

Will thought back to the last few days he'd seen Nick in the office and recalled thinking that the man seemed more drawn. Plus, he was always making excuses to slip off. It all made sense.

"Are we sure the source code didn't end up in the hands of the terrorists?"

"Yes, Nadir confirmed Omar never got the source code. His statements are corroborated by the fact that we found a flash drive containing the source code on him when we apprehended him outside of your office."

"What still concerns us is the plot that the terrorists were planning. Although we know that Omar is the man whose leading the effort to obtain this software, we don't know where he is. As long as he's at large, I think you are still in great danger," Leah told Will.

"Do you think he's responsible for the deaths of Vijay, Scott, and my brother?"

Her face showed mixed signs. "Nadir admitted that he knew Boris Kozlov was working for Omar. Based upon the evidence we already have, we know Kozlov killed Scott and Vijay."

Sarah lifted her hands to her mouth as she listened to Leah. A single tear had formed in her eye and it slowly trickled down her face. Distracted by the sight of it, Will suddenly noticed a nurse in the hallway who was walking slowly beside a patient hooked up to a medical device on wheels. She was cautioning the patient not to go too fast. Will watched the patient stubbornly argue. He imagined that must be what he looked like as he insisted he was fine to leave his hospital bed.

"So Kozlov killed James as well?" Will asked, returning his attention to the matter at hand.

"We aren't so sure that's the case," Leah replied, shaking her head. "We believe that another group is responsible for that."

"What do you mean, another group?" Will asked as he began to sit up in his bed again, wincing in pain. A steady stream of tears was now flowing down Sarah's face, and she began crying loud enough for everyone in the room to hear.

"At first we weren't sure if James and Cindy were killed or if what had happened was in fact an accident. We knew if they were killed, whoever did it was much more careful than Kozlov had been. It was a much more professional job."

Leah paused to take the thin blue tissue box on the shelf next to her and hand it to Sarah.

"Thank you," Sarah said and removed one of the tissues to wipe her eyes.

"This morning we got a huge break. One of the buildings next to Sander had a security camera running the day you were shot. It caught everything, including some crystal-clear images of the man who shot you."

Will and Tanner exchanged looks of surprise.

"Can we find him with this video?"

"Well, we compared the images to everyone in the ViCAP database and we have a positive identification," Leah announced. "His name is Paul Francis."

"Did you find him?" Sarah asked.

"We don't know where to find him, but we do know that he's a contract killer. He's number seven on the FBI's most wanted list. He's worked for foreign governments and others interested in overthrowing governments within foreign countries. We also have reason to believe private companies doing business both domestically and abroad have hired him when they have a problem."

"So are you saying some company believes James and I are 'a problem'?" Will asked.

"At this point we view this as a strong possibility," Leah replied.

"Well, we're going to find this guy, and grill him so that he can tell us exactly who hired him to kill me!" Will said, his voice rising to a near shout.

Outside the room, the police officer entered the doorway. Leah motioned to him and he turned and exited.

"Hold on there, Mr. Woltzberg. 'We' aren't going to do anything," Leah said. "You are going to stay in this hospital bed recovering from a serious gunshot wound, and I'm going to continue to work with other people in both the FBI and in Homeland Security to find Paul Francis."

Will nodded his head. He didn't want to argue. Yet he intensely disliked the idea of standing idly by.

Suddenly, the sound of Will's cell phone filled the room. Sarah jumped to her feet and retrieved it. "I don't recognize the number."

"Give it to me, please," Will said, extending his hand.

Sarah handed him the phone and he checked the caller ID. He immediately recognized the number. "Would you all excuse me?"

"Who is it?" Sarah demanded.

"Please, its business related. It's a very important client."

Will could tell from the look on Sarah's face that she didn't want to comply, but she reluctantly left the room.

Leah informed him, "I'll wait around for a minute, but if it's a long call, I have to get going."

"Tanner, please close that door behind you," Will said as Tanner was the last one to leave the room. With everyone gone, Will took the call. "Good afternoon, Monica."

"Will, I'm so glad you answered. I wasn't sure if you would, after all that you've been through."

"It's been an awful few days, to say the least."

"How are you feeling?"

"This is the best that I've felt so far. I told the doctor I could leave today, but he wants to keep me here a bit longer."

"Well, I need to talk to you. It's very important. It's about the vaccine we are working on."

A strange quaver made her voice thread, and Will realized it must be urgent. "Is there a problem?"

"I'm afraid that there is. It's quite serious, and I really need you to take a look at what we've found."

"Can you come to the hospital now?"

"I don't think that's the best place to discuss this. If anyone were to overhear us, well, I would hate for news of this potential pandemic to leak out."

Will nodded his head, feeling the fabric of the pillowcase against his cheek. I have to see what Monica has discovered, Will thought. Anything to do with the vaccine could jeopardize millions of lives. Where could they have a private meeting? Will glanced down at his flimsy hospital gown. They'd both agreed that the hospital was out. He'd also prefer if they didn't meet in an office setting since the idea of having to put on a suit made him cringe. He could go home, but that would be the first place people would look for him. His mind worked double time trying to think of a private setting where the two could meet. Suddenly he had it. Will shouted from his hospital bed loud enough to ensure it would penetrate the thick door. "Tanner!"

Tanner poked his head in. "Is everything okay?"

"Come in here and close the door."

Will waited as Tanner secured the door behind him. "You live about thirty minutes from here just outside the city, don't you?"

"Yes, why?"

"Monica," Will said into the phone. "Grab a pen and paper. This is where we need to meet."

Will relayed Tanner's address to Monica. "Meet me there in an hour. Are you sure you can bring everything you need to show me?"

"Yes, of course. Most of it is on my laptop anyway."

"Okay, see you in a few minutes."

Will ended the call and turned to Tanner. "Don't say a word about this to my wife. I'll explain all of this in a minute."

"Okay, I won't," Tanner said, but Will could see that he was confused.

"You can open it again," Will said, motioning toward the door to his room. Sarah was standing right outside as the door opened.

"What is going on in here?" she demanded curtly.

"That was Peter Hammill. He needs some information from my office. I'm going to have Tanner find it for him when he goes back. No big deal," Will said calmly. His tone and body language put Sarah at ease.

"You're sure everything's okay? You seemed quite concerned when you first answered the phone." Leah said.

"Wouldn't you be concerned if your CFO was just shot dead and you have his right-hand man trying to wear two hats?"

Leah nodded her head in agreement. "As long as everything's fine, I guess I'll be going." She reached the doorway and turned back to Will & Sarah. "If any of you need anything, don't hesitate to let me know."

With Leah gone, Will tried to adjust the pillows behind his head and winced in pain. He exaggerated his grimace enough to make an impact.

"Sarah, do you think you could ask the nurse for a couple of pain pills? My side is really acting up. I think all that talk upset it."

"Of course," Sarah said as she got up and headed over for the nurses' station. Moments later she returned with the pills.

When she placed them in his hand, Will looked down at them dubiously. "Oh, honey, I need some water for these. Actually, would you mind running down to the cafeteria to get me a bottled water? I'd like to have it here so I don't have to keep bothering someone for water."

"Okay, is there anything else you'd like from the café?"

"I'd love a turkey sandwich and fries, but we'd have to keep that our little secret, as I don't think the doctor would approve," Will said with a sly smile.

"No, he wouldn't." Sarah grabbed her black Coach purse off the floor next to the chair. She started for the door, then turned back to Will. She leaned over the bed and kissed him gently on his forehead. "I'm sorry if I've been difficult over the past few months," she said softly. "What's happened to you has really put things into perspective. I've taken things for granted. I've taken you for granted. I realize that now, and" she paused for a moment, her eyes firmly locked on Will "I just want all of this to be over so we can go back to the way we were."

Will took Sarah's hand as her eyes began to swell up with tears. Tanner turned and gazed uncomfortably out the window.

"I want this to be over too. Believe me, I want this all to be over more than anything. But until it is, I need you to be strong. I need you to watch your back, there are still people out there that want to hurt us. But most of all, I need you here with me to help me when things get tough. Now, why don't you go get that water before you start crying again?"

Sarah smiled warmly at him and whispered. "Yes, okay."

Just as she was about to head down the hallway, Will called to her. She turned and came back into the doorway.

"Honey, ask the officer out there to go with you. I don't want you going down there alone with everything that's happening. Tanner will stay here with me."

Sarah nodded her head and Will watched the conversation between her and the cop from his bed. A look of uncertainty crossed the officer's face. Would he go? What am I going to do if he stays here, Will thought. But after a moment, the cop took one look over his shoulder and said, "I'll be back in a few minutes."

* * *

As the two started off for the cafeteria, Sarah heard her cell phone ringing inside her purse. She took it out and saw Alan Burke on her ID screen. She quickly put the phone back. He had tried to call her numerous times since their encounter on his boat. Recalling the event nauseated her. Seeing what Will had been going through since James and Cindy had died made her realize how important he was to her, and how foolish she'd acted over the past few weeks. What would her boys think if they ever found out what she was doing? What would Will think? He'd always been faithful to her. As maddening as Will's commitment to his work was, he was even more committed to something else, his family. Her life was pretty good, she'd decided—as long as she didn't screw it up. She'd already made up her mind. If Will did somehow find out about her relationship with Alan, she would deny that anything had happened. Really nothing did happen, she thought, trying to justify the little white lie. She was not willing to jeopardize her marriage by confessing her relationship with Alan. And she would certainly not do anything so deplorable ever again.

* * *

Neither Tanner nor Will said a word until they were both sure Sarah and her escort were out of earshot.

"That was Monica. She's got something that she needs to tell us about the vaccine. She says it's important."

"And we're meeting her at my house?" Tanner asked, his face full of confusion.

"She wants to meet somewhere private, so no news will leak out, and I'd prefer not to meet at an office." He indicated what he was wearing. "For obvious reasons."

Tanner ran his fingers through his hair as he peered out into the hallway. "How the hell are you going to get out of here?"

"Just watch!"

Will sat up in the hospital bed and swung his feet onto the floor. A sharp pain tore through his midsection. His head felt like it was underwater, his mind woozy. I'm going to need these Vicodin after all, he thought as he rose to his feet. He held onto the bed for a moment to steady his balance, then gingerly headed for the bathroom. He popped the two Vicodin in his mouth and washed them down with a handful of water from the sink.

As he swallowed the pills, he looked at himself in the mirror. The face that looked back at him was pale and gaunt. A week's worth of patchy facial hair didn't help. It looked like he'd aged fifteen years in the past week. The sight of himself in the mirror made Will pause. Whoever had tried to kill him was still out there. It was going to be dangerous going out without someone watching his back. In the back of his mind he knew he was taking a foolish risk. Yet he knew he had to do this. This vaccine was going to be his chance to change the course of the human race, have his name memorialized in history. It was his chance to save millions of lives. Those lives might be lost if the vaccine wasn't produced quickly.

Will grabbed his clothes out of the thin closet by the door and disappeared back into the bathroom again to get dressed. That alone was an ordeal. Yet he found that if he minimized moving his abdomen, the process wasn't so bad.

"Let's go before Sarah gets back!" Tanner whispered as he handed Will his jacket and shoes. Will gingerly put them on, and they headed down the hallway. The nurses at the main station didn't even look up as they passed. In no time they stepped inside an elevator. They were in the clear.

* * *

"Jesus Christ, what do you mean, he got out of the hospital?" Charles screamed into the phone. His reaction drew the looks of other officers in the station as he sat straight up in his office chair. He pounded his desk with his fist and coffee splashed out of the cup on it. He got up to take a wad of napkins off a nearby desk, nearly spilling the rest of the cup with the phone cord. In his ear, Sarah's voice had reached a fevered pitch. After she'd provided all the information she could, he tried to calm her nerves.

"Sarah, look, you need to relax. Tanner was with him when you left. You know Tanner wouldn't leave him alone, not for a moment." Charles paused as he tried to sense whether he was succeeding in calming Sarah. "I have to go now, because the sooner we can begin looking for him, the sooner we'll find him, okay?"

Charles waited for agreement from Sarah, and quickly ended their call. What in the world could have pulled him out of a hospital bed? Charles thought. He figured he knew where Will was headed. Yet when he called SimSci, they said he hadn't shown up there. What was it Sarah had said? Charles tried to remember. Will had taken a phone call and he said it was business. He had disappeared immediately afterward. He had gone with Tanner, because how else could he have gotten away from the hospital? Certainly not on foot. Charles tried frantically to get inside his old friend's head.

As brilliant as Will was, he was also very practical. If the call was business related, he would probably meet whoever it was that called at the office. But Charles remembered the only clothes he had at the hospital were a pair of old jeans and a white tee shirt. He might invite the business associate back to the house. No, Charles thought, he would know that would be the first place that someone would look. The shooting would be fresh in his mind, so he probably wouldn't leave himself as a sitting duck in a public place like a restaurant. Tanner was driving him, could this be a clue?

Suddenly he had it. Charles turned to his computer and accessed the motor vehicles website. He ran a name, and pretty soon the information he needed appeared on the screen.

With the address in hand, he hurried for the door. He didn't know what was going on, but the circumstances seemed awfully suspicious. Too many people around SimSci had been getting killed lately.

Will might be walking right into a trap.

* * *

"She's not here yet," Tanner said as he turned into the empty driveway.

"We'll go in and wait. I'm sure she'll be here soon."

"Easy, let me get over there and help you."

With Tanner's help Will delicately got out of the car and headed for Tanner's house. As they approached the front door, Tanner fished in his jacket pocket for his key ring. He put his other hand on the door-knob. Will saw the surprise on his face when the knob turned freely, and the door opened inward.

Before Tanner could react, an arm thrust out from behind the door.

The gun in a man's hairy hand landed squarely on the top of Tanner's head. Will watched his knees buckle. The blow had enough force to knock him out cold. The man then grabbed Will before he could react. He was pulled into the house and pushed onto the floor. Adrenaline pumped through his veins, helping him to blunt the blazing pain that erupted in his midsection. He looked up into a pair of cold, menacing eyes. The man pulled him up and bound his hands behind his back with plastic bundling ties. Once his hands were bound, Will was thrown onto a couch in Tanner's living room. Pain scorched his temple as Will's head hit the hard leather arm rest of the couch.

The intruder headed back into the hallway. Moments later he returned, carrying Tanner over his shoulder like a sack of potatoes. He dropped him on the couch next to Will and went outside.

With the gunman outside, an eerie quiet filled the house broken only by the gentile patter of tiny drops of water from melting ice on the window sill outside. Will looked around the small living room. Furnishings were sparse. A brown leather couch and recliner rested a few feet away from an end table. The floors were bare hardwood, and a television was mounted on the wall. The television shared the wall with the doorway to the hallway that led to the front door. The only other way out of the room was through the kitchen to Will's left. The sole source of light was a window on Will's right. Suddenly, a silhouette appeared in the doorway connecting the living room to the kitchen. In the light Will recognized the appealing curves of Monica's slender waist and hips.

"Jesus Christ, Monica! Thank God you're here!" Will whispered, trying to keep the intruder from hearing him. "Quick, grab a knife from the kitchen and get this plastic restraint off of my hands! Someone else was just in the house!"

Monica walked over until she was towering over the two men.

"No need to whisper, Paul and I are friends. As a matter of fact, we are all friends."

Will's mouth hung open, and his eyes were narrow slits.

"Don't give me that perplexed look," Monica began. "You mean, you and your elaborate security entourage haven't put the pieces to this puzzle together yet?"

"What the hell are you talking about?"

"You've been a capitalist long enough to know only the strong survive. That's what makes this country so great."

"Do you know the man that's in here?"

A broad smile revealed Monica's perfect teeth. The evil smile gave Will goose bumps.

"So you've met Paul."

"Paul, is that Paul Francis?" Will asked as he heard the front door open. Paul came back inside. "I've just moved the car out of the driveway."

Will's mind was racing and a morbid realization began creeping in. "You killed James, didn't you?"

Monica chuckled and shook her head. "You are so gullible. You know, I could see that in you the first time I met you. But I didn't think you were this naïve. Jesus, Will. Did you really think I called you here to talk about the vaccine?"

When no response came, Monica continued. "I could care less about how many people in Asia die from this virus you've discovered. All that I care about is how many people in the United States and Europe are willing to pay for the vaccine. And all that I've wanted from you since the moment we met in Chicago is access to the engine that makes ViroPredict run."

"Is that what this is about? ViroPredict?"

She sneered at him. "That's what it's been about this whole time. You knew that, and you forced me to do things. Things that I prefer not to do."

He could no longer ignore what his mind was screaming. His throat tightened, and his voice was a whisper. "You killed James trying to get ViroPredict and now you're going to kill me. What do you think that will accomplish?"

"We've got to get this show on the road. We're taking too long," Paul said impatiently.

"Fine, I'm through with him anyway," Monica said as she turned away from Will in disgust.

* * *

Charles turned onto Tanner's street. He didn't see any car in his driveway. Either they're not here, or Paul did exactly what I would've done, Charles thought as he looked past Tanner's house for his car farther up the street. He checked the slip of paper for the information he had written down.

"Bingo," Charles said quietly as he spotted Tanner's car five hundred feet past his house. He parked his own vehicle and made his way to Tanner's front door. He was at the foot of the driveway when he stopped dead in his tracks.

* * *

"Wait Monica!"

Monica turned back toward Will. "It's too late to negotiate with me now. You know too much."

Through pain and puzzlement, Will understood his situation was grim. There'd be no pleading for his life, Monica's veins pumped cold blood. She wouldn't relent. My only hope is to buy time, he thought. Maybe help will come.

"Why, Monica? Why are you doing this to me? Why did you kill James?"

Monica walked over and looked down on him. "As you'll find out in a moment, life is short. What you do in that short time defines how you're remembered, if you're remembered at all." She opened her arms, indicating the world outside the windows. "Every day I look all around me at the weak people going about their lives, hating their jobs. They have a boss that they despise. They can't wait to get home from work. Then they come home to nagging spouses and whining kids. Next comes anticipation for the weekend, you know, shopping with the girls or poker with the guys. They spend their days wishing their life away. It really is pathetic."

She drew herself up to full height. "I refuse to be one of them. I'm not going to wish my life away and wake up one morning old and gray wondering how I'll be remembered. I'm not going to allow my mark on the world to be an anonymous gravestone for some punk to throw his empty beer bottle at. My legacy is going to be in the medicine cabinet of every household in the world. I will be remembered as the woman who built the world's largest drug company. Admired by doctors and CEOs, professors and researchers. I'll have paved the path of success for other women in business. And the wealth I'll accumulate by building this business will ensure I'm given as much respect alive as I will get when I am gone."

Will looked at her in disgust. She represented everything he hated in his field. "You're willing to kill to achieve this goal?"

"Nothing is handed to you in this life, Will. You have to take it. You weren't willing to sell me ViroPredict, so I'm going to take it," she informed him. "When there's no one left to run the company, your family will be forced to sell it. The chairman of our board, Alan Burke, is quite friendly with your wife Sarah. I think she'll be very pleased with the amount we're willing to pay for the company."

Monica was more evil than Paul, Will realized. She had painstakingly thought through every step of her plan to acquire Viro-Predict. Anyone who got in her way would be discarded. He knew he was about to become one of those people.

Paul reached inside his jacket and pulled out a garrote. "Get on your knees!"

When Will didn't respond, Paul grabbed him by his shirt and threw him onto the ground. Will gave out a sharp cry of pain.

"I said, get on your knees!"

Will struggled to his knees, and as soon as he did, Paul wrapped the garrote around his throat.

Will felt the thin, strong wire close around his throat, then felt Paul's arm in his back as the garrote tightened. The effects of the garrote were nearly instantaneous. After less than a minute Will began to feel lightheaded. Then a strange, soothing tingling overtook his mind. He dropped to his side and tried to swing his feet around to push Paul away, but he couldn't gain the leverage needed. The world began to slow around him and a sense of calm began to fill his mind as he felt his arms and legs began to spasm uncontrollably.

A shot rang out. Will felt the wire around his neck loosen. He crumpled to the floor and his lungs filled with air. Will turned and saw Paul on the ground clutching his chest, trying to get to his feet. From the hallway, Charles emerged, hands clutching a smoking gun. Charles closed on Paul, who had risen to his knees. Before he could, blood sprayed from Paul's mouth, and he fell face first onto the hardwood. Blood pooled beneath him so quickly it left no doubt in Will's mind as to whether or not Paul was still among the living.

"Are you all right?"

"Fine," Will said in between breaths.

"I saw that bastard from the window as I was approaching the house. What the hell are you doing here with him? Why are you here?"

"Behind you!" Will shouted.

Before Charles could turn, Monica buried a kitchen knife in his back. He fell forward, holding himself up with one hand, his weapon in the other. Sensing Charles' weakness, Monica lunged for the firearm.

Charles quickly pivoted and fired his gun. The bullet penetrated Monica's chest. A second bullet also reached its destination, followed by a third, then a forth. Monica's blue eyes widened as she staggered backward, arms flailing. Her final step was on top of Paul's body. It caused her to stumble, then land on top of him.

Shaken, Will could only mutter, "Are you okay?"

Charles didn't respond. Instead he crawled to a phone, leaving an ominous trail of blood in his wake. Just before he reached the phone he collapsed to the floor.

Realizing what his friend had meant to do, Will struggled to his feet. The ache in his side was now howling in its fiery intensity. Yet he finished the phone call that Charles couldn't make. Before long, the sound of approaching sirens filled the air.

CHAPTER 54

Will awoke to find his room full of people. Leah was standing on one side of him, Sarah and Tanner were seated on the other. The television on the hospital room wall was tuned to INN, and he could hear the anchor's voice from a speaker positioned somewhere near his head. Tanner was slumped down in his seat playing with his smart phone. He burst upright, though, when he saw Will was awake. Sarah also jumped to attention, quickly grasping Will's hand in hers.

"Oh God, Will," she said quietly. "Are you okay? How do you feel?"

With a throat of sandpaper, Will whispered, "I'm fine, really. But I'd love some water."

Sarah squeezed his right hand harder and handed him a cup of water in his left. The cold water felt like silk on his parched throat. Revived, Will asked about his best friend.

"Will, you need to rest. Don't worry about anything but getting yourself better," Sarah replied.

But Will persisted, "I'm responsible for what happened to Charles and I need to know if he is all right."

"Monica sank the knife in pretty deep," Leah began. "But he was very lucky. She didn't hit any vital organs. He's recovering down the hall right now. He should be out in a few days."

Relief swept over Will as he heard the news. "What about Monica? She didn't survive, did she?"

"There were more holes in her than a sponge at the bottom of the Pacific." Leah chuckled. "But all joking aside, sneaking out of here like that might have been the dumbest thing you've done in your life."

As Leah spoke, Will saw a headline flash across the bottom of the television:

Wildlife Expert Nigel Drake Dead at Age 36 from Rabies contracted in Thailand

He motioned to Tanner to turn up the volume on the television.

"We are confirming earlier reports that wildlife film maker Nigel Drake has died in Los Angeles International Airport. He had been returning from Thailand when his plane was quarantined. Thailand has recently been the center of a worldwide health emergency as tens of thousands of people there have died from a mysterious illness believed to be related to the rabies virus."

Will mustered the energy to shake his head in disbelief.

"It was a miracle that they caught that plane. I just don't know how long the entire world can stop allowing all travel to and from Thailand," Leah said, amazed.

"It just goes to show how badly we need to begin work on the vaccine," Tanner warned. "Worse, now we don't have a partner."

"There are other pharmaceutical companies out there. Sander isn't the only one. Finding one that's willing to work with us will be my top priority once I get out of here." Will said in a quiet but confident tone. "Are you comfortable holding down the fort until I'm able to return to work?"

"Yes, I'm fine. People are nervous, but I'm doing my best to keep them calm."

Will nodded his head in response.

As the group fell silent, Will could feel Sarah's eyes on him. "Could you all give me a moment? I'd like to talk to my wife for a moment."

The couple waited for the room to empty. "I can't believe you just got up and left like that. I was so worried," Sarah said, approaching Will.

"I had to. Monica had told me there was a problem with the vaccine. I was such a fool, falling right into her trap," Will said. That wasn't what he wanted to discuss with her though. He went on, "Before she was shot Monica said something curious. It's something that I need to ask you about."

"What is it?"

"She was probably just playing another mind game, but does the name Alan Burke mean anything to you?"

Sarah broke eye contact, and her grip on his hand weakened. Will read her body language and braced for the worse. "Yes, he was an old co-worker. I actually called him a few weeks ago. I gave him Nate's resume. I thought he may be able to help get Nate a job when he graduated. How on earth did his name come up?"

"She said that you were 'quite friendly' with him," Will commented, using his fingers as quotation fingers. "Are you sure nothing happened that I should know about?"

"I think he used to have a little crush on me. He still may. But nothing happened. That bitch was just trying to upset you."

"That's what I suspected," he said as he gently kissed the back of her hand then brought it to his chest.

"I love you."

EPILOGUE

A bright spring sun shone into Will's office at Simsci as he sat reading the *Wall Street Journal.* He felt as good as he had in weeks. The stitches had been removed days ago, and it was his first week back at work. For the first time in at least a decade, his desk was free from all clutter. The only paperwork was contained in folders, which were neatly placed in a silver rack.

A single coffee cup sat on one of a half dozen rediscovered coasters. Sarah and Tanner had teamed up to make his office spotless for his return to work. He was surprised how good it's appearance made him feel. It was like a fresh start.

His reading was interrupted by a knock on his door. Will peeked around his paper to see Tanner standing outside the office. Will waved him in.

"Howdy stranger," he said as he folded the *Journal* and held it out to Tanner so he could read it.

"The borders are still closed and the market was down another seven percent yesterday. The article says economists are predicting double-digit inflation as goods become more and more scarce. I don't think I've seen anything like this in my lifetime," Will said, pointing to the headline.

"The latest estimates show that the 'Thai-bes' pandemic has killed over one hundred million people around the globe. And the numbers outside Asia are getting worse, not better."

Tanner shook his head. "Is there any good news in there?"

"I'm afraid not."

"How long can you keep the boarders closed to everything? It's starting to look like a war zone in some places. You can't just stop everything from fruit to sneakers from coming into the country!"

"I can understand why they're doing it. The feds are trying to keep citizens safe." Will leaned forward and picked up his Rubix cube. He began to absently twist the cube around in his hand.

A look of skepticism was plain as day on Tanner's face. "But they're destroying our economy. I saw on the news that the President is beginning to deploy the National Guard in some areas of Texas."

"You haven't seen anything yet. Just wait until the vaccine is administered in the U.S."

The World Health Organization mandated every production facility capable of producing the vaccine begin production and continue to do so twenty-four-seven, until they were told they could do otherwise. Millions of doses of vaccine had been distributed to the most severely affected parts of the world. Will stood up and looked out his window.

As usual, the street outside was full of people walking from the subway to their offices. With the sun's rays slowly strengthening, some brave souls had ventured out with just their suit jackets and no overcoat.

Among the people on the street Will saw a young mother with two children by her side. Both children were bundled up in their warm winter jackets by the overly cautious mom. But that wasn't what caught Will's attention. Both the mom and the two children were wearing white masks on their faces. They weren't the only ones. Peppered within the pedestrians were people wearing the white masks that had been distributed to every American citizen by the CDC. Although the measure was precautionary, because the virus hadn't reached U.S. soil, there were plenty of conspiracy theorists who were swearing otherwise.

Will turned back toward Tanner. "Has the plan been finalized?"

"I believe so. I read that the Marines and National Guard will be mobilized to administer the shots, once the lottery winners are notified."

"Lottery winners?"

"Dates will be drawn on television. Only the people who were born on those dates will be allowed to get the vaccine."

Will shook his head. The two sat in silence for a moment as Will thought about the public reaction to a national lottery.

"You're doing that all wrong, you know," Tanner said, motioning toward the multi-colored cube Will was holding.

"You think you can do it better?" Will asked jokingly.

"I'm sure I can."

"Your noon appointment is here," Colleen said from the doorway.

He tossed the Rubix cube to Tanner as he looked at his Outlook calendar to see exactly who his mid-day meeting was with.

"It's not important. Tell them I'm going to be a little bit."

"You got it," Colleen said and turned back toward her desk.

"What about Al-Tabari?" Tanner asked, "Any word from Leah on his whereabouts?"

"Don't you read anything with your morning coffee?"

"I like to peruse the Arts and Entertainment section in the morning, I save the depressing news for later in the day."

Will navigated the web with a few quick mouse clicks and turned his monitor toward Tanner. The headline read:

Quiet Bama Town Rattled by Sleeper Cell Bust

Tanner's eyes were wide and mouth agape as he devoured the story. "How do you know that story is about Omar?"

Will flashed a knowing smile, "Leah told me."

Tanner sighed in relief, "So does that mean she thinks we're safe?"

She's nearly certain that we are. But she's going to be around for another couple of weeks to be sure. They want to be certain no new 'chatter' is heard."

"Are you going to tell everyone here that it's now safe to come to work? They'll surely be questions as to why the security is leaving."

"I can't say anything to anyone, remember this is all confidential. Leah told me she's made arrangements for a private security contractor to continue providing security after her and her team leave. The transition will be seamless."

Tanner tossed the Rubix cube back to Will. "You know this secret is safe with me."

"I know it is. Now get out there and start working to find the cure to the next big pandemic."

Will put the cube, still a jumbled mess, back on his desk. He rose from his seat to once again look out of the windows that formed one corner of his office. The mother and two children were still out there waiting patiently for the bus. He suddenly felt deep sadness. That's what he and James had dedicated their lives to, making sure innocent families like hers were protected. He would keep on fighting for them, even though he had to carry on alone. He would make sure that the next time an epidemic threatened to engulf the world, he would be prepared.

The phone rang, and he absentmindedly picked it up.

"So, is the hero still down for lunch?"

"Will smiled at Charles' familiar voice. "You bet I am."

"And you're buying right? You're not wiggling out of it."

"Yep, I'm buying," Will said sighing. "Actually, I think I'll be buying for a very long time."

ACKNOWLEDGEMENTS

There are a lot of people who, whether they realize it or not, have contributed to this work. They've influenced, inspired, and impacted my life in one way or another, and that influence has seeped into the words that you've just read. Without their assistance, encouragement, and influence this work would not exist today.

First and most importantly, without my wife Mindy holding things down at home, this work would not exist. My two children Brayden and Ava have provided me a whole new perspective on life and our world, and have motivated me to see this project through to completion. Thanks to Sharon Laine for doing one of the final edits of the book, and Bob Oshry for supporting earlier iterations. My mother and father raised me, and there is no bigger influence than that. Thanks to my friends who expect me to underachieve, its fuel on the fire. Martha, Dave, Quin, Ferris, Kevin, JB, CC, Monica, Nate & the FFL crew, Mattie, Jessica, Mark, college friends and past co-workers, cheers.

I could write a paragraph on each of these artists, but in the interest of brevity, I'll simply list their names, and some of their best work. Sage Francis, *A Healthy Distrust*, Roger Waters, *Amused to Death*, William Braunstein, *Black Metal*, Kai Hansen, *Land of the Free*,

Steven Frye, *The Power Broker*, Steve Martini, *The List*, Stephen King, *The Long Walk*, Glen Kaplan, *Evil, Inc*, Pro-Pain, *Contents Under Pressure*, Adam Green, *Spiral*, Charles Bothwell, *This is our Science*, Sick of it All, *Scratch the Surface*, Iron Maiden, *Seventh Son of a Seventh Son*, East Side, *Product of our Society*, Flip 22, *Another Level*, Phideaux Xavier, *Number Seven*, Peter Hammill, *Over*, Ra, *From One*, Sinch, *Clearing the Channel*, Tom Gabel, *Searching for a Former Clarity*.

Thanks to Dave Portnoy and the Barstoolsports.com team, for providing me good laughs when I needed them most over the past two years.

Finally, I owe a debt of gratitude to John Paine, without his guidance this book would not have been possible.

ABOUT THE AUTHOR:

Michael J. Andrews resides just outside of Boston, Massachusetts with his wife and two children, Brayden and Ava. A CPA in a past life, Mike now spends his time running an online business, and writing fiction. In between selling shoes online and refining his prose, he enjoys day trading and playing tennis. In the summer, he can be found among the crashing waves and dune grass devouring fiction in his gravity chair in Old Orchard Beach, Maine.

www.ingramcontent.com/pod-product-compliance
Lightning Source LLC
Chambersburg PA
CBHW071047250626
47159CB00002B/398